"IT'S THE KID!"

he said in a voice ~~like the~~ grunt of an animal.

"Boy, I'm gunna split you in two!"

"Whenever you're ready," said Ricardo.

The old outlaw changed his expression. "Between you and me, Kid . . ." he said.

He continued talking more and more persuasively, but in the middle of the sentence his hand jerked down for his gun. In the first thousandth part of a second, Ricardo saw that he had been trapped by this commonplace treachery.

The gun fired. And Ricardo saw the burst of sudden flame as he fell into darkness.

Books by Max Brand

Published by POCKET BOOKS

MAX BRAND

BORDER KID

PUBLISHED BY POCKET BOOKS NEW YORK

Distributed in Canada by PaperJacks Ltd., a Licensee
of the trademarks of Simon & Schuster, Inc.

POCKET BOOKS, a division of Simon & Schuster, Inc.
1230 Avenue of the Americas, New York, N.Y. 10020
In Canada distributed by PaperJacks Ltd.,
330 Steelcase Road, Markham, Ontario

Copyright 1928 by Dodd, Mead & Company, Inc.; copyright renewed
1956 by Dorothy Faust

Published by arrangement with Dodd, Mead & Company, Inc.

ISBN: 0-671-44716-5

First Pocket Books printing February, 1948

18   17   16   15   14   13   12   11   10

POCKET and colophon are trademarks of Simon & Schuster

Printed in Canada

CONTENTS

◉

BORDER KID

1

Yellow and White

Vespers was ringing faintly when William Benn crossed the piazza and turned down a Western street. His horse slackened from a dogtrot to a walk and Benn himself blinked, for before him was a living wall of gold that seemed to be rolling from the rooftops to the dust and advancing upon him with a rush. It was the red-gold light of the sun, now about to sink. William Benn, like all men who live by their wits, was superstitious; for he who cheats his fellows is convinced, in that hidden corner of his soul where conscience has its uncomfortable abode, that there must be some power which cannot be overreached.

William Benn was totally bad. He never had experienced a generous impulse. He rarely spoke a kind word except with malice aforethought. And he looked upon the cities of men as a wolf looks upon the folds of sheep. Moreover, it mattered not to William Benn whether he dined upon mutton or lamb. He was carnivorous; he was omnivorous. His soul was composed of chilled steel; his heart was adamant. And yet he was superstitious, and now he actually started in the saddle and jerked up his head.

"I am about to ride into some great good fortune!" said William Benn to himself.

So he let his horse go along slowly, not as one apt to meet good fortune with indifference, but as one unwilling to pass opportunity by. In this way he heard a sudden flurry of shouts, and when he turned the next corner he saw a pile of half a dozen youngsters struggling and writhing in the dust of the street. The pile now erupted, split apart, and tumbled away, and from beneath it rose a youth with hair like the red-gold of dancing flames. The reason for the scattering of his assailants was in his hand—a bright-bladed hunting knife.

1

He shook off some of the dust with which he was coated, as a dog shakes water out of its fur. Then he dropped his left hand jauntily upon his hip, waved the knife in his right, and spoke in Spanish somewhat as follows:

"After this, dogs and coyotes, I am going to hunt you in couples. I am going to find you not more than two at a time, and when I find you I am going to slice your ears and put red peppers in the cuts. I am going to rub pepper into your eyes, shake some more of it down your nostrils. I say this, I, Ricardo Perez. I am going to take off your hides and tan them, and cover a saddle with them."

It was a little more than a childish brawl. These were boys of sixteen or eighteen years, and though Ricardo Perez spoke Spanish, the fight had taken place in the American section of the town, and there was no doubt that the half circle which faced the Mexican youth was composed of white blood. One of the boys now picked up a stone and, in answer to the insults of Ricardo, threw it with such good aim that it struck him in the mouth. Ricardo spat blood.

"This is what you do," said Ricardo. "All the gringos are cowards. There is not one of you who will dare to come close to me. But you stand off like women and throw stones; and after a while you will get your older brothers and your fathers to come and help you to fight me. But even among them all, there is not one man who dares to stand to me by himself. You gringos are dogs, and the sons of dogs; you are mangy dogs. Some day I will tie together half a dozen of you. I will tie half a dozen of you together by the ears and then kick you into the river."

He stamped as he finished this speech. The dust puffed beneath the stroke of his foot, and the audience of young Americans started a little.

William Benn looked upon this scene partly with a superstitious eye for wonders and partly with the keen eye of a critic of humanity. He looked sharply up and down the street, but he saw nothing to attract his interest except this group of quarreling youngsters and the storm center—the lad with the flaming hair. He had blue eyes, as well, and looked as little like a Mexican as any man William Benn ever had seen; however, he knew that the old Castilian strain of Gothic blood was bound to show itself again and again in the Mexican.

Now he rode into the circle. He said to the young Americans:

2

"Six of you on one! That's fair play, I suppose?"

The oldest and largest stepped forward. He had the shoulders and the blunt jaw of a pugilist.

"He's a poison snake," said this boy. "He'll never fight with his hands. He has to have a gun or a knife. He's a murderer, that's what he is! He oughta be put into prison!"

Full of honest indignation was this voice.

"Well," said Benn to Ricardo Perez, "is it true that you're afraid to fight these boys with your hands?"

Ricardo hesitated only a fraction of a second. Then he answered: "I will fight two of them at once, with my bare hands! I will fight any two of them! But they are afraid to stand up to me!"

"Come, come," answered Benn, a little irritated by this. "You—big fellow—you're willing to fight Ricardo, I take it? Without any help?"

"Fight him?" snarled the American champion. "Why, I'll knock the stuffing out of him. I'll break him in two and feed his insides to the birds. But the sneak'll pull a knife if I get him cornered!"

"If he does," said William Benn deliberately, "I'll shoot him through the head. In order," he added with sardonic quiet, "in order to keep him from murdering another! Stand up, Ricardo."

Ricardo actually made two or three bold paces forward, with a bearing of wonderful confidence, as though he expected that the American boy would shrink away from him and try to run. But the other was a burly youth, and besides, he had obviously been taught to box, for he fell into a good position of defense, his posture correct, his weight evenly distributed on his toes, and his guard high. In those poised fists of his was gathered almost all the force which even full maturity would give him. In fact, he was nearer to twenty than to eighteen, and his pale-gray eyes now glittered with the fire of battle.

William Benn looked upon him approvingly. It might very well be that this splendid, strapping youngster was the good fortune of which he had felt the near presence!

Ricardo, marching toward his enemy, suddenly halted and actually wavered. He in turn doubled his fists, but the instant he did so it was apparent that he knew nothing of the new game. His ignorance was apparent to the trained eye of the American boy, who nodded, and said with satisfaction:

3

"I got you where I want you now, Ricardo. I'm gonna knock your head right off of you and——"

"Are you?" sneered Ricardo. "You are going to knock my head off and——"

He left his own sentence incomplete, for with the last word he leaped at the other, swayed to get beneath a driving fist—and was clipped by the American fairly upon the jaw. Nothing could resist the impetus of such a shock, and Ricardo pitched backward, struck the dust, and rolled over and over with a terrible cry.

It seemed to William Benn, his ears thrilling with that cry, that it contained more rage and horror and surprise than actual pain or fear; but the sound of it raised a howl from all the young Americans; they sounded like so many savage dogs, which have heard a cat yell in anguish. As for the American champion, he did not overlook this opportunity, but ran after his rolling enemy ready to plant a finishing blow the instant that Ricardo got up.

But he was not prepared for the manner of Ricardo's rising. It was not to the knee, and then staggeringly to the feet. Instead, young Perez hurled himself suddenly from hands and knees and feet and dived under the guard of the American and smote him in the stomach. Whether it was fist, hand, or knee that delivered the blow, even the quick eye of William Benn could not discover. But the effect was wonderful. The white champion remained standing, but he was doubled over, and his face was distorted with a breathless grin of agony.

"You'll stand up to me, you fool?" said Ricardo Perez.

And he struck the other across the face with his open hand. It was not a heavy blow. There was no sting in it except the insult, but the paralyzed nerves of the other fighter at that moment took possession of him. He fell into the dust and lay on his side, feebly kicking out with alternate feet and biting at the air like a dog at a bone.

Ricardo Perez stepped straight over the fallen body and walked toward the other youngsters. There was a trickle of blood still running from his mouth, but that stain was hardly perceptible, so sneering and cruel was his smile.

"Where's the next one?" he asked. "I want to pass you all through my hands, to-day. I have a judge to stand by and see fair play. To-day I'm going to put my mark on your hides; another day I'll begin to skin you!"

They shrank back before him. They had seen the awful

4

downfall of Goliath; he lay writhing, almost dying before their eyes.

"You yellow rats!" shouted Perez suddenly, and rushed.

The others did not wait for his coming; they turned and bolted in five different directions, and the instant they fled, Ricardo Perez stopped his pursuit. It was apparently the moral triumph that delighted him more than actually mauling one of them. Or perhaps he knew very well that there was strength enough in every one of these youths to beat him if it came to physical grips. At any rate, he was smiling faintly as he walked back to the fallen form of the other warrior.

William Benn looked on with the keenest attention while Perez actually raised the fallen hero and dusted off his clothes, and helped him to breathe again by patting him on the back.

"Now you know what I am," said Ricardo Perez. "But I like you better than the rest. You stood up and fought. I'm ready to be your friend!"

William Benn, astonished, saw them shake hands. Then the American went rather uncertainly on his way.

2

◉

He Is Like a Man

The golden wall of light no longer rolled down the street; in the distance the sky was turning crimson; but the ruffled hair of Ricardo Perez was still like a tangle of flame, and William Benn made sure that this was the pot of gold which fortune had placed in his way.

The young Mexican was now approaching him.

"I have said a good many bad things about the Americans," said Ricardo. "But is was only because those others are my enemies. You, señor, have been my friend. I thank you, and offer you my hand."

Benn took that hand. It was soft as the hand of a woman.

No labor of any kind had hardened it with calluses, though it was full of a nervous strength.

"I never judge a man by what he says but by what he does," said William Benn. "And I've seen you at work. How old are you, Ricardo?"

"Eighteen," said the other.

"Eighteen years old. And what's your work, then?"

"Work?" said Ricardo, rather blankly. Then he added quickly: "I'm preparing to go to work. One has to look around and decide what is the best thing to be done, señor!"

"Now," said William Benn, "I'm on the lookout for just such a young fellow as you seem to be. Suppose you come along with me, Ricardo?"

The boy looked at him with eyes as blue and mild as the eyes of a woman; and yet there was thought in them.

"I would have to ask the permission of my father!" said he.

"Let us go to see him, then."

"Perhaps he has not yet come back with the mules."

"Is he a muleteer?"

"Yes," said the boy, "he is an employer of mules."

This more dignified manner of stating the case made Benn smile a little to himself, but he was careful not to allow that smile to be visible to the youngster.

The boy led him through several side streets, and at last into a district where the scent altered to that which inevitably fills the air where people eat frijoles, tortillas, and roast kid. The pungency of bacon and frying, burning steaks was changed to a softer tone.

So they came at last to the house of Antonio Perez, and found Antonio himself seated in front of his door smoking cigarettes. The day had been very hot and Antonio Perez had marched a long distance, beating his mules along the way. Therefore he was tired. His eyes were blank. His shirt was opened at the throat and showed a hairy chest. His sleeves were rolled up over brawny arms to the elbow. His whole body drooped with relaxation, and his face looked ten years older than in the morning of a new day.

Yet he rose with a good deal of dignity to respond to the greeting of his boy and his boy's new friend.

In fact, there was a reason behind Antonio's air. It was no affectation; it was his sincere estimate of himself which endowed him with a liberal portion of self-reverence.

For in the old days he had been a laborer in a mine. He had toiled up the long ladders, carrying baskets of ore upon his back. That was in Mexico, of course. There was still a deep mark across his brow where the head band that braced the load had passed. After a time, this sturdy peon had decided that he would venture farther away to the north. He went north. In a foolish moment he crossed the path of a gendarme. He had to flee across the river into the strange land of the United States.

There he lived miserably for a while. But he was willing to work. His hands were very strong. By degrees he was able to save money—more money in a year than he could have saved in ten, south of the Rio Grande. He bought himself a mule. This doubled his earnings. He then wandered through the Navajo nation and found there and took for his wife a tall, supple, Navajo girl.

She made him a good wife and in due course of time, she presented him with three sons. The last was born in this small town, and here Antonio settled permanently. He increased his mules to three. With these he made what he regarded as a large income. It did not matter to him that his boys were ragged. He contrasted their state favorably with the nakedness in which he himself had been reared. And if their food was little other than beans and cornmeal, cooked in varying ways, the appetite in the Perez family was always keen enough to make every sort of cookery delicious.

Antonio Perez felt that he had climbed from a low level up to a mountain height, and the dignity of that achievement was impressed upon his face, his speech, his manners. He had a good many words of English. Even his wife could speak a few! But each of his wise sons could chatter in either tongue with wonderful ease. To hear their rapid talk was, to the father, like listening to the pleasant sound of cool, running water. He loved nothing so much as to hear them speak words which he himself did not understand. Then he would smile at his wife. If she were too busy to notice, he would close his eyes and register the expression in his mind, so as to tell her about it afterwards.

He had risen, therefore, and greeted his boy and the stranger. He had so much dignity about him that he gave a sharp glance at the red stain on the face of Ricardo, and yet he said not a word about it. Instead, he begged Señor Benn to dismount and honor him by stepping into his house. And he had a bottle of beer for the señor; and perhaps he would honor them by partaking of their supper, also?

Except the Irish, no race in the world is so hospitable as the Mexicans. But William Benn preferred to dismount and sit on the step of the house and talk to the master thereof. When Perez was bidden he sat down on his stool, again. He offered tobacco and papers. These were accepted; they smoked together.

"I have been admiring your son," said William Benn.

"Do you mean Ricardo?"

"Yes, I mean Ricardo."

"There is blood on his face," said the father thoughtfully.

"I saw him fight," said Benn, "like a wild cat."

"Ah!" murmured Perez.

The remark seemed of little interest to him.

"I have three other sons, also," said he. "Ricardo is only the youngest."

He called: "Pedro! Vicente! Juan!"

In the houses of poor people, children usually are obedient, because the parents have not time and strength to pamper the little ones. Arguments are cut short with a blow, not because of cruelty, but because of lack of energy.

Now three young men came hastily from around the corner of the house and stood in a row before their father. They stood silently. Each had observed the stranger and bowed courteously to him.

"My name is Benn," said he, understanding.

"This is my son Pedro; that is Vicente; that is Juan."

"They look like a strong trio," said William Benn.

"I shall not have to worry in my old age," declared the Mexican. He waved the boys away. "I like to show them," he explained simply. "It makes me feel very rich."

"That is true. I can understand that," declared William Benn. "They are very different from one another!"

"Pedro is a lion," answered the father. "I never have seen such a strong man. He does not know what fear is. Then there is Vicente. He was the one in the center. He is next to Pedro in age. You will have noticed that he has a beautiful face and that he is tall. That is because he takes after his mother. Vicente is like a tiger. He is terribly fierce. I have seen his eyes turn yellow. That smallest of the three is Juan.

8

Juan is like a fox. He is always thinking. I have seen him sit with his head on his hand for an hour. Some day he will be rich, unless he is hanged," said the father.

"You have had another wife?" said Benn.

"Why do you ask me that?"

"Because your fourth son, Ricardo, has yellow hair."

"He is not my son at all. I found him crying on my threshold, one warm summer night," said Antonio Perez. "And that is all that I can say."

Benn jerked up his head like an animal who smells danger before he sees it.

"You adopted him?"

"Never legally. There are papers to sign. What is the good of that? He has lived with us and eaten our food. I am his father and my wife is his mother, and the three boys are his brothers. That is enough for us to know."

"Of course it is," agreed William Benn. "I want to tell you why I want Ricardo. But first of all, will you tell me what you know about him? You said that one son is like a lion, and one is like a tiger, and one is like a fox. What is Ricardo like?"

This question made the muleteer reflect for some time. After a while he said, with his usual frankness: "I cannot lie to you, but I will tell you what I know about him. He is very lazy. He will not work. He tells lies all day long. He would rather tell a lie than tell the truth. He will not even learn how to use a knife, and the one that he carries is always dull. Besides this, sometimes he strums on a guitar. He is, as you have seen, beautiful; also, he is brave. But he is cruel and cold-hearted, and my wife and I cannot be sure that he loves us. I have told you these things because you speak kindly about my boy. I want you to know the truth about him."

"Perhaps," said Benn, who was more delighted with every word that he heard uttered, "perhaps you could say that he is more like a fox than Juan, even?"

"No, that is not true," responded the muleteer. "The truth about him is different from the truth about my other sons."

"In what way, my friend?"

"In this important way. They are all brave and strong and clever, like a lion, a tiger, or a fox, but Ricardo is like none of them. He is only like a man, and he commands the other three, although he is the youngest!"

9

A Question Answered

The guest remained for supper. Being a cosmopolitan, William Benn made himself at home. He talked about mules, and their loads, and the sureness with which they moved their narrow hoofs, and about their prices. And with Perez he agreed that no mules north of the Rio were equal to those bred south of that stream from good tough mustang mares and the asses of Andalusia.

He could have a pleasant manner in spite of his ugly face. Indeed, his whole body was ugly. His face was long and narrow, with a protruding jaw and an indentation running across the forehead, and when he smiled, his lips lifted at the corners a trifle, giving him the most sinister look in the world. His body, like his face, was long drawn out; and he had, in spite of that leanness, a neck corded with strength, and great hands, and long, thin feet which were incased in flexible boots. Sometimes, as he sat at the little table, his shoulders somewhat hunched, and his big hands stretched out to the food, he looked like a snapshot out of focus, so exaggerated appeared the length of the arms, the size of the hands.

However, this formidable appearance was masked in a genial manner as he talked to his host. The wife and the three sons kept back in the shadows as much as possible, never daring to speak while the gringo gentleman held forth. Only young Ricardo lingered near the board, unabashed, even after the others hastily had finished their meal and retired. He leaned an elbow on the edge of the table and looked continually into the face of William Benn, and Benn, far from appearing to resent this familiarity, smiled and nodded at the boy now and then, and carefully included him in all his remarks, and even drew out an opinion from Ricardo, from time to time.

Antonio Perez was elated by this gentleness. He produced

a bottle of fiery white brandy to crown the feast of beans and tortillas and red peppers, and William Benn drank off that terrible potion of distilled fire, and praised its flavor with a thoughtful, upward eye, and said that it made him think of happy days in Mexico City.

Afterwards, he opened the subject which had brought him to their house. He was, he said, a merchant who had dealings on both sides of the river, and therefore he needed to use, constantly, both Spanish and English. And, above all, he was handicapped by the lack of an assistant, who must have high qualifications. In the first place, his assistant must be young, to learn the business. In the second place, he must speak the two languages perfectly. In the third place, he must be brave. In the fourth place, he must be honest. And all these qualifications, he had seen at a glance, were possessed by young Perez. Forthwith, he invited the lucky Ricardo to accompany him and begin to work as a sort of junior partner, with a salary, to begin, of a hundred dollars a month.

"A hundred dollars a month!" breathed Antonio Perez, and his wild glance looked backward into his past, to the moment when he had been of an age with Ricardo, and when his back and his legs had ached so horribly from the labor in the mines, carrying up a man's load upon his youthful shoulders. And then he looked to his own present earnings, out of which he was forced to keep three mules, a house, a wife, and four growing young men—except for the seasons when his own three children were able to get employment. "A hundred dollars a month!" murmured Perez again.

Then, as though he misunderstood, William Benn added that this was only named as a sum to begin on, while young Ricardo was learning the business, and while he was being trained in the necessary knowledge. "For a successful merchant can't be made in a day," smiled Benn.

The father extended both his hands, to invite the opinion of Heaven upon such generosity, but young Ricardo put in:

"You want me because I am four things. Well, you heard me speak Spanish and English pretty well. You know that I'm young enough to learn. You saw me stand up to the six of them, and that may make you think I'm brave. But what makes you think I'm honest?"

Mr. Benn glanced down at the floor, and then looked up from beneath his brows, with the odd smile lifting the corners of his mouth.

"I know that you will be honest," he said, "because you are an upstanding boy; and because you are the son of honest Antonio Perez; and, above all, my boy, because I shall attach you to me by a hundred kindnesses which I have in mind at present!"

"Well——" said Ricardo, obviously unimpressed.

His father broke in: "Ricardo, you are talking like a fool! You hear me? Like a fool! Do you hear this kind señor promising a thousand gracious things to you? Saints! And all you do is talk! You talk of what? It is nonsense!"

Ricardo grew silent. But still his eyes were thoughtful. They dwelt fixedly upon William Benn and the uptilt at the corners of the mouth of the stranger.

Then he left the table and went to his foster mother. She was stirring about in a dark corner of the single room which was their house, and trying to clean up and put away, without disturbing the kind stranger who had come to them. He took her by the arm and led her outside the house, where the three foster brothers were gathered. They surrounded him— Pedro and Vicente pushing close up, and only the foxlike Juan holding off to a distance. He rarely committed himself; he never made himself a part and portion of a mass movement of any kind. "And what has happened? And are you going away with him? And will you really get a hundred dollars a month?" demanded Vicente, whose emotions were all on the tip of his tongue.

"You three run away," said Ricardo carelessly. "I'm not going to talk to you now. If you want something to do, walk over to the gringo's town and see what happens to you!"

He laughed a little as the three drew back, and Ricardo began to walk up and down, holding the hard, strong hand of his foster mother in his. Labor of the house and the field she had known for many years, and yet she was not bowed, and her step was still majestic and free.

"What do you think of him?" asked Ricardo.

"Of the stranger? Who thinks when Heaven sends a blessing?" she asked. "I do not think. Who thinks when he is hungry and food is put to his lips? He only eats!"

"And swallows poison," said the boy, "and puffs up like a toad and dies screaming, as Lopez Almagro did."

"Hah?" cried she. "Ricardo, what are you saying?"

"I don't know," murmured Ricardo. "I have brought you out here, because when you are in the house with my father,

12

you never can do any thinking. You only have a tongue to say the things that he expects you to say."

"You," said the woman, "are wicked! Besides, you know too much!"

Nevertheless, she laughed a little, her laughter no louder than a soft whisper.

"Now that you are here, with the stars as near as any person——" began the boy.

"What a silly way to speak, my son! The stars are far away. They are the lights in the tepees in the land of the departed——"

"You forget what the priest teaches you," he reminded her.

She crossed herself suddenly.

"That is true! However, what were you about to say, Ricardo?"

"That I want you to think for me. I cannot think this all out for myself!"

"I? Well, I shall think for you as well as I can," she replied. "But you had better trust everything to your father!"

"My father may be flattered," replied the boy. "When he is tickled with flattery, he cannot think at all. He would tell me to go with the stranger. But I don't want to go!"

"You do not want to leave us," said the woman gently, "and that is what any boy should feel about his home. Heaven knows that I have tried to make it a home—a true home for you!"

Ricardo took her heavy hand in his and raised it to his lips.

"Ah, well," sighed she. "But no true son of mine ever would have thought of doing that!"

"Listen to me," said Ricardo. "The rest are all excited. I mean, my father, Pedro, and Vicente, of course. Even Juan had eyes full of red light while he listened to that talk about so much money every month. Well, but I don't feel that way. I want you to hear what I say. This man, this Señor Benn, is not telling us everything that is in his mind. He is not telling us half of what is in his mind. I am sure, because I watched his face."

"Peace, peace, child," said the mother. "Are you old enough to read the mind of such a great and rich man?"

"Rich men are the same as me, from the skin inwards," said Ricardo. "When I looked into his eyes, he could bar the way to me and keep me outside and very far from an un-

13

derstanding of him. That is true. Nevertheless, I could try to understand. I did not like a great many things. Besides, he says that he is rich but we don't know it. He says that he is a great merchant. We never have seen him before. But most of all, I don't like the way that he looks up through his brows, and the way that his lips lift at the corners when he smiles."

"Now," said she, "I see that you are talking like a baby, Ricardo. Women and boys always are apt to think like that. But the face of a man never has anything to do with his heart. Look at your father. He looks as though he were always going to draw a knife, but, as a matter of fact, he has the heart of a lamb."

"You have had a great many years to learn about my father," said he. "But you never saw this other man before this evening."

"Ah, Ricardo," she replied finally, "how much you could do for us if you were to take this work—you who never have worked before! How much you could do for us! Because," she said, "you are the one who will lead up my three sons by the hand and place them in good comfortable houses! That is the hope of my life!"

Ricardo said nothing at all, for a moment. Then he sighed: "I think that is the answer for me!"

4

◉

"Bring Him Back"

When it was decided by the family that Ricardo was to accompany the stranger, William Benn would have started at once, but arrangements are not easily made by simple people. For two days the household was in an uproar, getting together a packet of clothes for Ricardo, and preparing him in every way that they could for the great journey. In fact, they were troubled to learn that the rich merchant hardly could tell them where the journey would take Ricardo, for William Benn said that he was forced to be constantly on the road.

He gave them an address in the town of El Real, however, to which he said that they might write; and finally Ricardo was made ready for the trip, and on the second morning he started off. The magnificence of William Benn appeared particularly in this start of the journey. The muleteer had determined to give his favorite foster child a mule to ride off into his new life; but when the last morning came, a fine bay mare was found outside the house, with a magnificent new saddle on her back, and a complete accouterment. It was a gift from William Benn to his new "assistant," for this was the title that he gave Ricardo to the family.

The Perez group poured into the street. The boys were very much affected; Antonio Perez allowed the tears to run down his face; only the mother retained her composure. She blessed Ricardo and embraced him. Then she said to William Benn: "This is not really my son, but I have given to him the work of my hands and the love of my heart. And who can tell? Heaven may have made him mine by that love and that work! If he should not seem at first what you expect him to be, have patience, kind señor. There are seeds planted in him, though it may take time for them to grow!"

William Benn listened to this sad little harangue with downward eyes and a nod, here and there. Secretly, he was in a fever to be gone from the town and the Perez family. Also, his first superstitious emotion had been somewhat dimmed by the passage of time, and he no longer was so sure that Ricardo of the flaming yellow hair might really be a pot of gold for him. However, what one commits himself to, one will not readily draw back from. William Benn said to himself, quietly: "The first hunch is the right one!"

So he stuck to his purpose.

He rode off down the street with Ricardo, who was so delighted with the fine new mare and with his own graceful horsemanship that he looked back only once to wave to those he left behind him, and so with Benn he turned the first winding corner of the way and disappeared from their eyes.

However, it is not right to follow them at once into the adventures which waited for Ricardo. We must turn back to the Perez family and see what happened to them after Ricardo departed.

For a few days, everything went as before, except that

15

the house was more silent, and this was caused by the gloomy behavior of Antonio Perez. He was so sad and occupied with thought that his three real sons began to look to one another and say: "We are nothing to our father. He cares only for Ricardo, because he has a white skin, and blue eyes, and yellow hair, like a gringo!"

The wife of Antonio had the same thought, and after some time, she came on her husband and found him dictating a letter, which young Juan was writing down, for that was an art which the muleteer never had mastered.

The letter was somewhat as follows:

I send my greetings and my love to my dear son, Ricardo. Send us word of yourself as often as your duties allow you to write. Pedro and Vicente both have been given places on a ranch. Their pay is not much, but they are learning to be men. All goes well with us, except that there is a silence in the house!

Then the wife interrupted the muleteer and took him to one side.

"Why do you not love your own children?" she said. "They are truly yours. If you doubt it, look at Pedro! He has a face like a lion, but he has your eyes. Or look at Vicente. When one hears him, his voice is yours, except that it is smoother. Or there is Juan. I admit that he is not so much like you, but he has a hundred of your ways, and you can see if you care to look! But you care for Ricardo and for no one else!"

Then Antonio Perez answered her:

"Now I know what you are thinking; but it is not true!"

"Ah," said the Navajo, "but you have not smiled since Ricardo left us!"

"Is that why you have such foolish ideas?" said her husband. He looked up to her and smiled indeed. But he was rather in awe of his wife, as he had been the first time that he saw her, standing tall and straight and beautiful in the cornfield, a sheaf in one arm, and a cutting knife in the other. In that manner she always appeared to his mind's eye, and so she would always stand before him, in spite of time and wrinkles, to her death day; for love, after all, is the only true enchanter. So Antonio looked up to her now with a little awe and heard her say:

"Whatever you speak to me will be the truth."

"It will," he answered. "And this is what I am going to tell you. When we heard the voice on our threshold sixteen years ago and I opened the door and saw the golden head of Ricardo, I guessed that he was a treasure sent to us. You may remember that I would not let him be sent away to an orphanage, as you wanted to do!"

"Heaven forgive me," said the woman. "I was a fool, but after all, I was afraid. We were poorer, then!"

"Exactly," said Antonio. "We were poorer then, but I guessed in the first instant that Heaven had sent the boy to us to be our fortune. And he has been! Is it not true that the day after he came to us I was given a contract which kept me busy for six months, and out of which we made enough to clothe the entire family, fill the corncrib, and put away some coins, besides?"

She nodded, with a smile. Such times of plenty were memorable seasons!

"And we have gone on safely from that moment. None of our children have been seriously ill. We have had no great bills from the doctor, and we have not had to call in the priest!"

The Navajo crossed herself devoutly.

"But now," said the father of the family: "Ricardo is gone, and I am afraid that our good fortune has gone away with him."

"No, no!" she replied. "He has gone off to become rich. We shall have a shower of gold from him!"

"It may be," said Antonio, "but give me the brandy bottle. I need a taste of it, because even to talk of these things has made my heart cold!"

He proved a false prophet for more than a month. Everything went on smoothly, though he was still so apprehensive that his wife often would say to him: "A watched window will crack!"

And then misfortune came. Juan grew ill. It was a high fever. The doctor had to come twice a day, and Antonio himself was taken on the seventh day, so that Vicente was called in from the ranch on which he worked. Vicente struggled to take care of the sick people—and he himself went down suddenly and lay sicker than all the rest.

When Pedro came in like the lion he was to help the rest,

17

he found that his father and his mother and his two brothers all lay prostrate.

He was the head of the house, and he had to work night and day. No one of the neighbors would come in because the fever was so contagious. Even the doctor did not like to come near them, and when he did arrive, he stayed the shortest possible time. He had a disinfectant stuffed up his nose with cotton. He never spoke a word for fear of drawing in the infected air, but he would sit at the table and hastily scratch out instructions, all the while breathing noisily through his cotton.

Pedro had to keep the house clean, do the marketing and the cooking, and above all, care for the delirious patients. It was a dreadful time, and Pedro grew as thin as a rail.

Juan, the first to sink, was also the first to rise. He looked more like a fox than ever, with his great, massive forehead, and his face which pinched to a sharp point at the chin. He staggered about and helped his exhausted brother. With the spirit of Hercules they toiled together. But it was very hard. All the money in the house was gone. Dreadful necessity sent Pedro forth, and he stood in the piazza and held out his hand before him and, with a burning face, solicited charity!

On the first day he brought home a handful of coins. On the second day there were fewer. On the third day he received almost nothing. Men pay for a novelty but they detest a nuisance.

This terrible time passed and the whole family recovered, but they were so dreadfully in debt that even when the three mules were sold they could not satisfy the doctor. However, they all went cheerfully to work. Pedro and Vicente returned to the ranch which had employed them before; Juan got work in the shop of a shoemaker, and Antonio went to labor in the little flour mill by the river. He was perfectly willing to do anything; nevertheless, his pride had received a mortal blow. His three mules had been to him like three separate kingdoms, which he ruled gently but firmly, a benevolent despot.

By constant labor they paid off all the debts and they bought two more mules which, however, were not as good as the others had usually been. But a week after they were bought, a fire started in the shed and gutted it and stifled the two poor mules in the smoke.

18

The next day Antonio could not stand. His head was dizzy. The doctor was called and said that they must keep him in dark and quiet with special food. In a word, he must go to the hospital. His wife turned pale, but away he was sent.

As she crouched by his bed, he said to her in a feeble whisper:

"You understand now that I was right. When we lost Ricardo, we lost the gift of Heaven! Send for him at once. Send one of our boys to bring him home again!"

5

◉

Some Strange Servitors

Now we must go back to Ricardo, for our chief business is to follow him in his travels, and his adventures, and all the strange things which he met during his young life.

When he rode out of town he felt like an antelope which has been turned loose from a lariat, or like a bird pitched out of a cage. He wanted to dash wildly across the hills, but the quiet, thoughtful face of his companion restrained him. William Benn did not speak a great deal then; neither did he talk much during the whole of the next two days, during which they were cutting across the country as straight as a bird flies. He was a man who seemed to have limitless thoughts, through which he wandered as some people wander through a wilderness; and constantly as they journeyed along, the eye of Benn was dim with that inward look which comes to people who are following intricate trails through their own minds.

Some day, thought Ricardo, he would be allowed to enter fully into the mind of his master and participate in these mysteries. But in the meantime, not a word was expressed to him about the important affairs of William Benn.

"This is a school," said Ricardo to himself, "in which I shall have to begin by learning a new language."

He had only the vaguest ideas about business of any kind, but he had read a good many tales, chiefly those of the Near East, in which a poor merchant travels from Damascus to Cairo and sells goods at a great profit, and in two or three efforts suddenly becomes wealthy enough to build a house with fountains and gardens! So wealthy become the merchants of the fairy tales that every now and again a whole shipload of rare goods—silks, spices, the finest bales of stuffs, and barrels of choice wines—could sink to the bottom, and still the lucky fellows grew wealthier and wealthier. So much had these tales grown into the mind of Ricardo that when he was smaller he often had wondered why Antonio Perez had such bad luck, for Antonio went out day after day with his three laden mules, and he returned home night after night, never having found abandoned treasure, never having encountered adventure! Growing older, the boy began to learn that business rarely produces results so suddenly, but still it remained involved in mystery. He continued to think in such terms of miracles as one finds only upon Wall Street, when markets rise and fall. So he waited for the revelation to come, waited impatiently, turning many possibilities through his mind.

They reached rough mountains and journeyed through them by trails which Ricardo knew that he never could remember, if ever he had to retrace his steps to the rear. Then, from a high point, he found himself looking sheer down upon a white town in a green plain, beside a river that lay across it as straight as a sword. Ricardo could see the bridge that arched the river. He even could see the reflection of the white stone pillars and arches; he could see the bell tower of the old mission church; and, straining his sharp eyes, he could see the big bells inside the lantern.

"That is El Real," said William Benn.

Then they began to descend. They followed a little stream that streaked down the mountain's sheer face, pointing towards the larger river that watered the plain below. But it could not go arrow straight, for now and again it was dashed aside by the rocks and jagged here and there, like a mountain sheep dropping down a precipice almost sheer.

So they came, down into the foothills. They were so close to the town, by this time, that the church bells plainly sounded, and seemed like melancholy cymbals struck heavily above them, in the sky. Here there were thick woods interspersed with gigantic boulders, and turning suddenly from the trail and going back around one of these monstrous stones, William Benn pressed on through a thicket which seemed absolutely impenetrable even to a man on foot—and might easily, indeed, have become so—yet Benn knew exactly what winding path to take so that a horse and rider actually could pass through the dense wood.

They came out into a charming glade. The forest gave back upon either hand and allowed a pleasant lawn through which ran the stream beside which they had been riding, and which now hung above them in white rags and tatters; but here its violence was subdued and it ran more gently. On the cliff it had sounded like a clashing of swords, but here it was rather like the murmuring and the plucking of harp strings, trying to recover lost music and old airs dissolved in time. Ricardo looked about him, delighted; but neither the tall and gloomy forehead of the woods, nor the white flags of spray set against the cliff, nor the soft green grass, like Irish turf, on which they rode, pleased him so much as the house which he saw.

It had been built on a broad rock hanging over the stream, as though the original builder had wanted to fortify it against attack by giving it loftier walls. But nature had defied his attempt, for a thousand climbing vines, rooting themselves resolutely in the crevices of the rock, now threw up their arms over the sides of the house and joined their fingers at the roof ridge. It smothered, partially, and shut away the windows and so gave the house a half-blind appearance. But with the sun glistening along the ripples of trees and the ten thousand blossoms quivering and breathing with beauty, Ricardo was so moved that he reined his fine bay mare to a halt and stared, agape.

"That is a place where a man could live!" said he.

"That is a place to live or die in," said William Benn, and something about his voice suggested to the boy a thought so harsh and so frightful that he looked sharply at his master, but did not receive the slightest hint of a word or a glance to enlarge the words.

"You see," added William Benn after a moment, "how I show you all my secrets. This house, for instance!"

The boy looked at him again, but it was always hard to

21

catch the eye of Benn, for either it was blankly turned inward, or else it stared into the distance, as if it saw thoughts reflected in the mirror of time.

"I didn't know," said Ricardo, "that merchants had to have so many secrets!"

"And how do we make money, then?" asked Benn harshly. "If there are no secrets, couldn't every fool in the world simply lean down and gather up handfuls of gold?"

"That is true!" said Ricardo.

There had been such sudden irritation in the voice of William Benn that Ricardo was afraid to speak to him again. They rode around the side of the house and found a small barn. It was really much more capacious than appeared at the first glance, since one passed down an incline, and half of the barn was sunk into the rock beneath the general surface of the ground.

Never was Ricardo Perez more amazed than by what he beheld in this barn. For he found three rows of box stalls, and in every row there were five stalls, and all but four of those stalls were now occupied. And by what horses!

Ricardo looked upon them with bewildered joy, for he had an instinct for good horseflesh, and this was a thoroughbred strain that he was looking upon. Lean and long of neck, sometimes they were as narrow as swords—but like swords, again, they looked tough and true.

Ricardo stared from one side to the other as he took his own bright bay mare to a stall.

"She's a weed," said Benn, looking in at her. "You can keep her if you like her. I bought her because she was good enough to bring you here! But you ought to learn to get the picture of a real horse in your mind. Beauty comes often enough. But service is a lot ahead of looks!"

A little hunchback was at work among the horses. Benn spoke to him shortly and sharply as "Lew," and the hunchback saluted and never answered a word. Always a salute for his master, but from the corner of his eye he tried to catch the attention of Ricardo with a wink, as much as to say: "We have to listen to this foolish man, but you and I know what rot it all is, don't we?"

Ricardo was slightly amused by this attitude. And he was half horrified by the deformity of the little man, and half pitying.

They left the barn and went to the house, where the door

opened at their approach, and Ricardo saw standing in the shadow the largest man he ever had seen in his life. One could hardly make him out, at first partly because he was a Negro, and partly because his proportions exceeded the expectation of the eye so greatly.

When Ricardo passed him, it was like passing a tower, or a vast, overhanging tree. The man must have been several inches over seven feet. He disguised this height somewhat by wearing thin felt slippers which had no heels, but this was a small paring from such a height. He was not pulled out of shape in one way or another, but appeared to be a perfectly normal man simply of excessive size. As to his weight, Ricardo would hardly have ventured a guess at it! The house was built with such exceeding strength that there was no creaking of floors or even of stairs under the striding of this monster, but nevertheless Ricardo felt a peculiar, slight tremor as the Negro walked. It was literally a crushing sense of bulk. The man could have taken a charging bull by the horns and snapped its neck!

This apparition grinned at his master, entering. His grin was like a flash of lightning in a black sky. Then he rolled his eyes down at Ricardo and took the hand of the boy in a paw which was like the hand of some Egyptian colossus, some black basalt monster which smiles across seven thousand years of desert. So Ricardo felt, looking up at the giant.

Then he went on down the hall with William Benn, who said cheerfully:

"Have you a chill in the middle of your back?"

"Exactly there!" admitted Ricardo, startled. "Why did you ask me that?"

"Because," replied William Benn, "I hope you will live for a long time in this house, but no matter how long you live here, you'll have that chill down the back the moment you have Selim behind you."

"Is he an Arab, or something like that?"

"I don't know. I think he picked the silly name out of a book. Everything about Selim is big, except his brain!"

6

◉

Why?

It was not a large house, but it was built with wonderful neatness and strength, which made Ricardo think of the lines of a ship. The rooms were small, also, and the ceilings low, so that the monstrous Selim seemed to graze them at the height of every step he took.

Up a narrow stairs, which turned quickly, Ricardo was taken to a little chamber which had a single window not more than two feet square, and yet one would not have complained of the lack of air any more than one would in a ship should a cabin have a port of such dimensions. Here the bed was built against the wall exactly like a ship's bunk; and there was even a slight curve to the floor, as though it were accommodated to the curve of a ship's deck!

"Put yourself up here, Ricardo," said William Benn. "You can be comfortable here!"

"I've never seen such a fine place!" exclaimed the boy.

He could have shouted in his enthusiasm, and William Benn brought him up short by saying tersely: "Who taught you English?"

"One listens," said Ricardo.

"One listens," said William Benn in the oddest tone. "But sometimes——"

He said no more. He went on abruptly to point out the clothes closet and the two small bookshelves which, as he said, would soon be filled from the books which were in the house.

"What books do you want to read?" he asked.

And Ricardo answered that he never had read a book in his life. This answer seemed to please the other immensely, and William Benn said with actual warmth: "Maybe I'm going to be able to fit the right sort of things into your brain, my boy. I'm going to try, and if you will do what I tell you, you'll be one of the richest men in the world before you finish!"

He said this with conviction, not in a rush of enthusiasm, but slowly and selecting his words, and Ricardo believed him, and his heart leaped at the promise. He did not doubt. Ever since he had met this man in the street of the village, he had been inclined to doubt him, but now he doubted no longer that William Benn, whatever might be his faults, was totally capable of doing what he pleased in the world—beginning with the life and the fortune of his new protégé.

They had dinner on a small veranda which overhung the river, and William Benn, while he waited for the meal, and even in pauses during it, would start up from his chair and pace backward and forward. He explained, with a short, harsh laugh, that the veranda was very like the bridge of a ship, and Ricardo could see that he was right. It was closed in with a series of small windows, and looking out through these, the river seemed to be rushing straight upon the house with a silent glide of speed; in a moment the water would appear to be standing, and it was the house which moved.

Selim waited on them at dinner. He was not a servant of formal manners, but conversed freely with them both and even lounged with a hand resting against the back of one of their chairs while he talked.

William Benn did not reprove this familiarity, but he said with a smile to Ricardo: "Were you ever waited on before?"

"No," said Ricardo, "but I have seen people eat in restaurants, and I've watched the waiters."

"So you know how the thing should be done?"

"Yes."

Benn said no more, but there was a glimmer of greater interest in his eye. "Have you eaten duff?" he asked, as the meal came to a close with the sweet.

"Never," said Ricardo, looking incuriously at the yellowish mass which was heaped upon his plate.

"This will be a treat for you, then," said Benn with great eagerness. "I remember a time off the pitch of the Horn——"

As he spoke, he tasted the plum duff, and instantly cried out in a terrible voice: "Wong!"

The gigantic Selim leaped backward as though that great voice were a thunderbolt which might cleave him in twain.

"Wong!" shouted Selim, but in spite of his size, he could not put the same authentic ring of command into his tones.

The door at the other end of the veranda opened, and Ricardo saw the ugliest little Chinaman he ever had laid eyes on. Even the hunchback was a handsome creature compared with the narrow and frozen malice which appeared in the thin face of the Oriental.

"Wong, you've spoiled it again!" exclaimed the master of the house.

The Chinaman chattered something unintelligible.

"Speak English, you dog!" boomed William Benn, and leaped across the room. Big Selim cowered back into a corner. The Chinaman slipped a hand into the loose bosom of his coat so that Ricardo instinctively gripped his own knife; but William Benn laid hold upon the long, glimmering, silken, braided pigtail of Wong. He raised his other hand, balled into a massive fist.

"I've a mind to beat your face flat!" he said.

The face of Wong worked, but he said not a word.

"And some day," went on Benn, "I *shall* beat you to a pulp. Now get back to your galley and thank your stars that you're not dying to-day!"

He jerked Wong around and kicked him with such force that the Chinaman crashed against the jamb of the door and dropped in a loose pile upon the floor. After a few moments, he stood up, but only after gathering himself together by degrees.

William Benn returned to the table. He was fairly yellow-green with wrath.

"The scoundrel!" exclaimed Benn. "The robbing scoundrel! Is there nobody in the world but me that can make plum duff? I've seen the times on shipboard when there was nothing but the duff to comfort a man and to warm the heart of him! I've seen the time when——"

He stopped short and bent to the eating of the food, but Ricardo, who had said nothing, felt sure that his new employer was watching him with critically searching glances from time to time to see in what manner he took the scene that he had just passed.

Carefully Ricardo strove to keep a mask upon his emotions. But strive as he might, he could not be sure that he was succeeding in maintaining a false front. For him there had been enough mysteries connected with William Benn before ever they arrived at this house, but since the arrival there was enough to make the head of an older man than young Perez spin. There was the singular situation of the house, fenced off with the impenetrable palisade on the one side, and by the tigerishly swift flow of the river on the other; there was the mystery of the barn and its box stalls—a very odd luxury in the West. Most important, too, was the quality of the horses in that stable, for Ricardo could guess that he had not seen a creature in the place that could be bought for less than a thousand dollars.

There was the house itself, its strange, boatlike construction; the talk of Benn about the sea; the monster Selim; the deformed Lew; the hideous face of Wong; and, above all, tying these elements together, he hardly could explain why, came the final outbreak of passion on the part of the master.

It was a formidable enough exhibition of fury, and yet, strange to say, it lifted a burden from the heart of Ricardo. There had been something concealed, he had felt from the first moment, in the nature of William Benn. If it were sheer physical brutality and no more, then Ricardo was happy. But yet he could not be sure. The savage passion of William Benn seemed to have been sharply controlled. The brutal kicking of Wong had seemed merely a careless gesture, dismissing the offending servant. Had not the wrath of the master been checked, what would he have done to the man?

With these thoughts running rapidly through his mind, Ricardo maintained a polite smile at the corners of his mouth, but he could not help measuring the distance to the windows, and the distance to the doors, with catlike glances.

Suddenly he was terrified.

William Benn reached across the table and touched his arm.

"You can't get out, Ricardo," said he. "If you tried to run for it, I could catch you, if I wanted to. And why should I want to? Perhaps I don't. But now I tell you this, my lad. As long as you're with me, be honest. If you're afraid, let it jump into your eyes, the way it does now. And if you're disgusted, as you were a minute ago, show that also. And if you're angry, show that. Because I'll let you know, in the first place, that I'd rather see the heart of a man as it is than have him try to put me off with lies! And there can be a lie in the eye as well as in the mouth."

After seeing a blow which had struck down Wong, this

was a sufficiently terrible speech, and all through it, William Benn kept his great, bony hand upon the arm of the boy. He did not grip it hard, but merely letting it lie there of its own weight, Ricardo had the sense of irresistible power holding him.

"You didn't like it," went on Benn in a quieter tone, leaning back in his chair. "You thought I was a brute. Perhaps I was. But all these fellows are rascals. How could I get ordinary men to work for me, living here at the end of the world without a chance to leave me?"

He shrugged his shoulders.

"They have to be kept in hand—or under foot, darn them! But they know that I never sleep!"

Then he added, more cheerfully still: "You've traveled far enough, for one day. It's time for you to tumble in, my lad. Turn in soon and tumble out early. You can never stand a proper watch unless you've slept yourself out."

Ricardo said good night and went straight up to his room, and he did not linger on the way! But he was wondering earnestly why it was that the three servants in this house could not leave it!

7

◉

The Veranda Roof

That night in his sleep, Ricardo had a nightmare. He dreamed that he was lying in the grip of a gigantic hand which encompassed all his body, and the thumb and forefinger were pressed over his throat, as though about to pinch his head off. He looked off at a distance and saw the face of the monster that held him. Darkness and mist lay between, but far away he could see the grim head of William Benn.

He awakened stiff with fright; that night he slept no more! He lay wide awake, staring at nothingness, for some time.

At last he got up and tried his door. It was fast locked! It made him strangely uneasy. He went to the window and looked down from it to the roof of the veranda—the bridge of Benn. Beneath and beyond that there was enough starlight to give him a glimmering outline of the river, but most of all he could hear its swift rushing. It was a sleepy, dreamy sound by day, but now it was like an ominous hissing in the ear of Ricardo; it was like a whisper of warning, rising momently louder and louder.

Ricardo leaned out the window and took stock of his situation. He was in the top story of the building, but the eaves projected well above the top of his window. Only by standing up most perilously on the outside of the window could he hope to reach the eaves. There was of course no reason why he should try to escape, except that the locking of his door had given him the sense of being in a prison. Looking down, the difficulty was not so great. There was a large and rather ornamental hood over the window under his own, and if he could get down to that, the roof of the veranda would be immediately beneath!

Suppose he were able to descend, could he climb up again to his chamber?

He considered the matter with the greatest care. The more he considered it, the more interested was he in the possibility. So down he ventured and made the journey with ease; then after shivering for a minute on the top of the veranda roof, and listening to the stamping and shouting of the far-off cataracts, he turned and climbed back to his room, with only a little more difficulty than he had managed the descent; for though he was neither very strong nor very enduring, having always avoided even the slightest tasks during his life, yet he was as light and active as a cat.

The first dawn light came shortly after his return. He felt much more at ease with himself and with his situation in the house since he had discovered that it was so possible to get in and out of his room. So he spent some time dressing carefully, and just as the early morning light turned a strong pink, he heard his lock turned, softly. And nothing more except, afterwards, a few tremors of the floor on which he stood—as though a gust of wind were at that moment shaking the place. But Ricardo stood still, transfixed; he knew that it was the passing step of Selim!

Now that his door was opened, he judged that it was

proper for him to leave the room when he pleased; so he went down through the house, which gave him more than ever the impression of a ship. When he reached the lower floor the odor of frying bacon came to him. Breakfast at this early hour seemed to be the rule in that odd household. He could not help sighing, when he remembered the lazy life he had led in the house of Perez. Then he went out through a side door and stood shivering in the morning chill, just in time to see a tall chestnut ridden furiously around the front of the house and put at a series of jumps. There was a fence, a wall, and an earthen mound, and the chestnut took them all gallantly, twisted around, and went back over the same course. Then Ricardo saw that the rider was William Benn.

The hunchback came out of the stable and took the horse as Benn dismounted.

"He's too soft; you'll have to work him harder," Benn said to the fellow.

"One man can't exercise ten horses," declared the stableman.

Benn made no answer, but he watched the horse being led away, and then turned toward the house. When he saw Ricardo, he checked himself a little as though in surprise. Then he came on and nodded to the boy.

"You don't make a long night of it," he commented crisply. "And that's a good thing. We keep early hours, here. Breakfast ought to be ready."

They went into the house again, and big Selim served them with bacon and eggs and coffee and toast. Ricardo ate heartily, for he was very hungry, and after breakfast he asked what he was to do first.

"You're anxious to begin learning the business, I see," said William Benn. "But take your time. You'd better use a day or two just looking around. There's no use trying to learn my business until you've learned me. Do whatever you like— but stay between the trees and the river!"

He said this with his faint smile that tipped up the corners of his mouth a little and always made Ricardo think of a demon mocking some poor Christian soul. However, he did not dream of disobeying. He walked around the house, studied the jumps, and tried to make friends with Lew, the stableman. But he could not get a word out of the little man, and when he retired to the house and strove to open a conversation with Selim, he was met by a similar silence. Yet he could see that they were greatly interested in him; he felt their glances following him whenever he was in view.

William Benn had left the place that morning. He did not come back at noon, and Ricardo ate alone, with big Selim stalking about the dining room and placing food before him in stark silence. After lunch, he slept for two hours, and then went down to the river with a fishing rod and tackle which he had found.

He caught nothing, but he killed the time until evening brought William Benn back on a tired, foaming horse. They had dinner together, with hardly ten words from Benn during that time; and afterwards they sat on the veranda— or else Benn walked back and forth along his "bridge," stopping abruptly at the windows, now and again, and peering at the sweep of the river.

Ricardo followed him up and down with his eyes. He would have given a very great deal to have learned what the business might be for which he was enlisted, or how to explain the strangeness of the three servants, or the grim manner of William Benn himself.

"Can you handle guns?" asked Benn after a time, halting abruptly before the boy.

"I'm not an expert."

"Go up the river to-morrow until you're close to the falls. Then start practicing. Selim will fill your pockets with ammunition. And maybe you can persuade him to go along and give you some lessons, eh?"

Ricardo agreed. And Benn explained:

"We have to ride into all sorts of dangerous places. And south of the border there are bandits who would hold you up and strip you of everything as gladly as a blackbird will sing. You have to learn to take care of yourself before you can ride with me!"

Ricardo fell into a study. In the first place, though it was not odd that a merchant should have to ride armed in this part of the world, it was very strange indeed that he should have to go up the river to the waterfalls in order to do his practicing. Unless, to be sure, William Benn wanted to be confident that the explosions of the gun would not be noticed by those who might pass by along the trail. But already Ricardo was beginning to feel that the mere asking of questions would take him nowhere. It did not seem to be

31

expected of him, and he felt a covert challenge from Benn to find out all he could for himself.

In the midst of these thoughts, Ricardo heard a step which he did not recognize. Certainly it was not the shuffling step of Lew, or the scuffle of Wong's slippers, or the floor-shaking stride of Selim. This was a brisk, decided, heel-first walk, and it brought out onto the veranda a middle-aged man with a tuft of gray at each temple that gave him a peculiar horned appearance. He was dressed like an ordinary cow-puncher, but Ricardo guessed that he was something more. At least, he was certain that he never should forget that keen, resolute pair of eyes.

William Benn, at the sight of the stranger, exclaimed: "Charlie, what on earth are you doing here?"

Charlie hesitated in the entrance to the veranda, looking not at Benn but at Ricardo.

"I came up because it was time to come."

Benn whirled upon Ricardo.

"Go up to your room!" he said tersely.

And Ricardo fled, without a further introduction.

In his room, however, he could not rest content; his very soul was on fire to hear what might pass between William Benn and the stranger who was called Charlie.

And, since he had prepared the way before and knew every step of it, he left the room via the window, and climbed swiftly down to the veranda roof. On it he moved with the utmost caution, for he could hear the voices of the two speaking excitedly beneath him.

It was a cold, clear, mountain night. The stars burned very low; a wind was leaping up the valley with pulses of strength, and then falling off again to murmurs. And Ricardo shivered as it struck him and chilled him to the bone.

He found, however, a better place than he had at first hoped for. He discovered that he could slip over the edge of the roof at the farthest corner and there he could stand entirely screened by the tangled branches of a climbing rose. The thorny limbs whipped and frayed him, from time to time, but he paid little attention to that annoyance; for after his first moment on the rail of the veranda, leaning and looking on at this dialogue, nothing else was of importance to him except the words which were passing between his accepted master and this newcomer.

"Cut the talking short," he heard William Benn say.

"The fact is that you wouldn't wait for me! You've chucked the job; or else you've blundered ahead with it and spoiled everything!"

"I've tackled the job alone. I had to," said Charlie. "Not alone. I had Sam and Mat with me."

"Where are they now?"

"Dead!" said Charlie.

8

◉

The Right Sort of Men

The announcement that the two men were dead threw William Benn into a passion. He paced the "bridge" unsteadily.

"I search the world to get the right sort of men," said he, "and I train them, and I spend money on them like water. And then you get your hands on them and spend them like greenbacks! By gosh, Charlie, I'll not carry on with this sort of handling on your part!"

Charlie sat in a chair near the inside wall; he kept erect in it, and Ricardo could guess that this was simply because the man had spent so many hours in the saddle that he was accustomed to bearing his own shoulder weight without slouching.

To the outburst of big William Benn the other made no rejoinder. He merely shrugged his shoulders and continued to watch his companion with a fixed stare, as one who sees what is before him, but also finds the time and energy to think of something else.

"Go on, then," said William Benn. "You lost the two of them?"

"I lost the pair of them."

"And what have you got in exchange?"

"Fifteen thousand."

"Fifteen thousand? They were worth ten thousand apiece!"

Young Ricardo listened with bulging eyes. In the business of William Benn and this other fellow, it appeared that human beings were set down at a cash price. He could not help wondering if his own blood, therefore, would be shed for a certain number of thousands! It cast another light upon the many kindnesses of his benefactor.

"Ten thousand is too high a price," said Charlie, "for any gent under thirty. You know that, Bill. Don't try to kid me out of it. I know the facts!"

"You got fifteen thousand. Don't tell me that you got it out of the Ranger bank?"

"That's where it came from."

He seemed to have settled himself to resist a tirade on this subject, and Ricardo caught his breath, expecting the same thing. But nothing was said by William Benn. Instead, he raised himself to his full height, and then a little upon his toes, and one clenched hand was raised quivering until it was level with the top of his head.

But he allowed that hand to fall without speaking a word. Words, after all, were feeble, compared with such a gesture.

"You took down fifteen thousand," he said, "and you knew that we could get half a million out of that place?"

"You want to make up your mind without listening to sense," said Charlie.

"Lemme hear the great Charles Perkins, then," said William Benn with irony. "Lemme hear all that was going on inside of your head, Charlie!"

"We had the night watchman fixed. You know that," said Charlie.

"Of course, I know that. I did the fixing!"

The truth began to break in upon the unwilling mind of Ricardo. This generous Benn, this kind benefactor, was simply a robber—and a robber, among other things, of a bank!

"I did the fixing and I did it cheap. As neat a job as I ever turned in my life," said Benn, with pride.

"It was too cheap to last," said Charlie.

"Who says that?"

"I say that. He wasn't satisfied. He began to see that the bank couldn't be had except through him. He came to me and wanted more money."

"You told him to be quiet, of course!"

"I didn't! I didn't tell him that. The reason was that he meant what he said."

"You let him bluff you?"

"Billy," said the other, quietly, "no one bluffs me, and you know it!"

William Benn shrugged his shoulders and took an impatient step or two up and down the room.

"Go on," said he. "What happened? You gave him more coin?"

"I gave him five hundred on the spot and I promised him a lot more!"

"You let him bleed you—and of course then he came back again."

"He did."

"I knew that!"

"When he came back," said Charlie Perkins softly, "I was half of a mind to chuck the entire job just for the sake of putting a slug of lead through him. And I wish that I had, the sneaking traitor!"

He added: "The whole job may teach you that if you want a man's job done, you've got to pay for a man. You've been out fishing again, and you've landed a soft-looking sucker, by my way of thinking!"

"You mean the greaser kid?" asked William Benn, carelessly.

Ricardo, flushing with anger, could guess that they were talking about him.

"I mean just that," said Charlie. "What's he good for? What are you going to do with him?"

"He may be a loss," admitted Benn, "but then again I may cut my way into a lot of money with that boy, Charlie. He has a touch of something rare about him. But go on with your yarn. I want to know how the boys died."

"You've got to wait for a minute, then. I say that the watchman began to drink, and when he began to drink, he began to talk."

"About what?"

"About money that he expected to have before long. He began to let people know that he expected to come into a fine bundle of hard cash, and when that happened, he would do his best to change his way of living. He'd buy a ranch and settle down and live like a white man!"

"And you let him talk like that?"

"I warned him not to. But he laughed at me. He began to know it all. A fool like that can't be handled—a cheap fool like that, Bill!"

"You throw it up to me because I bought him?"

"You'll see how much of him you bought before long!"

"Well, then, it went along like this: and you let the thing drift into shallow water. Great Scott, Charlie, couldn't you keep a lookout?"

"I was keeping a lookout day and night. I was wearing eyes in the back of my head, and sleeping no sounder than a wild cat. I wanted to go ahead and make the break before another day passed, but I wanted to wait for you, too."

"My fault, I suppose?" sneered William Benn.

"Of course, it was your fault! You should have known that your place was there, where the deal was cooking. Instead of that you were off gathering in another crop of suckers! You were getting this thin-handed beauty of a greaser boy! That was what kept you so occupied!"

William Benn shrugged his shoulders high and let his big head thrust out.

"Keep to your own work, Charlie. Don't horn into mine. Now what happens? You wanted to wait for me—but, after all, by gosh, you *didn't* wait for me!"

"Of course, I didn't. Because I saw, finally, that things were off balance, and that the fool watchman was all ready to break out talking. And that, as a matter of fact, was what actually happened!"

"Let's have it short and sweet, Charlie. I've had enough of the preliminaries."

"I got the boys together. We planted everything as carefully as we could. We had the combination of the small safe and we had the powder for the big safe."

"Powder?"

"Soup. You know what I mean."

"The watchman was going his rounds. He gave us the high sign. We went straight in through the front door. The watchman was to keep going the rounds and make sure that everything was all right on the outside. I sent the boys after the little safe, first of all. We gutted it. That's where the fifteen thousand came from, and that was only a small part of what was there."

"Go on. You wasted some time on the little safe and then you went for the big vault?"

"We went for that. I had the yellow soap to make the mold. Mat had the soup. And as we got up to the door of the big safe they opened on us!"

"Who did?"

"Why, there were eight men with repeating rifles in that bank, old son. The watchman had talked, all right. And finally he'd talked to the president. Another man than Ranger would have taken things easy and simply put on an extra guard, but Ranger, he wanted to use that bank as a trap and snap the lot of us. And he came close to doing it."

"Ranger's a fighting man, of course," said William Benn.

"He is," said the other, "but he's fought his last fight."

"He's done for?"

"He is. They blasted away at us from behind cover. The boys went down with their shooting irons in their hands. They didn't have a chance. The fellows had switched on a big ceiling light that showed us up perfectly, and the two lads went down almost with the first volley. I managed to smash that light in the ceiling with a lucky shot. Then I worked out of the bank. I lay for a minute alongside of one of those hounds and shot toward the safe, like I was one of them. There was such a racket, and the room was so full of smoke, that nobody could be sure of anything. I got through to the back door, and there who did I run into but the night watchman. I didn't waste a bullet on him. I smashed his head with the butt of my Colt."

"And then you rode for it, Charlie?"

"I did not. I waited an hour. Then I went to Ranger's town house. I knew pretty well that he'd be spending the night there instead of going back to his ranch. I rang the front-door bell and told the Mexican girl that came to answer it that I wanted to see Ranger about the robbery. Ranger himself came down into the hall.

"'I can tell you about the third man at the bank,' says I.

"'I want to know that,' says he. 'Who was he?'

"'Me!' says I. 'Fill your hand.'

"He made a quick draw, but I was ready for him, and I stopped his heart with my first shot. Then I started for home, and here I am!"

9

He Hunts by Night

No dweller in the southwest can be without some information concerning gun brawls, but though Ricardo had heard of battles before, he never had seen or heard the slayer confess as had Charles Perkins. With solid satisfaction Perkins related the killings. He had smashed the head of a watchman at a bank—a treacherous man, it appeared, but even that hardly made the slaying less brutal. Then he had gone to the home of the man who had dared to trap him, and had shot down that unfortunate in cold blood on the threshold of his house.

From the grim, contended face of Perkins, Ricardo looked to William Benn to see some signs of horror or bewilderment as a result of this narrative, but there was no trace of such a reaction. With gathered brows, Benn stared at his companion, but at the same time the corners of his mouth were tilted in that smile which had grown so familiarly hateful to Ricardo in the past few days. Afterward, to be sure, Benn changed his manner a little.

"Did anybody spot you?"

"I think the greaser girl might have known me," said the other carelessly.

"You think? Then you're down for murder!"

"Not the first," answered Charlie with a shrug of his shoulders.

"The first since you've been pulling with me," said Benn. "Charlie, I don't run things that way, and——"

"You don't run things that way," sneered Perkins. "You don't kill! No, you don't publish it, you mean to say. Man, man, do you think I'm all blind or half fool and that I don't know? I tell you, Bill, I know about the story of the Black Friday in Tucson when you started with Steve Chalmers——"

"Shut up!" snapped William Benn.

He was rigid with anger, and Perkins nodded with a grin.

"That's under your skin, I take it!" said he.

"When they run down your trail, what if they come here?" asked Benn.

"They'll never run down my trail. They never do."

" 'Never' is a long word, Charlie."

"D'you want me to retire, Bill?"

"You retire from me," said Benn.

Perkins rose.

"You make that final?" he snapped.

"I make that final."

"Darn you, then," answered Perkins, "I'll give you your split! And then I'll——"

He drew out his wallet as he spoke, but William Benn raised his hand.

"I don't want your money," said he.

"*My* money?" echoed the other in astonishment.

"Your money. I don't want any of your money, because I don't want any of your luck."

"My luck has never taken me up the river," said the other with satisfaction.

"It'll take you up Salt Creek, though, one of these days," remarked Benn. "I don't like your way of working. Four men died for the fifteen thousand you have in your pocket there."

There had been proof enough that William Benn was a criminal, a bank robber, a planner of one could hardly say how many other crimes. And from the talk of Perkins it was more than apparent that Benn had dipped his hands deep enough in the blood of his fellows, and yet as he stood before Perkins and disclaimed any share in that money which was so soaked with human blood, the heart of Ricardo warmed toward the big man who was his master.

Perkins merely sneered.

"This makes me seventy-five hundred in," he said.

"I suppose it does," answered Benn contemptuous. "You don't remember that Mat had a wife?"

"And what about her?" asked the other, harshly.

"Doesn't she come in for the share he would have had?"

"Darn him and her both," answered Perkins. "You take care of your own charities. I'll take care of mine. Mat was a bungler. I always told you he was a bungler!"

William Benn lifted his long, bony forefinger.

"Every dead man is a bungler," said he. "Some day men will be calling you a fool, too! But I'm tired of the talk and

I'm tired of you. Get out, Charlie. I never want to lay eyes on you again."

This he said without passion, but Ricardo held his breath. For, after all, this was defiance of one who had two murders freshly upon his hands. The light of a third murder showed green in the eyes of Perkins as he watched Benn.

Finally he broke out: "You can't bluff me and sham me, Bill. I don't take water from you. And I dunno but that I got as good a right to this here house as you have!"

"Are you going to brave me out like this, in my own house?" asked Benn savagely, striking twice on the top of the veranda table in the violence of his anger.

"And what if I do?" asked the other, growing more cool as Benn grew hot. "What if I do stand up to you? You don't like that, do you? But I tell you, Billy, you don't mean nothing to me. I've seen them that turned pale when they heard the mentioning of your name. I've seen them that could never meet your eye. But I ain't that way. I stand up to you. I meet your eye right now. There ain't a thing about you that means anything to me!"

As he delivered this defiance in a tone of contempt, sneering broadly and openly, Ricardo wondered with all his heart; for even that cold-eyed man, Perkins, fresh from his crimes and reeking from his murders, still seemed to him a mere name, a mere ghost of fear compared with the unspeakable terror that surrounded Benn.

He flinched as he clung to the sill of the window, waiting for a flash of fire to dart from the hand of the master of the house—while the other man pitched headlong to the floor, dead.

However, nothing like this happened. But the door behind Perkins suddenly framed the enormous form of the Negro, Selim, who slipped in like a vast stalking cat, picking up his feet with anxious care and placing them toes first, and holding his vast hands in readiness.

Perkins looked suddenly like a mere child, gesticulating on a stage, pretending to be a man, compared with the monster behind him.

William Benn said: "You're a brave fellow, Charlie, to stand up to me like this. I suppose you're inviting me to a fight. Is that it?"

"If you've got more heart in you than any mangy dog,"

declared Perkins, "how else could you take what I've said to you?"

"But," said Benn, "I never waste my time on murdering fellows like you. I leave you to others. All right, Selim. Take him."

He made a little gesture as he spoke the last words, and before they were out of his mouth, Selim leaped lightly from behind. There was no time for Perkins to take warning except by some electric premonition of the danger that was flying towards him. But now he whirled suddenly, reaching for a gun—and found himself wrapped around and around by the huge arms of the Negro.

There was a writhing, a long, gasping groan, and then— as Ricardo grew sick and his head swam—William Benn went on: "Don't kill him, Selim. I don't want to kill him."

For answer, Selim tossed the helpless form of his victim across his arm. He pointed an eloquent finger at Benn and then drew it across his throat.

"He hunts by night," said Selim.

His meaning was perfectly clear.

"He hunts by night," smiled Benn. "But at the same time, he knows that my house is full of cats all ready to catch such rats as he. Take him away, Selim. I'll go with you!"

Selim turned and went from the veranda, and William Benn went after him, lighting a cigarette.

So that odd scene came to an end, and Ricardo Perez leaned back against the wall and, clutching at the vine, he drew in long breaths and made sure that he was not going to faint after all. For when the tension had ended, he felt it most of all.

His head cleared rapidly, however, for the cool wind up the valley was fanning the mists from his brain, and he was able to think matters over with some degree of precision. Quite enough had been said for him to realize why he had been wanted by Benn in the first place. He was to be the food which Benn fed into the mouth of danger, as he had fed the last two, in charge of Perkins. And after some preliminary training, he would be put to work on crooked business of some sort. That very day, had not his master urged him to begin to practice the use of the revolver?

There was a peculiar temptation to remain in the house, return quietly to his room and to bed, and then let affairs take their own course. Since William Benn intended to use him for no good end, was it not true that he was justified, on his side, in letting matters drift as they would and then separating himself from Benn at the critical moment, while his hands still were free?

But, he began to see, as he thought the matter over and recalled the devilish smile and the bloodless face of Benn, that once thoroughly committed to the hands of that monster it would be extremely difficult to break away from him thereafter.

So thought Ricardo, at least, and with that he made up his mind to leave at once. He would only return to his chamber and put together a bundle of necessities for the journey. After that, he certainly would not attempt to so much as take a horse, but would strike off on the long homeward journey on foot.

So he set about climbing back up the roof, and found that he was so thoroughly chilled and unnerved that he once or twice almost lost his grip and ended his life on the instant.

However, he was naturally active and sure, and so at last he had his hands on the sill of his window and drew himself in to safety.

There he leaned against the wall for a moment, breathing hard, and finally collected himself and lighted his lamp. No sooner was the chimney pressed down into the guards and the flame turned up than he knew that he was not alone in the room. Something waited in the farther corner, and watched him with serious eyes!

10

◉

What Was Benn's Business?

He remained for an instant leaning above the lamp gathering his nerves and setting his teeth; and the white flame of battle which burns in the hearts of the brave burned up fierce and steady in the heart of Ricardo. Quietly he slipped his knife into his hand, then he whirled on his heel and flung himself straight at that waiting danger.

He saw it only as he leaped, with knife raised—and it was the long, ugly, bloodless face of William Benn! A long arm shot out to meet him. A fist of steel caught him fairly between the eyes; he buckled backward and fell heavily on his back.

His face and throat and chest were wet and cold when he wakened. He lay on the bed, and William Benn sat beside him, smoking. The boy sat up; a trickle of blood ran down from a cut between his eyes.

"It's better to bleed than to bruise," said William Benn. "If the knuckle hadn't cut the skin, your face would have puffed up like a balloon. How does your head feel?"

Ricardo looked cautiously at the big man. He was trying to make out whether this casual tone was the effect of irony or of a really friendly forgiveness. His very mind was read by William Benn, who said: "You wonder what's going on inside my head. I'll tell you, my lad. Young boys are like tom cats. They have to walk out in the evening. And so it was with my young friend Ricardo. He walked out. He came back a little late, and as he lighted his lamp, he felt that there was something in the room with him. Now, some boys would scream and jump for the door. Some might even dive out the window at a time like that. But the tiger jumps at the thing that makes a noise in its cave. Afterward, it asks questions. And so Ricardo stiffened as he felt a thing in the room, and then he jumped for my throat. Is that it? And he hardly saw me as he was in mid-air. Am I right, Ricardo?"

Ricardo sat up on the edge of the bed, his head still a little hazy from the effects of that tremendous blow, but rapidly clearing. There was a slight stiffness inside his coat and he knew, with wonder, that while he lay senseless, his knife had been restored to its sheath.

"Yes," he said, "that's true. There was something in the corner. It scared me."

"And so," said the other, "we balance accounts. I forgive you for drawing the knife on me, and you forgive me for knocking you down. Is that right?"

"Yes," said Ricardo.

"And fair?"

"Yes," said the boy.

"No hard feelings remaining behind?"

Ricardo looked up steadily into the ugly face of his master.

"How can I tell?" said he. "How can I tell what goes on inside your mind?"

"Is that it?" asked the other. "Well, you'll have my own word for it. I say that I have no hard feelings about it. What about you?"

Ricardo hesitated. And then he saw that he had waited too long to tell a pleasant lie.

"I don't know," he replied.

"You understand," went on the big man, "that if I hadn't bowled you over, you would have sunk that knife right through my throat?"

Ricardo said nothing.

"My neck is not made of iron, you know," went on the older man.

"No," said Ricardo mechanically.

"Well, let that slide for a moment. There's another thing that you and I should talk about a little. I asked you to stay in your room. Sent you up to your room rather harshly, I think."

Ricardo made no comment on this statement.

"But you didn't choose to stay here. You went out through the window. Well, I understand that. Young boys have to walk out."

He laughed. He had, at times, a peculiar, soundless laughter, which gave to his face an expression even more uncanny than the smile.

"You walked out. But where did you walk?"

Ricardo, feeling that danger lay ahead, set his teeth. Then he looked boldly at his master.

"I wanted to see the horses," he said. "It was too early to go to sleep. So I went out and took a look at the horses."

"Naturally. You like horses, don't you?"

"I do."

"Did you talk to Lew about them?"

"I didn't want to bother him. Besides, I was supposed to be in bed."

"Of course you were! I like to have a boy who speaks out frankly when he's done something wrong. Not very wrong, mind you!"

44

"No," said Ricardo. "I didn't think that it was very wrong."

"And you were wise not to talk to Lew. He's got a crabbed disposition. He's a rascal, is that same Lew. Like you, my boy, he carries a knife. But even a sharper knife than yours, I'd say!"

And the wicked smile tilted the corners of the mouth of William Benn.

"Thanks," said Ricardo. "I'll remember that."

"And," said William Benn, "I wouldn't let Lew think that you hang about the stables, spying on the horses. He wouldn't like that, either. He's touchy, in fact. He's as touchy as a cat!"

He rose and went to the door.

"Good night, Ricardo," said he cheerfully.

"Good night," said the boy.

With the door half open, the big man turned as by an after-thought and rested a hand on the foot of the bed.

"By the way, Ricardo," said he, "while you were going to the stable and back, did you stop anywhere?"

Ricardo lifted his head. He had fancied himself at the end of this dangerous questioning, and this shocked him for a moment so that he could not answer.

And, before he had a chance to regain his equilibrium, the big man continued:

"Did you stop, for instance, on the outside of the veranda? Did you do that, Ricardo?"

Ricardo felt his face turn white. His heart fairly stopped.

William Benn quietly closed the door and came back into the room.

"And while you were outside the veranda, did you hear me talking with my—friend?"

Ricardo could not speak.

"Answer!" said Benn in a terrible voice.

"Yes!" said the boy, and passed his hand inside his coat.

For he felt sure that he was about to die, and it was as impossible for him to surrender meekly to any odds as it is for a wild cat to die in the pack of hounds with claws still sheathed, mildly recognizing and accepting fate.

So he gripped his knife handle, and he waited desperately with his eyes upon the face of William Benn.

He thought, at first, that Benn would rush straight upon him and beat him to the floor—and then a grip of those

45

terrible hands would end 'his life. But Benn did not stir; it was merely that his eyes had changed and grown more awful, and that the peculiar smile was on his lips again.

"You heard how much?" he asked.

And Ricardo answered: "I heard that you planned a robbery. That Charles Perkins killed two men."

"You heard that?"

"Yes," said Ricardo, bracing himself. Then he added: "And I heard you break with Perkins because you wouldn't have blood money."

He stood, as it were, upon the brink of a precipice. The slightest misstep would be death. And his stepping had to be done with words. Therefore, he held his breath and waited. He was ready for the struggle; but he knew how it must end.

Then it seemed to Ricardo that the pressure upon his nerves and upon his brain was less. He felt that something dangerous in the big man was relaxing, though, to be sure, his manner had not altered.

"You heard a great deal, for a young man," said William Benn. "You heard that I'm a robber and not a merchant?"

"I know that you're not a merchant," said Ricardo.

"And suppose I give you liberty to go back to your home?" said William Benn.

"I know what you mean," answered the boy. "Well, if that happens, I'll do no talking."

"Are you able to keep your mouth still?" asked the other with a sudden return of his violence.

"Yes," said Ricardo. "I've kept secrets for years!"

And he looked straight back into the eyes of William Benn.

The latter obviously had come to a point at which he hesitated.

He went to the window and looked out and Ricardo actually considered leaping at him from behind. Somehow, he was able to put that thought out of his mind.

Then William Benn turned sharply around on him.

"I want to talk to you again," said he. "In a way, my life lies in your hand. And there you have a window open. But, if I were you, I would not try to go through that window again tonight. In the morning we'll have a chance to talk things over again. Good night, Ricardo!"

He left the room, and Ricardo ran to the window and

46

looked out. Now, before the master had a chance to give the alarm or post a watch, was his time to escape.

But suddenly he knew that he could not do it. His nerve was drained away. He went back to his bed and flung himself upon it. So totally was he exhausted that his body was shaking. He closed his eyes and tried to think about the perils of his position, but instead of thought, sleep rushed suddenly over his mind in a dark, all-subduing wave.

11

◉

Your Natural Gentleman

But when the morning came, Ricardo was totally himself. He even felt a certain gayety as he dressed, looking forward to the dangerous meeting with William Benn. When he went down to breakfast, he found that a stranger was with Benn, waiting for him, and he was introduced to Doctor Humphry Clauson. He was a dapper, small man, with the head of a scholar and thoughtful, farsighted eyes. It was he who did most of the talking during the breakfast, keeping the conversational ball rolling with perfect ease and courtesy so that his manner awed Ricardo almost as much as the fierce strength of William Benn.

Then, as they finished their coffee, they turned the talk back upon Ricardo himself. It was Benn who brought up the subject with his usual directness, for he said: "Now, doctor, we'd better get down to cases. What's to be done with Ricardo Perez?"

The doctor looked in his thoughtful way at Ricardo, and suddenly the boy was filled with fear by the impersonal nature of that gaze.

"One likes to have all the facts at hand before making up one's mind," remarked the doctor. "There's nothing worse than trying to make a decision before all the testimony is in."

"And what information do you want?" asked William Benn. "I have enough, I take it," he went on. "I know that Ricardo eavesdropped, for instance. That goes for something!"

"Of course it does," admitted the other. "Ricardo eavesdropped. I rather like that myself."

"You like it?" muttered William Benn. "Do you know what you're saying, doctor?"

"I think I do. It showed that the lad has pluck and spirit."

"I knew that before. I brought him along because of that," said William Benn.

The doctor, through a pause, looked earnestly at Ricardo; and the boy felt very much as though he were an anatomical specimen being studied with interest because of its very peculiarities.

"If he's worth saving, he's worth knowing," said the doctor. "But we don't even know who he is."

"He's the adopted son of a muleteer," answered Benn. "His name is Ricardo Perez. I thought I told you that before."

"Of course you did. But, as far as I can see, that means nothing at all."

"And why not, if you please?"

"Because," said the doctor, "the probability is that there is not a drop of Mexican blood in his veins. He's an American, no doubt. But the color of his eyes and hair—Irish, I'd say, predominantly."

Ricardo opened those blue eyes very wide. He never had thought of such a thing as this!

"Irish? Not greaser? I tell you, doctor," insisted William Benn, "that there are lots of Mexicans who have blue eyes and fair hair."

Then Ricardo tilted back his head.

"I *am* a Mexican," said he. "I would not be a gringo!"

He knew that this, beyond a doubt, was a dangerous speech. Nevertheless, a sense of patriotism forced him to make it.

"You hear him talk for himself," remarked Benn.

"I hear, of course," replied the doctor. "However, that's not finished."

He took out a cigar case and opened it upon a dozen black cigars, no thicker than a pencil. He offered one to William Benn, who refused it with almost a shudder.

"Those villainous things will poison you," he assured his guest.

The doctor lighted one and puffed at it with loving care.

"What he thinks about himself is obviously important," said he, "but now let's get at the bottom of the matter. Mr. Perez, did any one ever tell you that you are a Mexican?"

"Why," answered Ricardo, "of course I'm a Mexican! I've grown up with a Mexican family."

"They found you on their doorstep?"

"Yes."

"Did they know who put you there?"

"No."

"Tell me—do Mexicans often abandon their children?"

"No. Never, I believe."

"I believe the same. No matter how many come, each is the gift of Heaven and must be treated as such. But now get on with this question. In the Mexican section of the town, a child is found wailing at a closed door. A Mexican, therefore, had left the child there, because only a Mexican would be apt to be passing through that portion of the town after dark. A Mexican left the child there, but, obviously again, it was not a Mexican youngster."

"A point that I don't follow," said William Benn.

"A point that is not true!" said Ricardo fiercely.

"Be quiet, young man," said the doctor, with more irritation in his words than in his voice. "I am trying to do for you some simple thinking that you should have been able to do for yourself, long ago! I say that for several reasons you are not Mexican. We've just agreed that Mexicans don't abandon their children. And, even if they did, how many chances are there that the abandoned child would have fair hair and blue eyes?"

"I've pointed out that there are plenty of light Mexicans!" said William Benn. "Don't be stubborn as a mule, doctor."

"Most of those pale Mexicans still have a touch of smoke in their eyes," answered the doctor. "And their skin is apt to be sallow. But young Perez has the true Nordic look. Ricardo, tell me—you know your town pretty well?"

"I know it," said Ricardo confidently, "from top to bottom. But I don't know the town as well as I know that I am a Mexican, and that I won't be anything else!"

"A patriot," said the doctor sneering faintly. "Well, Ricardo, did you know a single other Mexican in that town with blue eyes?"

49

Ricardo glanced into his mind with a studious frown. Then he grew alarmed.

"No," he said hurriedly, "not one I——"

He paused with a gasp, as he realized what this admission meant. Then he cried: "But you've already said that white men would not be around the Mexican part of the town during the night!"

"I have. But those same Mexicans are free and easy. They don't love work for its own sake. Is that true?"

"They work enough to live," said Ricardo haughtily. "And that is enough for them. They are not worshipers of dollars!"

William Benn scowled at this, but the doctor merely laughed pleasantly and went on: "Those same gallant Mexicans are not above sticking up a stage, now and then, or shooting up a party of travelers, and holding some of them for ransom?"

"There are villains in every country," answered Ricardo. "But the Mexican is naturally adventurous and brave. He loves danger. Therefore, he might commit such crimes!"

"You defend them well enough," nodded the doctor. "However, I want you to admit that such things are possible. Suppose a band—I don't know what band, naturally—had run off with a family, or a part of a family, to hold for ransom. They find a young child of what?"

"Four years, perhaps," said Ricardo, intensely interested in the narrative in spite of himself.

"A child of four. They don't want to roughride into the mountains with a baby like that. Too big to be carried in the arms and too small to sit in a saddle, of course. So the leader hands the little one to a follower. 'Get rid of it,' says he. And, like the good robber in the fairy story, of course the follower relents. He will not kill the boy. He'll simply drop him into the middle of a Mexican town and let him take his luck. That is the same as death, so far as the purpose of the bandit leader is concerned."

"A very complicated explanation," said William Benn.

"Find a simpler one that is half as logical," said the doctor. "But what's the matter with young Perez? He looks ill!"

Ricardo, in fact, had risen slowly from his chair. He steadied himself for a moment, gripping the back of it.

"I'm going up to my room—for a moment," said he.

And slowly he walked away through the door.

"I don't follow that, either," said William Benn. "Nor do I see the point of the questions you've been asking him! *Is* there any point?"

"For a really great man," said the doctor, "you are obtuse! Why did you bring me here?"

"To take your opinion as to what this youngster is worth— if anything. He must either be used or knocked on the head. I wanted your opinion. Instead, you begin to build up yarns about his birth!"

"And by doing that," answered the other, "I've gained everything that I wanted to know."

He laughed triumphantly in the puzzled face of Benn.

"In the first place, I've discovered that the boy is enormously proud. Proud as an eagle. Proud as a lion, William!"

"He's proud enough. But what of that?"

"Take the average youngster, and you'd find that he could very easily swing his allegiance from a nation like Mexico, which isn't exactly at the crest of the wave, to a rich people like the Americans. But this Ricardo Perez, the adopted son of a muleteer, finds it difficult to do. He hardly can manage it at all. It makes him ill."

"An absurd affectation," said William Benn. "No man is sensitive as all that."

"He turned white," said the doctor calmly. "Don't shut your mind to the truth. At this moment he's in his room in an agony, confronting his change of race, holding his head in his hands, hating me for showing him the probable facts!"

"And what is the great importance of all this, doctor?"

"I'm a believer in blood, Benn. And I believe that the lad is taking this affair as a gentleman would."

"Perhaps you're right," said Benn more harshly than ever. "I wanted a clever thief, and a brave robber, and a handy crook. I've picked up a natural gentleman, instead!"

"And who," asked the doctor calmly, "makes a better thief, a braver robber, and a more talented criminal in all directions than your natural gentleman?"

12

A Modern Robin Hood?

This point was made quietly, but it stunned William Benn to silence. He stared at his companion; and then at last he shook his head.

"The kid knows too much," he declared. "I can't have him around. And yet——"

"Well?"

"The fact is that I have a superstitious feeling about him. There's no use going into details. But somehow I got an impression, when I found him, that I'd found a pot of gold."

"At the end of the rainbow, eh?" smiled the doctor. "Well, Benn, this is your business more than mine. You go about it exactly as you please. I'm perfectly indifferent, but I've tried to point out the facts to you. If you can keep him in your hand—why, you might make a fortune out of him!"

"A gentleman!" muttered Benn, chiefly to himself. "The lazy, ragged son of a muleteer!"

"A gentleman too lazy to work," said the doctor. "In the old days, they used to go to war. Now and again you'll find them, today, buccaneering on Wall Street, say. And besides that, they have their representatives in the underworld."

"You may be right," said William Benn. "The first hunch is the best one. I thought I found gold; perhaps I've found diamonds! Open up to me, old fellow. What would you do with him?"

"He speaks perfect English. Even his Mexican is almost too close to pure Castilian to make him the son of a muleteer!"

"That's explained easily enough. He has ears."

"And he had the sense to pick and choose. I would finish his education, if I were you."

William Benn exclaimed with impatience:

"Spend eight years putting him through schools?"

"Not a bit, but spend eight months, say polishing his manners, giving him just a touch of books, making him familiar with the ways of the world. It won't be hard! It's never a struggle to teach a hawk to fly!"

William Benn frowned and shook his head again.

"And who will teach him? And what should he be taught?" he asked.

"One should keep the Mexican flavor," said the doctor thoughtfully. "By all means, one should keep that, because he'll be working in the States, largely, I suppose. And there's nothing that gives an edge to a gentleman's position in the States like a foreign flavor. We Americans are a little suspicious of native high-breeding. We take it for granted that a grown man ought to have calluses on his hands; we like a dash of roughness. Foreigners are different. We're inclined to look up to them. They supply, in a way, our taste for a nobility."

"Are you going to make him a nobleman?" asked William Benn, grinning in his peculiar, fiendish fashion.

"I'm thinking of it," said the other. "But I don't know. Suppose, for instance, that we simply make him a member of a fine old Spanish family."

The door opened. Ricardo entered the room.

"How much have you heard?" asked Benn, without anger.

"That I'm to be a member of a fine old Spanish family," answered the boy, and laughed. It was not mirth or enjoyment that rang in his laughter, but a peculiar bitterness.

He added: "And suppose that after all it turns out to be wrong—and I learn that I *am* a Mexican?"

"Then," said Benn, "your skin will still be whole."

Ricardo shrugged his shoulders.

"Well," he said, "I'll never turn back. You can show me the way!"

"Exactly," said the doctor. "I expected that! And I think, my young friend, that William Benn will show you the way to a very gay life!"

"Am I to send him to Spain to make him a Spaniard?" asked Benn, with his grin. Then he added, striking his hands noisily together: "There's another chance—by Heaven, I have it! We'll ring in old Mancos! I have a hold on him. He'll have a visit from a nephew or a cousin from Spain. A young Señor Mancos will arrive—Ricardo Mancos of Andalusia, eh?"

William Benn leaned back in his chair and, for the first time, Ricardo heard frank, booming laughter from his lips.

"An excellent idea," said the doctor. "In the house of Mancos he could learn everything that he needs to know—except what you and I and a few others will teach him. In a year, William, he'll be ready to graduate!"

Ricardo, hearing himself cast about, as it were, from hand to hand, made no comment; for he began to feel that he had been caught in a current so strong that no effort of his own could set him free.

Now that the decision was made, William Benn turned to the boy and said to him gravely: "You can pick and choose for yourself. I don't ask for any oaths or promises. You see how the thing stands. If you say the word, I'll back up and let you loose. You can return to your foster father's pig-sty. You can grow up as an honest man. You can work as a cow-puncher, and spend your fifty dollars a month on the last Saturday night, and pawn your watch for cigarette money to last you to the next pay day. Or you can break ground in a mine, and break your back at the same time swinging a singlejack. On the other hand, you can make up your mind to be a crook—as I am—as the doctor is. We live easy, have plenty of ready cash, and every day is a game.

"You wonder what I'm to get out of making you a crook. I'll tell you. I set you up in business. I teach you the trade. I give you an education. In return for that, you pay me fifty percent of everything that passes through your hands inside the next five years, and besides that, you're to do what I tell you.

"Suppose you accept my offer, you may double cross me later on. Well, I can't prevent that, but the minute you try to knife me, you have trouble on your hands. You've seen Selim, and Wong, and Lew. You've met the doctor. You know a little about me. But that's not all. I'm an organizer, young fellow. I have a machine at my back, and if I have any reason to suspect you, I'll smash you. Be sure of that! I'll smash you flat as pancakes.

"Now I've laid my cards on the table. I always do in a case like this. I don't force your hand. There's the door. If you want to be an honest man, get out. If you want to stay with me, you know what it leads to. I'll tell you one last thing. *If* you stay with me, the machine then works with you and for you. Nobody that plays the game with me is a pauper. Lew, for instance, has five thousand in the bank. I'm rich enough to retire. I won't because the game is too much fun.

"I think that's about all. Now, what do you say?"

Of course, young Ricardo listened to his talk, but what he had really heard was that reference to his foster father's house, and to the labor in the fields; and, whatever else he was, Ricardo was a boy who hated work. He sat for a time with his fingers locked together. One wind of desire blew him hot, and another wind of desire blew him cold. If ever the good and evil geniuses of a man stood at his elbow and whispered words of counter-advice, they stood now beside Ricardo and poured their uncanny wisdom upon his heart.

He looked at the other two. They were studiously avoiding him. The doctor, puffing slowly at his unspeakable cigar, looked upward toward the ceiling, where the thin blue-white rings were dissolving in rank mist; and William Benn had folded his arms and looked straight before him with that fiendish smile upon his lips. A fiend, indeed, and a tempter!

Then Ricardo closed his eyes and thought of the kindness and of the honesty of Antonio Perez, and how it had made his life a thing of gold; and just as he made up his mind upon that point, he thought of the dark and crowded hut on a summer's night, when the stove had just died down, but the rank odors of food still lingered everywhere, and even the hot and dusty street seemed a paradise by comparison.

He opened his eyes again and viewed the comfort and the cleanliness of the room in which he sat now. Selim, with miraculous softness, was clearing away the breakfast dishes, never letting them clink—lest the noise should break in upon the thoughts of this boy! Suppose a day should come when he, Ricardo, had three such clever servants as Lew and Wong and Selim!

Besides, there are ways and ways of leading a lawless life, and does not every one know about the gentle and noble brigands who take only from the rich and give ever to the poor? Are there not modern Robin Hoods?

So thought Ricardo, and suddenly he started up from the table and answered: "I'll go with you, William Benn!"

The big man relaxed suddenly, and it was apparent to

Ricardo that William Benn had worn the smile merely to mask the real anxiety which he felt, for this appeared to be an important matter to the criminal—far more important than Ricardo could understand.

The great hand went out, and the long arm. The hand of Ricardo was seized upon.

"Now, kid," said William Benn, "you and I are going to find the end of the rainbow together."

"You might remember me when you split up the profits," said the doctor, with a faint smile.

And he, also, shook hands with Ricardo.

"If you're a strong man, as I think you are," said he, "you'll never regret to-day. If you're a weak fellow, you'll have some pangs and—go to death on account of them. I wish you luck, Ricardo—Mancos!"

And they laughed together, all three, Ricardo a little hysterically.

13

◉

What Comes of Playing with Fire

The town of El Real was American in situation more than in fact, and it, therefore, possessed more Mexican than American ideals. For this reason, the position of Señor Don Edgardo Mancos was not affected by his business. He ran a large gaming house, and yet he lived among the elect on the broad-backed hill at the rear of the town, and there was no member of the community more respected than Don Edgardo. The large and solemn front of his house was like a guarantee of character; and the large and imposing front of Señor Mancos in person was another reënforcement of the same ideal.

Perhaps because he had such a business as the gaming house, he made sure that his whole establishment was run upon a most impressive basis of gentility. The house *mozos* were carefully schooled in the ways of dignity and of silence. They moved like shadows through the mansion of the gambler, and Don Edgardo was almost like a magician: he waved, and mysterious hands performed services for him.

On this day he had just risen after his siesta, which he took with truly Mexican regularity in the middle of the day. The ceremony of his rising was accomplished in the following fashion.

First, in the chamber beneath his own, his butler, who was a good musician, played a lively air on a muted violin. When the gentle strains had penetrated into the slumber of the master of the house, his body servant entered the room and carried in a silver basin filled with cool water, a wash cloth, a soft towel, and a fan. He first moistened the face and hands of the master, and then fanned him until most of the water had evaporated. This occupied some moments, during which the violinist in the room beneath played a stronger air and upon an unmuted instrument. Finally, with the towel, the servant completed the drying of Don Edgardo's face and hands and next offered him a cigarette, which the gambler smoked at leisure, and then accepted the assistance of his man to get to his feet—a proceeding which had to be accomplished with due slowness, so as not to throw the blood into the head of Mancos. He was finally assisted toward the door, and so, as he went down the stairs again, he could be his usual smiling, cheerful self—though always his cheer was checked and maintained within limits.

It was in the very midst of this usual ceremony—it was, in fact, while the fanning was still in progress and the noble blood of the don was being cooled to the proper point that the violin music suddenly ceased, and then the butler himself, after a hasty rap, appeared at the door of the room.

Don Edgardo was so angry that he could not speak. He merely cast a freezing glance at the servant, who gasped out: "Pardon, señor. Señor the doctor has just come."

"Away with the señor doctor!" said Don Edgardo. "What doctor do you mean?"

"Doctor Clauson, señor."

At this, the eyes of Mancos opened. He rolled suddenly from the couch to his feet and strode toward the door, his body servant following with a towel frantically waving.

"The doctor!" said Don Edgardo, and stood at the head of the stairs, wavering.

There was only one man in the world who guessed how important a hold upon him was maintained by Doctor Humphry Clauson, and by William Benn. That man was the butler and, glancing suspiciously aside at the anxious expression of the other, Don Edgardo told himself that here, at least, he need not fear treason. There was only a sort of fierce concern in the eye of the butler, as though he were chiefly asking what he could do in order to accommodate his master—even if it were to the extent of drawing a sharp knife and fighting in his behalf!

So Don Edgardo went down the stairs and found the doctor, who stood up and advanced to greet him.

Don Edgardo managed a smile, but it went out at the first touch of their hands.

"Now, Doctor Clauson," said he, "I suppose you know that a visit from you to my house is not exactly to be expected unless there is something very important on hand?"

"There is something," said the doctor, "which no one in the world, I suppose, is more concerned in than you are!"

"And what is that, if you please? Will you have a cigarette?"

"I'll light a cigar, if I may?"

Don Edgardo shuddered, but he veiled his emotion by bowing elaborately.

"Of course you may."

"This has to do with your family," said the doctor, through the first acrid cloud of that smoke.

"Ah, indeed!"

"And with a branch of it now living in Mexico."

"All the Mancos," said the gambler, "live in Mexico, with the exception of the few who are now keeping the old house in Madrid."

"You still keep up a house there?"

"We still do," said Don Edgardo, with a magnificent wave of the hand. "We always feel that at least one of the family should be near to the King of Spain!"

"Quite so," said the doctor. "I suppose one of the older members of the family?"

"The oldest, Don Felipe. My brother José Mancos was there for a few years, before he went to Mexico."

"He's an older brother?"

58

"Yes. He lives in the Mexican wilderness."

"In fact," said the doctor, "I believe that what I have to tell you has to do with him."

"Is that possible?"

"Because I think it is his son who is now in the city."

"His son! In El Real?"

"Exactly."

"That is impossible," said the other. "He had only one son, who died, I believe, a few years ago."

"I cannot be mistaken," said the doctor. "And now, I want to call to your attention that your brother José was married some twenty years ago to a——"

"It was twenty-five years ago, my friend."

"If you please. He was married to an Irish beauty——"

"Impossible again! He married, I believe, a young Spanish heiress."

"Once more, I assure you that I cannot be mistaken. He married a blue-eyed, golden-haired daughter of Ireland."

Don Edgardo scowled and waited. He began to see that this was something out of the ordinary, and he determined to hold his fire.

"And their son, who is now a boy of between eighteen and twenty," went on the doctor, "inherited the color of his mother's hair, and of her eyes."

"A blue-eyed Mancos!" sneered Don Edgardo. "Such a thing is not to be thought of!"

"Nevertheless, it is true. You see, I have information which cannot be gainsaid."

"Very odd," said Don Edgardo.

"I knew you would be surprised."

"Very!"

"And you will be further surprised to know that young Ricardo—which is his name——"

"Christoforo——" began Mancos, but then stopped himself, and waited again.

"Young Ricardo," insisted the doctor, "is coming to spend some months with you! Here, you understand, in your house and as a member of the family!"

At this, the other recoiled; he stepped back with such violence that his plump jowls quivered.

"Are you serious?" he asked.

"I am."

59

"This is nonsense!" cried the Mexican angrily.

"It is true. I came ahead to prepare you."

"The whole town will know that it is a lie!" cried Edgardo.

"Not if your brother José really lives in a wilderness. Who can know anything about him? Who in El Real, at least?"

The other began to bite his lip nervously.

"Doctor Clauson," he said finally, "I always have been a friend to you. I want you to understand me. I don't desire to have any trouble with you or with William Benn——"

"That's it," said the doctor mildly. "Of course, you know what Benn is. When he gets an idea into his head, he'll die to execute it!"

"I know that very well—Heaven help me!" sighed the gambler.

"Heaven helped you one day when he brought Benn into your life, I believe."

"I have paid for it, ten times over!"

"The little matter of your life? You have paid the value of that ten times over?"

The Mexican was silenced, but his eyes were rolling frantically, as though in search of release from this inhuman pressure. However, the doctor did not relent.

"As you know," said he, "William Benn is freehanded if he thinks that the other man is going to play straight and fair. He doesn't want to press you into a corner, but he insists that you shall give his protégé a place and look forward to the time when you will have a use for this blue-eyed young man yourself. In the meantime, Benn hopes that you will be able to educate the youngster, teach him good manners, perfect Spanish, and look after him as a tutor—or a father who could not afford a tutor—would do!"

The gambler stared straight at the doctor. In fact, he was unable to speak for a moment.

Then he gasped: "If there were no other reason, I can't take him because I cannot explain him to my wife!"

"That's a thing that we'll have to change. You can see, Don Edgardo, that there's a great deal hanging upon this affair. And we look to you!"

"Tell me!" said the Mexican suddenly. "Is it a gently bred boy that you are speaking of?"

"I know nothing about him except that I am sure that you can fit him into your household."

Suddenly the gambler threw both hands wildly above his head.

"I have played with fire," he groaned, "and now fire will burn me to the heart!"

14

◉

The Foster Brothers' Search

Of the three sons of Antonio Perez who were sent out on the quest of the trail of Ricardo, the first to go was the eldest, Pedro. It was not hard to go to El Real by the railroad, and he rode on top of a box car and when he arrived he searched for a week, high and low, and found nothing that could be considered a sign of Ricardo. Vicente followed and made the second attempt and he failed in turn, and then it was hardly considered that the youngest son, Juan, could succeed in such a search, but his mother it was who insisted, because she had a great deal of faith in the cleverness of her youngest boy. Besides, Antonio was still very ill, and though Pedro and Vicente had recovered from their sickness, they found it hard to get anything other than odd jobs—the house was bare of money, and there was not a day when the mother did not expect that the landlord would come and turn them out of the place and seize upon their poor furnishing to satisfy his claims for the rent. So she sat down and talked seriously with Juan, and he dropped his thin, pointed chin upon his fist and looked at her curiously, and drank in every word.

"Well," said Juan, when she finished, "Pedro and Vicente are a great deal stronger than I, and they're a little older. But I suppose that my eyes are as sharp as theirs are. I'll try to find Ricardo; but I don't think I'll have any luck."

"And why?" she asked him sadly.

"Because," said he, "if Ricardo wanted us to know where

he is, he would have written to us a long time ago. And we haven't had a word from him."

"Do you think that he's forgotten us?" asked the mother, more drearily than ever. "Why should he do that?"

"He isn't one of us," answered Juan. "And he's living with a rich man. Why should he think about us?"

"Because we love him!" said she, with a sob in her throat.

"I've noticed," said Juan, "that a calf forgets its mother before the mother forgets the calf. But I'll go and try to find Ricardo."

"And what will you say when you see him?"

"That I don't know," answered the boy. "His face will tell me how to talk to him, I suppose!"

"May Heaven inspire you!" said the mother. "Because his father says that, wherever Ricardo may be, he is our fortune; certainly we have had no pleasure or happiness since he left us."

To this Juan returned no answer except to bid her farewell; and that same day he reached El Real by the railroad, as his two brothers had reached it before him. He determined from the first that he would not bother to merely ask questions. His brothers had attempted that; but if Ricardo were wearing another name, of what use was it to ask for him under the title of Perez? So for two days he drifted through the streets of El Real, his foxlike face filled with cunning attention; and in the afternoon of the second day he saw none other than William Benn ride down a street.

Juan was so filled with emotion that he ran straight out from the pavement and under the nose of the horse, which was reined up with a sudden violence. And Juan clung to Benn's stirrup-leather and gasped out "Señor, señor! I have come to find my brother! Will you tell me where I may find him?"

William Benn looked down on him in such a way that a chill passed to the very toes of the boy.

"Of course, I can tell you," he said after a moment, in which his expression cleared a little. "Better than that, I'll take you to him."

"Ah, señor," said the boy, "and thank Heaven that this is so, but let me go to him soon. I have a great story of sad news to tell him."

"Wait for me here," said William Benn. "I'll be back here again a little after sundown. Before it is dark, at least. Then I'll take you to him. There, by those poplars," he added, and pointed to some trees in a vacant field near by. "I'll meet you there. Just now I am too busy!"

When he rode on, Juan turned the matter quietly in his mind. The manner of the riding of William Benn had not been that of a man desperately bent on important business—too important even to direct him to the place where he could find his brother. As for conducting Juan personally to the house of his brother—that seemed too great a condescension from so important a man as Señor Benn.

So Juan waited, but he did not wait by the poplars. Instead, he took a place at the side of the neighboring shed and, as the sun set, he watched the poplars with keenest interest. A cat at the hole of a mouse with the scent of game on its edges could not have been more patient than was Juan. The sun sank, the sky turned golden and rose, and then Juan saw two shadowy forms which left the vicinity of a canteen and slipped noiselessly across toward the poplars. The movement of the stalker is unmistakable, so Juan waited no longer. He understood, now, what sort of a reception had been planned for him by William Benn in the dusk of the day by the poplars.

He went off to a restaurant and there he ate a great heaped plate of frijoles, seasoned with the hottest peppers in the world and helped down with slim, clammy tortillas. Afterward he sat for a little while, his brain numb from the terrific strength of the peppers which he had eaten, his tongue numb from the same reason, and electric prickles scourging his throat. He smoked a cigarette and waited until the burning became intolerable. And when it was such an anguish that he could not endure it for another moment, and the moisture stood in beads upon his forehead, then he called for a glass of cold beer. It was brought, the sides frosted with the pleasant chill, and this Juan drank in one long, slow, steady draft, flooding his throat through endless seconds of joy with the cold liquor.

When he had finished this draft, he lighted another cigarette and settled for the consideration of his problem, but he found that his brain did not work well after a full meal, so he went off and found a sleeping place in the hay of a barn. He crawled out the next morning in the pink of the dawn, his head clear, his determination like steel. Only, he wished with all his heart that Vicente, the tiger, and Pedro, the lion, could be with him during this time of trial, for he knew that he was in the gravest danger.

And if he were in danger merely because he asked after the whereabouts of Ricardo, what of Ricardo himself? What grisly secrets would the trail uncover? It made Juan blink even his bright eyes. It made him shudder as though he had sensed a snake sliding quickly on his heels.

Then he steadied himself and started in his pursuit of knowledge. His two brothers had had only the name of William Benn to ask after. But he had something more. He could ask the loiterers in the street what they knew about the big man who had ridden along on a splendid horse in the middle of the afternoon of the day before.

And this produced results at once. Men knew, for instance, that this rider was rich, that he was a gringo, and that he was a friend of Edgardo Mancos; men knew that he had fine horses and many followers, but no one seemed quite sure of his business. Perhaps he was a horse dealer. Perhaps he was a shipper of cattle.

"Or a merchant?" asked Juan.

"Well, friend, you can see for yourself that he does not have a shop or a business place in El Real!"

This answer needed a little thinking over. But what Juan knew, now, was that he had a definite name of a resident of El Real on which he could peg something. It was one point on the chart; and with nothing but the North Star to guide him from this moment on, he was reasonably sure that he would eventually be able to find some trace of his vanished brother.

He sat down, then, to the watching of the house of Edgardo Mancos. It was not hard to manage that, on account of a thick hedge opposite that house, and on the second day of his watching, in the later part of the morning, he was rewarded by seeing big William Benn turn a horse into the gravel-strewn driveway of the Mancos house and disappear in its yard.

Juan was a timid soul, but now he did not hesitate. He got up and ran straight across the road; and then he fled down the driveway and dipped to the side, through a hole in the boundary hedge, until he came to the rear of the garden.

There were ample grounds around the house of Edgardo Mancos, for land was not so precious in El Real that a man could not spread his elbows almost at pleasure. So Mancos had laid out a very considerable garden, chiefly in cactus and evergreens, and such things as made some show of foliage and color without actually demanding much water.

Juan found that there was plenty of cover behind which he could stalk William Benn, but also that the foliage everywhere was dry and crackling, and he went with his heart continually in his mouth. Benn had not dismounted in the stable yard of the place, but still continued, and Juan saw the head and shoulders of his quarry working away into the mazes of the winding hedges. There were so many paths, so many loops and windings of hedge, that Juan was almost afraid to go deeper for fear lest he should not be able to get out of the maze.

In this state of mind, he was even more silent of foot than usual, and so he came back to the end of the garden and looked, through a small gap in the bottom of the hedge, at an inclosure of lawn in the center of which stood what looked like a little summerhouse, and in the summerhouse sat a man over a book, and there was paper beside him; and beside the summerhouse, still in the saddle, was William Benn.

The rider waved. The man stood up from his book and stepped into the sunlight. It was Ricardo Perez! For who could be disguised that had such flame-colored hair and such blue eyes and such a white skin?

Juan looked at him with a sudden leaping of the heart. He knew and always had known that his two brothers and his mother and his father all loved Ricardo more than they loved anything else in the world; for there never had been any jealousy shown by the real children of Perez toward this beautiful and brilliant foster child. But Juan himself always felt that he had reserved judgment, and that Ricardo looked a little too good to be true.

But now he knew, with a thrust of joy and sorrow through his heart, that he loved Ricardo, also, not less than all the rest.

⊙

15

A Mancos Is Graceful

But if it had not been for that flaming hair, Juan felt that he never could have known his foster brother, so completely was Ricardo altered from the self that he had been. Or, at least, so greatly did he appear changed by the disappearance of the rags in which the family of Perez always were dressed. He looked to Juan like a rich young man of aristocratic blood!

He held his breath in the wonder of this discovery. Then he heard the two speak together, their voices plainly audible.

"What are you working at this morning?" said William Benn.

The boy held up a sheet of paper.

"Locks," said he.

William Benn chuckled.

"You have to know a lock before you can learn how to open it," he said. "And there's no key to knowledge as important as the key that will open a lock. Where's the doctor?"

"He's inside. He's coming out here in a short time."

"And how does the time go with you, Ricardo, my boy?"

"Slowly," said he. "I'm still anxious to get out and try what I've learned."

"All in good time," said the other. "We can't conquer the world in a day. But how do you get on in the house?"

"Do you mean with Don Edgardo?"

"Yes. And with his wife?"

"He hates me, because I'm a constant danger to him."

"How is that?"

"Suppose that one day a man comes who really knew José Mancos and his son! That would be embarrassing!"

"Then Edgardo could turn you out and swear that you had imposed on him!"

"He would have to, of course. But would everyone believe him? He has introduced me to all his friends—because you've made him do it! What will they say of him if I turn out a sham?"

"That's no worry of ours. Use Edgardo Mancos while you can, and use his name, too!"

"That's reasonable," said Ricardo. "But it may be dangerous."

"Danger is the seasoning that makes this sort of a life go down."

Ricardo nodded again and laughed.

"I like it better every day," said he. "But it's growing a little thick. Yesterday a man came up from the Mexican mountains and called on Don Edgardo to say that he was an old friend of his brother, José. Don Edgardo was still pale when he got rid of the man and came rushing to me. He wanted me to run away and hide."

"You refused, of course?"

"Until I had your orders, of course."

"That's entirely right. You're getting entirely too much from Mancos to break off with him just yet. Does he still give you lessons?"

"He's in an agony about me every minute of the day," said Ricardo, smiling maliciously. "As a matter of fact, he has to give me a lesson in deportment every time I budge out of the house. If it's only for a walk down the street, or in the piazza in the evening, he has to show me how to walk, how to stop, how to bow to different classes of his friends. I have developed several styles. To the servants in the house I must be contemptuous, and alternately harsh and kind. Beat a dog ten times and pat him once. That's the way of Edgardo Mancos. Then there are friends. Last of all, there are superiors. Outside of this, there is the way one must act to gringos. I have to learn all these classes. I am kept bowing and scraping, and shaking hands with just the right pressure. He has a dancing teacher who comes every day for a whole hour and works on me. Every Mancos is graceful."

William Benn nodded.

"And the señora?"

"She is always either very cold or very hot. Sometimes she starts when she looks at me, and says that no son of a Mancos could have my hair or eyes; but then again, she forgets about that and she treats me really as though I were her nephew.

She can be kind, though she has learned from her husband to turn up her nose at nine tenths of the world."

"Tell me, Ricardo, you have no regrets about this life?"

"I've buried every regret. I'll never look conscience in the face again," said Ricardo carelessly.

"Keep to the straight line," said William Benn. "It may be that you will have something to do, before long. Something to make you rich for life, do you hear?"

"I hear you," nodded Ricardo.

"You go about to parties in the evening, don't you still?"

"Yes."

"Not Mexicans only—some whites?"

"Half and half," said Ricardo, laughing frankly. "Some of these American families grow dizzy when they hear about the age of a long line like the Mancos. The young men sneer a little. But the girls and the mothers listen!"

"That's exactly what I wanted to hear," said Benn. "And now tell me if you've met the daughter of John Ranger."

"The murdered man?"

At this, William Benn scowled, and Juan was frightened by the alteration in the face of the big man.

"Why do you say it like that? He was given a chance to fill his hand. He failed."

"It's always murder," answered Ricardo, "when a trained fighter draws a gun on an ordinary man."

"Ranger had been in a hundred fights!" exclaimed Benn.

"He hadn't a chance," said Ricardo, "and I think you know it. Consider the average honest business man. He goes shooting, now and then, and he does his firing at game. That's not real practice. Now and then he steps into a range and blazes away at porcelain ducks. And then he will think that he's ready for a fight. His courage may be high enough, but he has no chance against a professional, has he?"

"You can't get on in the world if you begin to split hairs at this rate," Benn informed the boy.

"But consider this," said Ricardo. "I usually work a couple of hours a day with a rifle and a revolver; and the doctor has been giving me a good deal of shotgun work, lately."

"That's it—that's it!" exclaimed Benn with enthusiasm. "Surety is better than speed, and there's nothing in the world as good as a shotgun for surety. Ricardo—there's another thing I want to talk to you about. I want to ask you a few questions about your brothers."

68

"Yes?" said Ricardo, and Juan listened in vain for any warmth in that voice, watched in vain for any brightening of his foster brother's face.

"Tell me about them."

"Pedro is the biggest and the strongest. He's brave and steady and a Hercules. Vicente is not quite so strong and he's not half so steady. But he has flashes when he'd burn down a stone wall! Juan is the youngest. He's cleverer than the rest. He's like a fox."

"He is," agreed William Benn, "and he's in the town."

Ricardo did not stir a muscle, did not exclaim a syllable.

"I'll tell you how it is," said Benn. "He met me on the street. He wanted to see you. But that can't be."

"And why not?"

"Because I don't want you upset."

"Suppose that the family has a need of me?" asked Ricardo.

"Let them scrape enough together to take care of themselves. Four grown men and one strong woman—what could put them in a hole?"

"I don't know," answered Ricardo. "But Juan is in town?"

"Yes. I put him off with a trick, and he saw through it. However, that's aside from the point. I began to talk to you about young Maud Ranger and you immediately started to tell me about the murder of her father—whereas that was a fair fight by every Western rule! Now, my boy, I want you, the next time that you have a chance, to pay some attention to Maud Ranger."

"She's a baby," said Ricardo. "She's—why, hardly more than seventeen or eighteen years old!"

"And you," said the criminal, "are a wise old man of what? Twenty, it is now, isn't it?"

Ricardo shrugged his shoulders.

"She sits in a corner. She's as still as a stone," said he. "Who would want to talk to such a girl?"

"You young fool!" exclaimed Benn. "Am I to do your thinking for you or not?"

Ricardo was silent; but his respect and his surrender were obvious, even from a distance.

"The doctor and I are working hard on you, my boy," went on Benn. "We never worked so hard on any other person. And now I think that I have a chance to use you. But you tell me that the girl is a stone. Let me tell you that she doesn't have to talk. She has something which will supply the place of silly chatter. She has several millions in property. Does that give the stone a dash of blood and color, my young friend?"

Ricardo was thoughtful.

"She's pretty enough," said he, in a coldly casual tone. "What do you want me to do?"

"You conceited young puppy," grinned William Benn, "I want you to try to get her in your hand. She's old enough to marry, and we're all old enough to spend her money, I suppose?"

"But," said Ricardo, "isn't that robbing the cradle? You said that you never would do that."

"Robbing the cradle? You never find millions in a cradle, unless there are man-eating dogs around to watch it. She has a guardian-uncle who will be the tallest wall that you ever tried to climb over. Don't make any doubt of it. The taking of the Ranger girl will be as hard a job as you ever tackled in your life! And you'll never find a better paying one, either! I'll tell you another thing. You'll no sooner start with her than you'll find an obstacle. Find out for yourself. Then come to me and we'll talk over a way around it. That's all for to-day. Good-by, Ricardo."

He rode off down the winding path, and Juan, through the hole in the hedge, watched him go.

16
◉

The Foster Brothers

When Juan had watched William Benn out of sight, and seen his foster brother turn again to his work in the summer-house, he began to advance, but never a fox crept upon a rabbit warren with more care than Juan showed now—a rabbit warren watched by guardian men and savage dogs!

He crept from shrub to shrub, and at last he stood up outside the railing of the little house in such a position that a wooden pillar assisted by a young cypress shut him off from the view of any one coming toward him from the house. Rising there, silent as a shadow, Juan looked earnestly and curiously at the bowed head of his brother, and the sheets of paper and the books which lay before him, the paper covered with swift, legible writing, and the books with their crowded pages of type. Juan had to close his eyes and look again, reassuring himself that the student actually was the Ricardo of their family, and that it was no fairy tale that the lazy, ragged Ricardo of the village was now this studious and gentlemanly youth!

He shook his head, and as he did so, Ricardo came out of his chair as a wild cat comes out of a nap at a scent of danger, head up, eyes fiercely alert.

He saw Juan, and the expression of his eyes changed a little, though it seemed to Juan that they remained equally impersonal and aloof.

But he caught Juan by both elbows and drew him into the house and forced him into a chair and stood over him, laughing.

How had Juan come there? How had he found him? How wonderful it was that they should meet in this manner! How like Juan to have turned up like this, at the least expected moment!

But though these exclamations ran out fast as water from the lips of Ricardo, it cannot be said that Juan was satisfied. He remembered the real Ricardo of the old days, taciturn, speaking rather with a single glance, a single flashing word that revealed much. This conversation was not the same.

He said simply: "I saw William Benn come into this place, and so I followed him."

"And how long have you been here?"

"I've only just come," lied Juan, who never told the truth when a lie was available. "I waited near the house. When he did not come out of the garden, I followed down here, and at last I saw you in this little house just as he was riding away. Of course I came on again."

The gleam of satisfaction in the eye of Ricardo could not be disguised.

"You've only just come? Well, Juan, I have ten thousand things to tell you. But first tell me everything about mother and father and Vicente and our great Pedro!"

The voice had a little ring to it, but not the ring of truth;

the cunning ear of Juan, sharpened by his own affection for all of those names, perceived the truth quietly. Ricardo was playing a part!

"Every one has been sick," said Juan. "All the money has been used up. Father is in the hospital, almost dead with worry and sickness. Mother is worn out. Vicente and Pedro can only get a scrap of work here and there. And of course where they can get little to do, I can get nothing. We have lived like dogs since you went away from us, Ricardo!"

Ricardo cried out softly in dismay and apparent grief. He seized a wallet and cast it upon the table. He turned it upside down and shook it and out of it fell several notes.

"Here are fifty dollars, nearly. All that I have in the world. Take it back to them, Juan, and I'll find a way to send more after you!"

"This would be like gold from Heaven to them," said Juan, taking the money with reluctant fingers.

He himself never had touched so much at one time. He looked gravely at Ricardo.

"I don't think that my mother would take this much from you," said he.

"And why not?" cried Ricardo, making words flow again. "Of course she will take it, and afterward I'll try to find a little more and send it after you to her. Of course I shall find more! Money? I'll make it grow on trees!"

And he laughed, but there was more exultant expectancy in his laughter than apology.

"And I wish to heaven that I could go there myself and give a hand in taking care of everything," said Ricardo. "But you see how it is with me, and that I'm as busy as can be. I work like a slave, Juan. Even our father never worked so hard in the old days when he was in the mines—you know how fond he is of talking about those hard times. But I have to be at it early and late."

"And what do you study, Ricardo?"

"Everything that will help me in my work for Señor Benn."

"And what is his business, Ricardo?"

"He is an exporter and importer. That means that he handles all sorts of things. I have to learn about them. And then there's mathematics, and such things—you see?"

He pointed to several sheets covered with figures.

"Poor Ricardo," said Juan, feeling the iron enter his soul. "Then you haven't found an easy place?"

"Ah, no, no!" said Ricardo. "I often sigh for the happy, sunny, lazy times in the village. Often I'm about to throw all of this away and go back and play with you and the rest."

"And fight with the gringos?" asked Juan.

"The gringos? Yes, yes," said Ricardo hurriedly. "But now, let me tell you the best thing that you could do."

"Yes."

"Go straight back home with this money. Assure my mother that there is more to come and——"

Juan rose and stacked the money in a neat pile, placed it on the table, and laid the edge of a book upon it to keep the bills from fluttering away.

"You're right," said he, "I must go back, but I don't think that I can take this money."

Ricardo frowned at him. There had been a time when the frown of Ricardo meant a great deal to Juan, but now grief and anger nerved him.

"And why not?" asked Ricardo.

"Because," said Juan, "as far as I know, we always have lived on honest money!"

The two stared grimly at one another.

"So!" said Ricardo at the last.

His foster brother did not answer. Already he had said enough. Now he held out his hand.

"I suppose we should say good-by," said he.

His heart ached more than ever; but he gathered his pride and his grief about him and spoke with dignity.

"Well," answered Ricardo brusquely, "perhaps you're right. Good-by, then, brother."

They shook hands, and Juan noticed that the grip of Ricardo, as ever, was soft as the touch of a woman, but with a subtle suggestion of steely strength in it.

Juan turned on his heel and went off, blindly, for his eyes were thick with tears. He had gone outside of the summerhouse and reached the first hedge when a swift step came behind him and a hand fell on his shoulder.

He turned. He could not speak.

"Juan!" cried Ricardo, and threw out his hands. And Juan fell into his arms and wept heavily on his shoulder.

He was led back to the summerhouse, he hardly knew how. There he sat in a chair and wiped the moisture from his eyes. He heard Ricardo saying:

"You were here before. You heard William Benn talking to me?"

"I heard every word that he said."

"Well, then, you know that I lied to you."

"Alas, yes," said Juan bitterly. "I know that, and I know how many other things!"

"Tell me what you know?"

"I know what you are studying to be."

"Tell me what?"

"A scoundrel, and a thief."

He threw back his head, almost as though he expected a blow in return for his words, but Ricardo was merely nodding and smiling. There was infinite pain in his smile. It made him look older and too wise for his years.

Then Juan caught both the hands of his foster brother and cried to him: "Come back with me! Come back to us. We love you. This William Benn only wants to use you. I heard him talk. There is very little good in him, I am sure. Come back with me, Ricardo. *Dios, Dios,* how my mother would weep with joy to see you, and Vicente and Pedro! And my father would be well in one day! We have had no good luck since you left us. Neither have you, for I see what has happened to you and what you are trying to be here!"

Then Ricardo answered:

"What you say may be very true. But I'll tell you something, Juan. You have a great brain in your head. You will understand. It is a story some one told me about a man who learned to breathe so extremely fast that at last he could live under water. Do you understand? He could live under water and breathe the air like a fish. But once he went into the water, he never could return to the dry land again. That is true of me also. I have learned how to be a bad man. You see and understand everything, Juan, and therefore you saw to-day that I had cut even you and my family out of my heart. I was determined to live only for the new life. And still I am determined to lead that life. Nothing that you could say would persuade me to do any other thing."

"Not if my father and mother and Vicente and Pedro and I all fell on our knees and begged of you?"

"Not even then! Heaven forgive me!"

"Ah," murmured Juan, "Heaven will forgive you, because even I can understand! You have become a free man. Because you are trying to do only one thing. You have given yourself up to follow evil and William Benn is your teacher."

"Ricardo!" called a voice among the hedges.

"Go quickly," said Ricardo. "That is the doctor coming. He is such a demon that if he saw tears in my eyes, he would guess everything. Good-by. Take this money. Don't say no, unless you want to break my heart. Tell mother and father that one day I shall come back and cover them with gold."

"Ah, Ricardo," said the other boy, "leave the gold behind you and only bring back yourself."

17

◉

Advice from the Doctor

When the doctor came to Ricardo he said: "Do you know a man with bushy, sunburned eyebrows, and a scar puckering one cheek?"

"I don't know. That sounds familiar."

"There is a man like that at the house. He wants to talk to you. You had better see him, then, if he knows you?"

"How can he know me," said the boy, "if he asked for a Mancos?"

"That's true, of course. And he talks as if he had two meanings in his words. I had better tell him that you cannot see him to-day, but that to-morrow you will be happy—say to-morrow evening?"

"Very well."

The doctor went away, and came back where Ricardo stared blindly at his books, and made no headway.

Doctor Humphry Clauson always went quickly to the point. Now he said:

"You're invited to-night to a supper where there will be a crowd of young Americans and a few Mexicans."

"I don't like that," answered Ricardo. "When the crowd is chiefly gringo, there is——"

75

"You'd better not use that word," said the doctor dryly.

"I always forget. Well, when the people are chiefly American, they act as though they looked down on the Mexicans. As though we were not good enough for them."

"There you go again. Once I proved to you that there is not one chance in a thousand that you are Mexican."

"My mother and my father are Mexican," said the boy stubbornly, "and I shall not change my blood till they do."

"You are an obstinate young fellow," replied the doctor carelessly. "But I don't care for that. Only I don't like to see you get emotional like this."

"Very well," said the boy obediently. "What's to do?"

"The greatest thing you probably ever will have a chance to do. You're going to the supper and you're going to dance."

"Very well. I'll go, if it's important."

"You're young, Ricardo, and that's important. Young girls like young men, as a rule. At least at dances."

"Yes," said the boy, "I'm young."

"You're handsome."

"That's true," said Ricardo, not vainly, but accepting a fact.

"You dance well."

"Yes, I do."

"You can talk to girls."

"Of course."

"In addition, you come from the celebrated old family of Mancos."

"Of course," grinned Ricardo.

"You have a look of Benn, when you smile like that," chuckled the doctor. "Very well. At this party you'll find among the guests Maud Ranger."

Ricardo grunted.

"Benn talked to me a little about her," he admitted. "How much money has she?"

"About seven millions, as nearly as we can work it out. Perhaps a shade more, not much less."

"That's three hundred and fifty thousand a year," murmured Ricardo. "A man could live on half of that."

"Heaven gave you a brain," smiled the doctor. "You can multiply seven by five and give away half to your friends!"

"Of course."

"Now, then, I want to tell you about this girl."

Ricardo exclaimed: "Do you know everything? If I ask you

the name of a star, you can tell me. If I ask you a question out of a book, you always know. And yet you know about people, too. You even know about young girls."

"I send my mind," answered the doctor, "wherever my business leads me. But to continue with Maud Ranger. She's eighteen. She's a pretty thing and——"

"Rather lean," said Ricardo.

"All the better," said the doctor. "It gives her room to grow. A sleek girl makes a fat woman. You want angles in the young, Ricardo."

Ricardo scribbled on a piece of paper.

"What are you doing?" asked the doctor.

"I'm making a note of that."

The doctor merely laughed.

"Very well," said he. "You may smile at me all you want to, my lad, but let me give you some footnotes before you meet that girl."

"Yes," said Ricardo.

"She has seven millions. Every one knows it. Ever since her father's death she's been going religiously to parties, and yet, though she's been very kind to the young men, she's never become engaged; and in this century of quick action, that's a strange thing."

Ricardo waited.

"The young blades have fallen in love in rapid succession with her, and her money," said the doctor, "But they have very bad luck.

"Three young fellows who have been courting her have died suddenly, and strangely, all of wounds received in gun fights—opponents unknown!"

Ricardo snapped his fingers.

"I see how it is," said he. "One of her lovers is blocking off the others, and using a gun to do it."

"A very good guess," said the doctor. "But though young men in love are capable of one murder, most of them hardly seem capable of three!"

"There's a difference between a fair fight and a murder."

"You can put it as you please. The point that I make is that the thing is very strange."

"Of course it is."

"But consider again how extremely strange it is. Three men dead. And not so many months in between. Consider another thing. This girl lived like a child at home till her father's

77

death. She never went out. Suddenly she begins to start abroad. She goes everywhere she's asked. She's very kind to all the young men. And what do you make of that, Ricardo?"

"It doesn't seem much of a riddle. Her father was a hard man, and kept a curb on his daughter. Some fathers do that, don't they?"

"Naturally."

"And so after his death, she's been enjoying her liberty. Isn't that an explanation?"

"That's a sort of explanation, of course."

"I suppose," went on Ricardo, "that she's like a filly that's been kept in a small pasture. Throw down the bars and she'll run all over the country."

"Everything that you say," answered the other, "is apt to be true in most cases, but it just happens that in this instance you're completely wrong. This Maud Ranger is as quiet and modest a girl as ever stepped. She was tremendously fond of her father, and no one can understand why she should not have remained quietly at home and mourned for him during a longer period. In fact, it's quite a mystery. I'm warning you before ever you see her. Because, sooner or later, if she looks on you with any favor at all, you're going to step into trouble, my lad, and that trouble may be the end of you, unless Benn and I can be of help in the pinch. In fact, you're risking your life, as it appears to me, by paying your attention to the girl. You can draw out of the deal, if you wish."

"In fact," said Ricardo, setting his teeth hard, "I'm interested for the first time. I'll be there to-night."

"That's ended," commented the doctor abruptly. "And how has the work been going to-day?"

"There it is."

Clauson looked over the heaped papers, sifting them through his fingers.

"You did this to-day?"

"Yes."

"When did you begin?"

"At six."

"At six this morning!"

"Yes."

"That makes a long day. No rest?"

"Yes. Of course I spent a couple of hours in the hills, shooting."

"And books the rest of the time?"

"Yes."

"How does your head feel?"

"Clear as a bell."

The doctor whistled.

"Come up to the house with me," said he. "Benn is wrong in forcing you ahead so soon. Another year, and I'd have you safely ready for great things. There are plenty of brains in this old world of ours, but very few of those who own them are willing to work with them long hours every day. Work is the grindstone that puts an edge to the knife. By gad, I'm moralizing like an old woman. Come along."

They gathered up the books and strolled up the path.

"You're thoughtful, Ricardo?"

"I'm thinking of my family."

"*Your* family?" asked the doctor with a certain emphasis.

"Oh, whoever they are—my foster family, if you want to put it that way. At any rate, I'm thinking of them. I want to do something for them."

"A reasonable idea," agreed the doctor. "I'm glad that you have it!"

A sudden bitterness rushed upon Ricardo.

"Why are you?" he exclaimed. "You care nothing for any one. Why do you say you're glad I want to help them?"

"Because," said the doctor, with his cold smile, "a man who is all bad by that very fact has diffused his talents over too great a field. He lacks edge. Which you will have, my boy!"

And he began to laugh, but softly, and to himself; for in the midst of the most heated conversation, the doctor always seemed more than half alone.

18

Ricardo Dances—and Fights

It was settled straightway that five hundred dollars should be dispatched at once to succor the family of Ricardo. And for that purpose this sum would be like a fortune to Antonio Perez. It would furnish him with a pair of good mules, pay most of his debts, and, in short, reëstablish him at a single stroke.

"If I can find some way of thanking you——" began Ricardo with emotion, when the doctor cut him off by saying, with the driest of voices: "Don't bother about the words, my lad. Save them for Benn. He's financing you. But now that you've provided for your family, take yourself in hand and prepare for Maud Ranger."

There had been frank doubts in the mind of Ricardo, but whatever scruples had troubled him before were now pushed into the background. And though, from some viewpoints, it was as wicked a piece of cold-blooded villainy as any youth could have engaged in, he partly salved his conscience by murmuring to himself that he was merely another in the countless army of fortune hunters. And as for the evil in the doctor and William Benn, he satisfied himself that men who were willing to rescue his suffering family in this generous manner could not be all bad.

So a political machine is run by a boss who carefully distributes little shares of kindness and favor until a whole district is bound to him by party spirit and by a sort of pseudo affection.

But the greatness of the results which they had in mind was enough to kill any scruples in Ricardo. When he walked into the house where the party was given that night, it was not only that strange red-gold hair of his that seemed on fire, but the whole man was in a flame; and when he saw

Maud Ranger he told himself that he was seeing not merely a woman, but seven millions of dollars!

She was paying a great deal of attention to a true son of the Western range—a big-boned man of toil, with the crooked legs of one who rides much. He had a sun-blackened face, with a sort of troubled redness breaking through on the cheek bones and the point of the nose. He had the look of a man who has fronted all sorts of weathers. He was quite dizzy with the attentions of Maud Ranger, and Ricardo observed her with the keenest interest. There was more to her than he had thought, more character, more keenness of eye, and more good looks, though her beauty was decidedly qualified by her independent, almost mannish bearing. She looked able to rope a steer or ride a pitching broncho as well as any man. Her grip in shaking hands was like that of a man, and her eye was as straight and direct. She introduced her companion and the latter fixed upon the dapper Ricardo an unfavoring glance.

"Are you a Mexican?" he asked.

Ricardo smiled coldly upon the burly youth. For many and many a month, now, he had lived a strictly laborious existence, and if he were encouraged to go out among the youngsters of the town, it was always rather with the purpose of polishing his manners a little than of giving him pleasure. He was still at school, so to speak, when he went out to play.

But now he felt that the period of his novitiate was completed. He had been sent out by the doctor with only these final marching orders: "Do things your own way. Follow your own ideas. You're not in leading strings. But show the girl that you're a man."

This blunt question from the cowman now made the old flame leap in the heart of the boy, as it had leaped in the old days, when he ranged the streets of the village like a tiger, looking for prey.

He turned upon the other and said: "It depends on what you mean by the word. When an American asks that question, sometimes he means Spanish—Castilian Spanish—and sometimes he means half-breed, and sometimes Indian, and sometimes—greaser!"

He set off the last word by itself, and spoke it slowly and softly, while a provoking smile of invitation appeared

81

upon the lips of Ricardo. The man of the range stared fixedly at him.

"I'll explain things to you later on," he said pointedly.

"Thank you," said Ricardo, and smiled again.

He drifted away. He had no desire to talk to Maud Ranger, now; he was sunning himself in the promise of trouble that lay before him. It was almost by sheerest chance, that he suddenly found himself face to face with the girl, later on.

She said to him in her direct way: "Are you going to have trouble with Dick Jones?"

"I hope not!" said Ricardo, but the light in his eyes belied him. It was as yellow as the flame of his hair.

They danced together. She wanted to know about his early life. She had heard that he was raised in the wilderness of Mexico's mountains. So he told her what Benn and the doctor had taught him to say. He told her about wild hunts—all imagined by William Benn and worded by the doctor. He told her of life in a rambling house in the wilderness, savage men, savage horses, dim trails, constant peril.

She listened to these tales with such interest that they sat out the following dance together.

"I want to tell you about Dick Jones," she said. "I hope you'll have no trouble with him. He has a name for being hard and—a little dangerous."

He thanked her for the warning, and watched her move away—and presently she was dancing with Dick Jones, and laughing up to that big, rough fellow.

Ricardo went out into the garden and sat down on top of a four-foot pillar. He leaped on it like a cat, and settled down with his knees hugged against his breast. He was more and more content. Life under the régime of William Benn had been very strenuous, but now the excitement was commencing, and the pulses of Ricardo were singing. He could have laughed aloud, but instead, he merely looked up at the stars and hummed softly to himself.

Others drifted through the garden between dances. They took little notice of him; for he had become known as a youth of naïve unconsciousness; but they pointed him out and chuckled as they went by. A wild young Mexican, said they.

Then a hand tapped on the foot of Ricardo. He drew back his thoughts from the stars and discovered that the garden was still, and the music was throbbing in the house once more. He looked into the face of Dick Jones.

"We could have our little chin now," said Dick Jones.

"We could," said Ricardo.

"About greasers," said Dick Jones.

"And gringos," said Ricardo.

"I could talk to you better if you was down here on the ground," added the cow-puncher.

Ricardo descended to the ground.

"How do you begin the talk?" he asked.

"With a straight left—to the head!" gasped Dick Jones, and drove a hand of iron at the face of Ricardo. But it missed by the narrowest of margins, as a striking hand misses a butterfly, or a whirling leaf. Then the two tangled together and spun about—separated—and Dick Jones staggered back and leaned against the pillar, his hands helpless at his sides, his head canted over on one shoulder like a broken reed.

After a moment he gasped: "What's happened? Where've I been?"

Then he saw Ricardo, and his brain cleared a little. He put up his hands.

"You greaser yaller dog!" said Dick, and came in uncertainly. Ricardo knocked down the feeble arms and poised his right hand; a cruel keenness was in his eyes, but he forbore to strike.

"You'd better go home and wash the blood from your face," said Ricardo.

Dick Jones touched his face with his hand; it came away, wet and sticky.

"I guess you've made a mess of me," he said frankly. "You got a wonderful pair of fists, kid. I thought that a pair of wild broncs was savagin' me. I'd better go home before the girls see me. So long, Mancos! You done me up proper, and I got no grudge against you."

Ricardo accepted the proffered hand with a feeling of wonder. He could not imagine his own wild nature submitting with such careless ease, and yet he could not help admiring the attitude of Dick Jones.

He saw the latter start off, and then he returned to the house himself and washed the stains from his hands; and a mild and genial warmth of content filled the heart of Ricardo as he went back among the dancers. It was a cheerful party and most diverting. Then suddenly he was talking with Maud Ranger again.

"You're not dancing much," she said. "Are you having a dull time?"

"Not a bit," he answered. "I'm looking on and admiring."

"It's like a chocolate cake with the chocolate settled in streaks," she observed. "The Americans are foolish, and the Mexicans are grave. I haven't seen Dick Jones, have you?"

"I think some one called him away," said Ricardo.

"You've barked a knuckle of your right hand," she remarked.

"I brushed against a thorn in the garden," replied he.

He looked straight at her, blankly, but he could see that she understood, and he also could see that she was surprised and pleased. It puzzled Ricardo a great deal, but since he had come there, expecting to be baffled, he waited, ready to observe and try to solve the riddle. In the meantime, he was to be agreeable, but that was a small effort. For from the moment of his return to the house, Maud Ranger monopolized him. They danced together, sat out together, walked in the garden together.

And yet no man tried to interfere with this monopoly; indeed, it seemed to Ricardo that two or three youngsters cast at him glances of grim content, and that he felt was strange. For certainly she was the prettiest girl at the dance. He considered her more critically, but still he found nothing wrong.

There was something rather masculine about her frank directness, to be sure, but that hardly could be held against her. She talked rather more like a friendly man than like a pretty girl; one did not need to make flattering advances to her. And she was trying to draw him out on familiar ground into talk about his native Mexico; then she told of her father's ranch, which must be much the same sort of country. Some day he should come to visit them. He would be delighted. Then why not soon? No reason against it. And in five minutes it was arranged.

◉

19

Uncle William Speaks

The doctor was complimentary when he heard from Ricardo what had been accomplished.

"You've opened the door," he said. "But you're too young to go inside alone, of course. We'll have to send someone with you—and who shall that be? I must see Benn. Go to bed, my lad. You've done a grand bit of work. Go to bed. We'll do your thinking for you!"

With this assurance, Ricardo turned in and slept; and in the morning he opened his eyes to find the long, lean face of William Benn silhouetted against the light of the window. Ricardo braced himself up on his elbows.

"Hullo," said he, "why didn't you sing out when you came?"

"When you have a stake horse," said the other, "you never bother his sleeping time. When do you go to the post?"

"I ride out this afternoon."

"With her?"

"Yes."

William Benn closed his eyes.

"It's too good to be true," he sighed. "And how did you take with her?"

"I don't know what you mean by that."

"I mean—a boy and a girl catch, or they don't. Like a cold. What did she think of you?"

Ricardo considered.

"She thought that I might be useful."

"Is that all?"

"I suppose so."

"You can't make a stone statue warm up all in a minute," said the criminal. "Take your time, though, and keep the fire up. How did she affect you?"

"I don't know," said Ricardo. "I wasn't talking to a girl. I was talking to seven millions, of course."

"Ah," said William Benn, "that would spoil everything! Let me tell you something. You are falling in love! You are getting deeper and deeper in love every minute. Never forget for a moment you've got to convince her of that."

"I don't know how to manage that!" answered Ricardo.

"Perhaps not. I'll tie you to a fellow who'll tell you how to act."

He raised his voice:

"Lew!"

The door of the bedroom opened instantly and closed without sound. Inside it stood the hunchback, Lew, his pale, unhealthy face grinning at them. He jerked his head in greeting at Ricardo.

"Come here, Lew," said William Benn.

The hunchback came closer. He picked up a chair and put it down beside William Benn. Then he sat in it, always keeping his eyes fixed upon the boy. He had a face like a frog. He was more ugly than a Hun of Attila, and what made him more frightful than ever was the mirth which seemed to be struggling in him now.

"Lew is going out with you to the girl's place," said Benn.

"But I was invited by myself!" said Ricardo.

"That makes no difference. Of course you can't go anywhere without your man to take care of you. Lew's a valet, when he wants to be, eh?"

At this, Lew grinned a ghastly grin and winked solemnly at the boy. It seemed that he was laughing both with and at the youth.

"And he's a handy man, too," said William Benn. "He'll take care of you and take care of your horses. He'll always be near. You can take my word for that. Lew will always be near!"

They were both smiling—the evil smile of William Benn and the hideous grimace of the dwarf.

"I thought of sending Wong along with you," continued the director of operations. "But I changed my mind about that. The reason is that Wong needs a heavy hand to keep him in order. But Lew is always in order. Eh, Lew?"

Lew grinned still wider.

"The kid has to pretend to be in love with her," went on

Benn seriously. "How'll he go about it, Lew? You'll have to tell him from time to time."

"Sure," said the hunchback. "I know all about that!"

William Benn looked down at that lump of self-satisfied deformity, and even Benn shuddered a little.

But he said: "You boss Lew, Ricardo. You understand? But when it comes to a pinch, do what Lew tells you to do. Because he'll never be wrong!"

"I'll tame her for you in three days," said Lew. "I know all about women!"

This time he actually laughed, and his huge head rolled in glee.

"Go down and trim up the horses," said Benn to the dwarf.

Lew rose. He assisted himself from the chair by leaning a little and so rising to his feet with the help of an upward thrust of his finger tips. For his arms dangled a vast distance. He looked to Ricardo like a tall man who has been shrunk and doubled up in the trunk and bowed and deformed in the legs.

After he had left, Benn said: "You'll find him useful. Besides, he'll set you off. The uglier he is, the better you'll appear. Take his advice about everything. He's as wise as a spider!"

So Ricardo was prepared for his visit with much good advice, and when he descended and mounted the horse— Lew holding his stirrup—William Benn and the doctor both shook hands with him.

"We'll both be close at hand," they told him. "And Lew will always know where to find us. When in doubt, ask him to get us."

He went off from them, keeping his horse at a jog down the street. And Lew followed two lengths behind him, whistling shrill and small through his teeth. When they arrived at Maud Ranger's, they found that she was prepared to start; and with her was a grim, gray-headed man already in the saddle. He was introduced to Ricardo as William Ranger, the uncle of Maud. He shook hands with a stiff grip and a straight, keen look. There was no doubt but that the girl had her manners from her father's side of her family.

The trail began to wind over the hills in broad loops, as soon as they left the white walls of El Real, and when they were fairly in the open country they struck on at a smart gait. All were well mounted; they fairly flew and put the long miles rapidly behind them.

At such a pace there was little chance for conversation, but it happened that swinging down a long slope the girl shot her horse well ahead, and her uncle drew up a little— Ricardo followed suit.

And suddenly he was addressed gruffly:

"Young man, d'you know why Maud has brought you out here?"

"Yes," said Ricardo innocently, "because she wanted to show me her ranch, which she says must be like the country where I was raised."

"Did she indeed!" muttered William Ranger. "Now, I'll tell you the truth. She's brought you out here because she wants to start you on a longer trail!"

"A trail?" echoed Ricardo.

"A trail that you'll never run to the end of, and if you do, Heaven help you. That's to put it shortly. The mischief is in the girl, I think. She imagines that one brave man can do what the law can't manage. Madness! Sheer madness!"

"I don't understand," said Ricardo.

"Do you understand that she had a father?" asked William Ranger, as bluntly as ever.

"Yes."

"And that her father died?"

"Yes."

"And that the man who murdered him was Charles Perkins?"

"I think I've heard that."

"Now then—the wisest man hunters that wear the badges of Uncle Sam have been working to get at Charles Perkins ever since the killing. And they've failed. They've never seen more than his dust as he rode out of range of their guns. One thing is certain—that the scoundrel is too clever and has too many friends to be taken easily even by expert trailers and fighters with all the resources of the law at their backs. But this ridiculous girl imagines that a single man might succeed where posses have failed!"

Ricardo nodded.

"I understand——" he murmured.

He could understand many, many things, in fact, which had been suddenly revealed by the impatience of Ranger. Maud was like a man hunting for cutting tools. That was why she searched among the young men—she had changed her way of living so that she might have greater opportunities of coming in contact with the youngsters of the county—and combing among them, she had attracted the ones who appeared to her to be fighting men. And when they were flattered to a point of high interest, then she would reveal what she hoped.

The pursuit and the death or capture of Charles Perkins!

Ricardo thought back to the interview which he had spied upon, between Benn and Perkins, on the arrival of the gunman; and he wondered what emotion would fill his breast if ever he should stand weapon in hand before that monster among monsters?

"You understand?" repeated William Ranger. "Then you see what a fool she's making of herself—and yet she'll try the same dodge with you. And I suppose you'll be like the rest of the lads, and sheer off from the adventure?"

"I don't know," murmured Ricardo. "Of course, there's this to say: The posses have failed—but a posse makes a lot of noise when it's on a trail. Besides, Perkins would run from six men, but he'd never run from one!"

William Ranger drew his horse a little farther to the side. He scrutinized Ricardo with a savage disbelief.

"Young fellow," said he, "do you mean to tell me that you'd undertake such a work as that?"

"I don't know," said Ricardo. "The idea is just beginning to take hold on me."

20

◉

Cats Eat Rats

The ranch was not a whit impressive. It was simply a wretched old shack onto which two wings had been built to give added room as it was needed. It looked at first glance as though no two boards were of the same dimensions or type of timber, and the rambling size of the house merely increased its appearance of poverty. The trampling hoofs of horses and cattle had ironed away all tokens of green life up to the very door of the place, before which stood two long hitching racks, the wood deeply gnawed and the ground pawed into holes beneath the crossbars. One would have said that a heavy wind blew constantly here and whipped out the very roots of the grasses before they caught hold.

The house did not stand by itself. A bunk house stood nearby. There were a few sheds, two great barns, and no fewer than ten stacks of hay or straw, now with a winter-old cap of moldering brown upon each one. The winter feeding pens made a network of rusted barbed wire and staggering posts and boards near the stacks.

"We have to feed a lot in the winter if it comes a hard year," explained Maud Ranger to Ricardo.

She pointed about her. The mountains were like a sea chopped one way by a storm wind and another by a current; they crowded their heads close together; the forest slipped from their steep shoulders; bald rocks glistened above timber line; and two summits were veined with white in the upper canyons, one was brilliantly capped with snow!

"You can see for yourself," she said. "The lighter snows generally are filtered down through the trees and not so many come down to the level of the lower valleys, like this one. But now and then everything is deep with snow; a thaw and a hard freeze, and we're apt to have thousands of cows on our hands. That's a hard job, you know. Do you know a good deal about cows?"

Ricardo hesitated an instant. He felt that now he was actually on a cow ranch, it would be dangerous to pretend.

"No," he said. "I don't."

She was as sharp and as rough as a man in her talk.

"But I thought that you came from a cow country?" she said.

"I do. But everybody in a cow country doesn't ride herd, you know."

She frowned, and looked squarely at him.

"What sort of work did you do down in your country?" she asked.

"A Mexican, you know," said the boy, "is supposed to grow up to be a gentleman, not a laborer."

"Ah?" she murmured.

She was not at all contented with this lofty reply, but she said no more about it, though once or twice her glances darted in a sort of honest indignation at Ricardo.

William Ranger had fallen back from the side of the boy and his niece. He appeared to find the hunchback more attractive for conversation.

In the meantime, they moved on to the house; after the first glance, the building itself was of less and less importance. The broken mountains filled the eye of the mind too completely.

"No one ever thought of working cows in this country," said Maud Ranger. "Everyone was only thinking of breaking through from one side to the other. People simply cursed and hated this range; in the winter, for years, it was considered to be impassable. But my father came here and settled down. He was not afraid!"

She let her voice swell a little, as she said that.

"He's famous, isn't he?" asked Ricardo, with as much of an air of interest as he could summon.

"No, he isn't," she replied sharply. "He ought to be! See what he did. He showed the way. Now there are twenty big ranches scattered through these mountains. Thousands of cows. But he's not famous. When he went into banking he got a lot more notoriety, he had his name in the papers more. But this is his real work. And who cared about it? Who cared a rap about it? Bah! How many posses are out now, hunting for the murderer? And yet it isn't as if he were an unknown man. Everyone knows that it's Charles Perkins. Everyone knows where Charles Perkins is to be found, and yet no one will dare to go get him!"

She clenched both her hands. She was trembling. And Ricardo, braced and prepared as he had been for such a statement from her, was astounded now. He had put her down as a cool-minded girl, with a stubborn streak in her which wanted revenge for her father's death, but he had opened a door on a furnace to-day, a red whirl and leaping of flames.

"He did this!" said the girl.

She held out her hands in such a way that one would have thought she meant that her father had built the huge mountains, and she added at once: "No one would have lived with them, you see, if he hadn't shown the way. I was raised here!" she concluded. "In the old days, we were shut off all winter.

That was before dad spent so much to break a road through. I'm sorry he did. The old days were the best. You had to go isolated for months. No newspaper. No mail unless a rider struggled down through the lower passes once in a while. You were shut in, here. It used to be terribly cold. What fires on winter nights! The whole house used to shake, the flames went in such crowds, herding up the chimneys, and roaring! Every fire had its own voice. I could tell them apart by their muttering, and by their hissing!"

She laughed, and, her laughter breaking off suddenly, she struck her hands together. It was not as dramatic an act in the performance as in the description. But she had turned pale and her eyes seemed set in hollows of deep shadow out of which she looked sadly at the boy.

"I can imagine," said Ricardo stupidly. "Of course it was exciting to be winter-bound like that!"

"He did such things!" broke in the girl, riding over his comment. "He *was* such things! And what does the world care? Oh, what does it care? Every evening, Charles Perkins rides down from the hills to Back Creek, and rides into it, and rules the place. The police know where he is. But they won't try to get him. They're afraid! They're afraid!"

Her uncle rode suddenly up to them.

"You better hurry on, Maud!" said he in the bluffest of voices. "We can't loiter all evening on the road!"

She did not answer. Her head was pressed down a little so that the brim of her hat covered the upper part of her face, and Ricardo could guess that she was crying. He could remember, once, hearing a broken-hearted man sob—a brave and a strong man who, nevertheless, sobbed. It had been a moment of horror—a thing not even to think of. But the tears of that man affected him with no more force than this moment's weakness in the girl. She was no weak type, letting sorrows flow through her to a ready expression. He looked at her in bewilderment, realizing that all he had thought of her was wrong indeed. Enormous passions worked in her. And Ricardo was quite overawed.

William Ranger pressed close to Ricardo and said to him ominously: "That's a subject that is going to wreck the brain of Maud one of these days. We try to keep away from it. Do you understand?"

"You try to keep away from it?" replied Ricardo, tipping up his head. "But why don't you do something about it then?"

A hot exclamation of anger came on the lips of William Ranger, but he suppressed it at once.

"You're a stranger," he said. "You don't know what you're talking about. Perhaps you've never heard of Back Creek before?"

And Ricardo had to be silent, admitting that the name was new. Besides, he received a sudden keen glance from Lew, which he took as a warning.

So they got to the house and tethered their horses at the rack. A Negro boy came and led them away, Lew going along to give his matchless care to the span which were under his charge.

Then Ricardo was shown up to his room. It was a corner of the second story. It looked full to the northeast, and as she led him to it, Maud Ranger pointed out through the window.

"There's Back Mountain. You see the snow on the top of it, turning to flame, now, like the hair on your head. That's Back Mountain. Back Creek lies on the knee of it. You can't see the town from here. But you can know it is there. Every day I look and know it is there. And every evening time I know that he's riding down into the place—waving his hand to his friends—and laughing and joking with them—and asking for news—and scoffing at the law and the fools who do what the law bids! Every evening!"

She caught her breath, and hurried suddenly from the room, and Ricardo sat down on the edge of the bed and rolled a cigarette and lighted it, and looked vaguely out the window at the head of Back Mountain, now like a torch in the sky.

Lew, bringing up the pack, found him there, and Lew sat down and stretched.

"You brought her on," said Lew, nodding. "You done a good bit of work there. I thought you were playing too dumb at first. But you were right. Sometimes it's better to let them talk by themselves if they got plenty to say! It'll come out sooner or later."

Ricardo said bluntly: "Do you think she's sane? Do you think that she's out of her mind, a little?"

"All women are," said the hunchback. "Their brains are no good. They got wits, like a cat, but they got no mind. Look at her. She's on fire like Back Mountain!"

He jerked his thumb over his shoulder.

"Do you know about it?" asked Ricardo. "Is it true that Perkins rides down to Back Creek every evening—and no one touches him?"

"Of course it's true," said the dwarf. "Where else would he be going? Where else would he be safe?"

"But how can he be safe anywhere?" asked the boy.

"Cats eat rats," said the hunchback. "They don't dine on one another!"

21

⊙

Back Creek and Back Mountain

He would not talk any more about Back Creek.

"You ask the girl to tell you about it," said he. "That's the best way; because it'll show that you mean business. I thought that it would take a little time, but now you got the game in your own hands!"

He rubbed his own bony claws together.

"I don't understand," said Ricardo patiently.

"I'm gunna explain," remarked Lew. "Don't you worry. I'll show you where you stand. How is things now? Well, the girl is kind of desperate. Her old man was sacred to her. He died. Nobody took a scalp to get even. She feels the way that an Indian girl would feel. That's right and nacheral enough. She was raised half wild. Now she looks over to Back Mountain and it makes her think of Charlie Perkins, and she pretty near loses her mind. You take a girl, and you'll always find that she's more likely to carry on with what her dad was doing. This girl wants to do the same thing. She wants to make the ranch flourish. But first of all, she wants to revenge the death of the old man. I seen through it all to-day. She ain't really crazy, but she'd pretty near sell her soul to plant Charlie Perkins under the ground. Now she's heated up so bad that you'd better bring around a show-down pronto. That's the best way! Right after dinner you open up with questions.

That'll make the uncle see red. He'll try to force your hand. 'What are you gunna do about this here thing?' he'll say. 'I'm gunna go and try to kill Charlie Perkins,' you'll say. 'Why should you do that?' the uncle will ask. 'Because I love Maud Ranger!' you say. 'Bah!' says her uncle. 'You love her as much as seven million dollars' worth, don't you?' You stick to your guns. Play right out in the open, apparently. That's the way to bluff them."

Ricardo was on his feet, the cigarette fuming unnoticed between his fingers, his mouth twisted hard.

"It's too fast!" said he. "I can't rush on and talk like that. I hardly know her!"

"Of course you don't," said Lew.

He sat in the chair with his knees embraced in his long arms, grinning like an ape and rocking himself slowly back and forth.

"Of course, you don't know her! It was love at first sight with you. When you talk about her, she sets you on fire! You'll stand up before 'em all and tell 'em that. You'll pretty near convince 'em, because you got the makin's of a good, first-rate, hundred-percent liar in you! You lie smooth, nacheral, and easy. You gotta flow of words. That means a lot. It puts the brains to sleep!"

He laughed silently. It seemed to Ricardo that this creature was more hideous than William Benn, more terrible than the pale, inhuman face of the doctor. Yet he knew that this was only a demi-devil, contrasted with the superior art and malice of the other two.

However, he was under orders to follow the advice of the hunchback, and he set his teeth and determined to pass through the ordeal.

At dinner there were four at the table—Maud, himself, William Ranger, and the latter's wife. She was a square lump of a woman with a great curved nose set in the middle of a red face. Her husband was a good-looking man; it seemed a miracle that he would be married to such a cartoon of a woman. Moreover, she had few graces, but like all the Rangers and those associated with that family she was wonderfully blunt and to the point in everything that she had to say.

She carried on the main burden of the conversation after dinner began, by telling how she had ridden up "The Five-mile Trail" on a balky horse.

"I could turn him around, but I couldn't start him ahead.

I had a spade bit on the brute and with that I could make him back. So, finally, I started backing him up that trail. He tucked his tail between his legs like a scared dog and still he had to back because that spade bit was murdering his mouth and jaw. I backed him up that trail for about half a mile, I think, and all the time he was pretty sure that he was only a step from falling over the edge. He'll never balk again. After I finished with that lop-eared fool, he stood and shook for ten minutes. When he had his legs under him I rode on. He'll never say no again!"

And she stabbed her fork viciously into a section of carrot.

"We'll do the Five-mile Trail to-morrow," said Maud Ranger.

"Who'll do the Five-mile Trail?" snapped her aunt.

"I was speaking to Mr. Mancos," replied Maud coldly.

"That's a funny name," said the older woman. "Mancos. That's a Spanish name. How'd you come by such a name as that, young man?"

"Mr. Mancos is from Mexico," said Maud.

"What? With his eyes—and his hair—and his pink cheeks?" said Theodora Ranger.

She put down her formidable fork and glared at him.

"Bah!" said Theodora Ranger. "Mexico my foot!" she added, still staring.

"There's the Castilian strain," explained Maud, coloring a little. "You know that there was a lot of Gothic blood in northern Spain——"

"Gothic foot!" said Mrs. Ranger, who seemed to reserve that expression as a sort of heavy artillery to express her scorn of the notions of others. "Young man, if you're not white, I'm an Indian!"

Ricardo was so angry that he was on the verge of telling her that she was almost the right color to belong to that breed, and certainly she was more than sufficiently ugly to grace a tepee of the most savage Apache.

He said nothing. His face was pink, streaked with white, so great was his anger; for ever since the first conversation in which the doctor had pointed out the probability that he was an American, he had been extremely touchy on the point. He only felt that it was giving away his nationality; he could not think of it as a claiming of his real right.

"You'll ride the Five-mile Trail and break your two precious necks," said Mrs. Ranger. "Unless you take mules!"

"Leave them alone, Theodora," urged her husband. "They're not old enough to be argued with."

"You came out to see the place, did you?" asked Mrs. Ranger.

Ricardo nodded, and Mrs. Ranger leaned her powerful chin upon her hand and regarded him with leonine calm.

"You're fond of natural scenery, I suppose?" she said.

"Oh, yes," said Ricardo.

"And mountains?"

"Yes."

"And rocks?"

He saw that he was being baited and did not respond.

"Mostly the mountains, you like, I suppose?" said Mrs. Ranger.

And at that, he struck back at her with a smile on his lips.

"Back Mountain is a wonderful old peak," said he. "I like Back Mountain especially."

Mrs. Ranger glanced at her niece and bit her lip. Then, as covertly as she could, she shook her head at their new guest, but Ricardo had seen the girl shiver and jerk up her head. He went on blandly:

"I'd like to know about the village on it, too—and how it is that in such a place they can laugh at the law. Can you tell me anything about it, Mrs. Ranger?"

She was so angry that she grew purplish, only the concern she felt for her niece kept her in control.

"I'll show you a map of the mountain *after* dinner," she said pointedly.

Maud Ranger clasped her hands on the edge of the table.

"I'll tell you all about it," she said in a slow voice.

"You'll do nothing of the kind," insisted Mrs. Ranger. "You go on with your dinner!"

Maud Ranger shook her head slightly.

"I can tell you," she said, fixing her glance upon Ricardo.

And he thought it was the strangest look he ever had seen on the face of woman or man, there was so much cruelty in it, and pity, and curiosity, and pain, and hope. And all these qualities were in her voice, though she kept that low. And Ricardo listened as to dangerous music.

"I can tell you all about it," she repeated. "The town of Back Creek is dumped down in a tangle of wild forest and rocks. Nearly all the people who live there are on the spot because they can't live any other place. There are always a couple of hundred scoundrels there. Several times a sheriff has taken a posse out there, but the wanted men scatter through the trees and the rocks, and the others keep them supplied with food. They're an organized community to protect crime. They *live* on crime!"

"You'd better postpone the rest of the story!" said Mrs. Ranger, giving Ricardo a dreadful glance.

"But how can they live on crime in the middle of the mountains? Do they rustle cattle?" asked Ricardo.

"They live on the money that the freshest of the crop bring in. The crooks carry their money with them. They pay for the protection they get. And that money passes through the village. It's the blood that keeps it alive. And that's the reason that Charles Perkins went there!"

Mrs. Ranger pushed back her chair a little, and it screeched on the floor, for she was a heavy woman.

"Maud!" she exclaimed.

"Well?" said the girl.

"I'm not going to have you start that thing again!"

"Can you tell me why I'm not to answer questions about Back Mountain?"

"You know perfectly well what you're leading up to!"

Maud Ranger said nothing, and her aunt, growing more angry, pointed deliberately at Ricardo.

"Besides," she said, "you're losing your wits, appealing to a pretty baby like this!"

22

◉

Maud Ranger's Promise

It was a distinctly unpleasant climax. Ricardo looked down at the table and wished for something to say. Dinner was at an end. Everyone sat stiff and collected for trouble. Maud Ranger did not make an immediate reply to her blunt aunt, and the latter carried on with the attack which she began.

She said to Ricardo: "Young man, do you know why you've been brought up here?"

"Yes," said Ricardo. "We were talking about my own home country. It's a good deal like this. Miss Ranger kindly thought that I would be interested to see——"

"Bah!" exclaimed Mrs. Ranger. "The truth is——"

"Theodora," broke in her husband, "I think that you've gone about far enough. There's no use dragging in the horrors at this point."

"I've started it. Now let me finish it," she insisted. "I'm not going to go through another dreadful farce. Mr. Mancos, will you listen to me?"

Ricardo watched her, making his expression as polite as possible, but all the time he was keeping covert watch upon the girl, to see how she took this affair, and he was hardly surprised to see that she was perfectly cool under fire.

"*I* know what Maud is up to," said the older woman, striking her clenched hand, though lightly, on the edge of the table. "You'll be shown around the place for a day or two, but after that you'll have the idea put to you in so many shapes that pretty soon you'll begin to take it seriously. Do you know what the crazy girl's idea is, Mr. Mancos?"

Ricardo was silent. After all, there was not much that he could say.

"It's simply this: That the sheriffs and the posses are helpless to get at Perkins because, when they come, their numbers send the warning before them. And then everyone assists Perkins to get off into the tall timber. But if a single man went to the town, he'd have no difficulty in getting at that murderer! In one word, Mr. Mancos, she hopes that *you're* the man who will undertake such a job. She hopes that *you* are going to meet and stand up to Charles Perkins singlehanded. And if that's not madness, I'd like to know what is!"

She went on angrily:

"Maud, I want you to say whether or not I'm right! Confess! It'll be good for your soul. You wanted to send this poor infant against that fiend of a Perkins. Am I correct?"

Ricardo looked keenly at Maud. She was staring down at her clasped hands as she replied in an even voice: "What else can I do, except to hunt through the world for brave men and see if one of them will fight for me, because I can't fight for myself?"

"Staring, raving nonsense!" exclaimed Mrs. Ranger.

"Theodora," said her husband sternly, "you'll have to stop it. You mustn't carry on like this any longer!"

"What would you do?" she asked. "Would you have a pink-and-white softy like this boy sent out to have his head blown off his shoulders to suit the silly whim of Maud? But you see, Mr. Mancos, that she's honest enough to confess at once!"

Ricardo did not make any comment, he was too busy trying to arrange words in his mind for this critical moment.

And Maud Ranger gave him no rest. "It's true. I'd noticed you before, but I don't suppose that I would have been so very excited if it hadn't been for what happened to Dick Jones. They don't understand what I mean, but you do."

"What Dick Jones?" asked Mrs. Ranger in her harsh voice. "You mean that wild man from Montana? There would have been a possible man for you, Maud, I admit."

"He had a little trouble with Mr. Mancos," said the girl, "and when it was over, Dick went home."

"You mean he wasn't fit to be seen?" asked Mrs. Ranger, with her usual bluntness. "You mean that this boy whacked Dick out of shape?"

Maud looked at her aunt with the faintest of smiles.

"No, it just happened that he was called away. And Mr. Mancos had a barked knuckle—because he'd grazed against the wall in the garden——"

She paused and turned her glance toward Ricardo. All three of them stared at him. He colored a little, and then Mrs. Ranger burst out: "I don't know that that makes it any better. What's against nature is not to be admired. How *could* this boy beat Dick Jones, unless he's a freak? Oh, well, I don't want to insult him. But I wish that you'd tell me exactly what happened between you and Jones, Mr. Mancos!"

"We agreed," said Ricardo, "that we couldn't agree. He—er—went home. That is all there is to it."

"Are you modest?" asked the blunt lady of the house. "But at any rate, that doesn't matter. You know about Charles Perkins, I suppose?"

"Yes."

"And now that you know why Maud has brought you up here, what are you going to do about it?"

"I suppose," said Ricardo, "that I'd better go to have a look at Mr. Perkins, if I can!"

100

"You *can* easily enough," exclaimed the virago. "You can look once, at least. But——"

"I think you might stop bullying," said Maud Ranger. "You've dragged my affairs out into the full light of day. Now I think you might leave them there. You've done what harm you could do!"

This cold speech had no effect upon Mrs. Ranger, who exclaimed: "And if you *did* find Charles Perkins, what do you think you would do to him, young man?"

He answered gently: "I would kill him if I could."

"Kill him!" said Mrs. Ranger scornfully. "And with what? With a pebble from your sling? Do you carry a gun, perhaps, Mr. Mancos?"

"I carry an old gun for shooting rabbits," said Ricardo.

He had grown angrier and angrier as the scorn of Mrs. Ranger and her disbelief were poured out upon him.

Now he stretched out his hand and under it there appeared a Colt .45, which he laid on the table before his hostess.

The others were startled a little by his unusual gesture. But then they began to notice many points of interest about the weapon—as that it possessed no trigger, and the sights had been filed off, and the gun had a peculiar look of battered care, like a well-polished antique.

"Who gave you that gun?" asked Mrs. Ranger.

"I bought it new," answered the boy.

"Well," gasped his hostess, "it's like something out of a book. But it's a man's gun! You *are* a trained fighter, then? But what's induced you to come up here to fight for Maud Ranger?"

Crimson poured over the face of Ricardo.

He could not speak.

"Out with it!" said the cruel Theodora.

"That question—ah, well—it's because——"

Ricardo stumbled and blundered again.

"You have no right to ask that!" he said at last.

"Bah!" snapped Mrs. Ranger. "Haven't I? But I have, though! It's because you can see seven million dollars as clearly as any man!"

"Aunt Theodora!" cried the girl, starting from her chair.

Ricardo had risen also. He was white—the truth is sometimes a poisoned arrow—but he retained his dignity.

"It was not the love of money that made me want to serve her!" he said.

101

And the lie came gravely from his lips.

"Not love of money. Love of her, then?" mocked Mrs. Ranger. "Love at first sight, I suppose!"

Maud Ranger broke in: "Aunt Theodora, I won't stand another word of this. You've insulted me repeatedly. You've begun to insult an invited guest. I don't know what you're thinking of!"

"Great Heavens!" said the aunt. "If you had the wit of a blackbird, you'd understand. I was wrong. This boy is not a pink-and-white little fool. He's a trained fortune hunter. And he wants you!"

The tortured girl cried out in a passion: "And what if he does? And what if he does? You and the rest sit quietly by. It doesn't matter to you if justice is sound asleep. You don't care. I've worked and prayed and hoped to find the man who would bring justice to Perkins. And if Ricardo Mancos can do it——"

"Wait a moment!" exclaimed William Ranger, rising at last in alarm. "What are you about to say?"

"What you've driven me to say!" she answered.

"I'm not driving you!" exclaimed Theodora Ranger. "Don't be silly. Don't say anything rash!"

But the girl hurried to Ricardo and stood before him very close.

"Are you honest? Are you fair and square?" she asked him.

He had to strain every ounce of strength in his soul to meet that searching glance.

"I hope I am," said he.

"Then—if you kill Charles Perkins—I don't know that you'd want me; but you could have me if you did——"

"Maud!" shouted her aunt.

"It's no use talking now," said the girl. "I've given my promise. You've badgered me and mocked me. And you know that there's one sacred thing in this filthy world, and that's my word of honor! Do you hear, Mr. Mancos? I confess everything. You're only a fighting machine to me. I got you up here, hoping that I could bribe you to take the trail of Perkins. And I'm willing to bribe you with all that I have and all that I am! I give you my word of honor. I swear to Heaven that this is the truth!"

She turned and ran from the room and left a gasping silence behind her. Then William Ranger said: "Young man, you've heard that promise. But if you should ever attempt to hold her to that promise I can assure you we all would——"

Nothing irritates a man so much as to know that he has played a low part, and Ricardo knew that he had lied, and been a grave-faced sneak. Now he took a quick step and caught Mr. Ranger by the wrist:

"I've been bullied and insulted by your wife," said he. "But she's a woman. You're a man—at least, I hope so!"

And he left the room as quickly as the girl had done. He could hear Mrs. Ranger saying, as the door closed behind him: "There *is* poison in him!"

23

◉

A Seven-Million-Dollar Mine

When Ricardo reached his room he was met at once by the grinning face of the dwarf, Lew, and the sight shocked and injured him; as though the devil that had been working in him at the supper table was here reduced to the flesh.

"Why are you here?" asked Ricardo. "The bunk house is for you, I suppose!"

Lew merely nodded.

"Of course, it is," he answered. "But I dropped in to spend a minute chatting with you, and I thought that maybe you'd want this."

He had taken out a flask, from which he poured two fingers of amber liquor into a tumbler. Ricardo took it; it was strong brandy, and he allowed the fumes to mount to his head. It relaxed him. He slipped into a chair and supported his forehead on the heel of the palm of his left hand.

"That's correct," said Lew. "Always, you have the right hand free, you understand? But you needed that drink. It'll do you good! The way that you been workin'!"

"What do you know?" asked Ricardo.

"On the way up to your room, I just stopped for a minute outside the dining-room window. Of course, I seen what happened inside, and I heard."

Ricardo stared blankly at him.

"You got brains," said Lew. "I told you what to do and what to say, but you cut everything fine, and made them bring the game to you! Well, that was brains. When that old fool of an aunt of the girl started to talk, I thought that you'd get sore and sling something back at her. Not you! I couldn't help admirin' the sad and silent kind of dignity you showed. It was a grand bluff. I seen that minute that you have the making of a grand little old poker player in you! I'm gunna teach you the game myself, lad. I'm gunna take you in hand. We're gunna make you a polished performer. What with the doctor, and Benn, and Wong, and the Negro, and me, we're gunna make you a performer, all right, and a stake horse, at that!"

This speech flowed so cheerfully and rapidly from the lips of the hunchback that Ricardo had no need to answer. And now, as he raised his head, the dwarf went on: "It makes you a little sick, just now. Always that way, at first, and particularly when you're workin' against a woman. Take an up-standin', fine wild-hearted girl like Maud. It sort of turns you to think of double crossing her. But then, she's let herself in for it. She played the fool, and fools have gotta pay, in this here world of ours!"

He struck his hands suddenly together with fierce exultation and exclaimed.

"Now we got them in our hands. Seven millions! And a fine wife for you. It's the grandest thing that ever come out of the brain of Benn. He's a great man. I always knew he was, but this beats everything! Seven million dollars!"

He whispered it, with an indrawn breath.

Then he added, savagely: "You heard what she asked? Are you honest? Are you fair and square? Well, you see what that means?"

"I know that I'm a liar," said Ricardo. "Is that what you mean?"

"It means that if she gets an inkling of what you really are, then the deal is off. But, once married to her, you have her in your pocket. You have her, and the rest is easy sailing!"

"I want to be alone," said Ricardo.

104

"Sure you do," said Lew. "Besides, I've got to go and report to the boss. He's gunna eat his heart out till he hears how you got through the first evening here."

He went back toward the window.

"Shall I leave you the flask, kid?"

"No, thank you."

"That's right. Leave the stuff alone. Just a jolt when your blood gets cold. That's all it's good for. Tell me one thing. When do you want to start?"

"The sooner the better."

"To-morrow morning, then, if the boss says so. The doctor has gone on ahead, I think. I'll be back before dawn and let you know everything exact!"

He disappeared through the window. There was only a faint scratching sound for an instant. When Ricardo went to the window and leaned out, there was no sight of the dwarf.

So the boy undressed, and turned in. His conscience, after all, was no powerful engine, and it could not avail to keep him awake. The last fumes of the brandy deadened his nervous brain; he smiled with numb lips at the praise which the hunchback had showered upon him; again he felt that he had committed himself to a mighty current. At last he slept, and dreamed that William Benn had come to him in the guise of a winged dragon, and snatched him up, and borne him across the world in resistless flight.

Then he awakened, with a tapping at his shoulder. The dwarf was leaning above him; the room was still black with night, but the window was a gray square.

"I seen Benn. It's fixed and right. You start on to-day. You take me along with you. You better get up and get ready to start now. We oughta be on the trail by dawn!"

Dragging himself out of his slumber, Ricardo dressed. His clothes were damp and cold; he went down through the chilly house and out under a windy sky. Flags of clouds were hung from the southern mountains; those to the east were black with the day coming up swiftly behind them.

"It's a mean day, ain't it?" grinned Lew. "But the darker the day, the better the start. The day ain't half as dark as when we're gunna meet up with Charlie Perkins. You can lay to that!"

By the time the packs were made up, and the horses saddled, the sun was nearly up and life was stirring on the ranch. From the kitchen chimney smoke poured white and thick, and in that kitchen they sat down to fried bacon, and cold bread, and huge mugs of coffee.

When they finished, they went out to their horses, which stood head down at the hitching rack, pointing their rumps toward the increasing blast. The fingers of Ricardo were half numbed before he could work them into his riding gloves, and as he swung into the saddle, Maud Ranger came out to him. She held his horse by the head and talked up to him.

"I've tried to think it out all night," she said. "I've told myself over and over that you're dreadfully young. And now I want to tell you that if it's only pride that's driving you on to try a thing where all the odds are against you—get off your horse again and go back to bed. *I* would never reproach you!"

He shook his head.

"I only want to get on the trail," he said.

She abandoned the head of the horse, stepped closer to him and gripped his glove hand.

"Good luck!" she said.

Then Ricardo took off his hat to her, and the wind blew the yellow flame of his hair forward and fluttering about his face. And so he turned off and started on the trail to Back Mountain with the dwarf riding a little behind him.

When they were out of sight of the house, and dipping down into the first valley, Lew came at his left hand.

"All that you gotta think of is riding straight ahead for Back Creek," said Lew. "Other brains is gunna take you up and handle the job for you, once you're there. All you need is to flash yourself as a crook. Understand?"

Ricardo nodded.

"You been doing a little safe cracking, kid. That's the job that you've just cleaned up on. You gotta have a wad to flash. Here you are!"

He took out a wallet and passed it to Ricardo. Inside, the boy saw the fluttering edges of a sheaf of bills.

"There's about three thousand in that," said Lew. "But you don't have to say how little. You've cleaned up. That's the idea. And you're heading for Back Creek so's to let the fuss die down before you come out into the world again. Is that right?"

"Yes," said Ricardo, nodding again.

"The main idea is to be free and easy of everything except talk. A little silence is fine salt for any sort of conversation that you have to have in Back Creek. But always act scared, a little. Don't sit down with your back to the door. Stand up, rather. Keep your right hand always free. Look people over before you talk to them, and look like you got something in your mind."

"Has there been a bank robbery lately?" asked Ricardo.

"There's always been a safe cracked, big or little, not long before, and it happens that just a few days ago there was a job done in Wyoming and a couple of bank clerks were planted under the sod after the shooting was over."

"Could we come from Wyoming here so quickly?"

"By train, sure! Then we hopped off the train and we got the pair of hosses, and we started drifting for Back Creek. That's all. You don't have to say even that. But that's your story. Benn says that's the thing for you to have in your mind!"

That ended the talk. They began to ride through a tangle of broken ravines, only now and then following some very dim cowpath, but usually pushing ahead like boats through a wild sea. But the dwarf seemed to know his way perfectly.

"I've been here before," said he. "That was before I met with Bill Benn and learned how to laugh at the law. That was when I was a young fool!"

Their horses were good; the guide was perfect; and they made such good time that at last they were in sight of a rugged hillside above which the huge front of Back Mountain sprang up to his gleaming snows.

"There's Back Creek," said the hunchback, "and that's where we gotta dig the mine that's got seven million salted away in the ground. Spit on your hands, kid, and wish us all good luck!"

24

Ricardo Rides Outside

The site of Back Creek was a little shoulder which had been carved out of the ribs of the mountain by the action of the creek itself. It was not a well-leveled shoulder. In fact, is was sprinkled over with gigantic boulders which often looked more like human habitations than the odd-shaped shanties and shacks which had been thrown together here and there among the rocks. The roar of the foaming creek dominated all other sounds. And the single street of the village ran a twisting course, like a tormented mountain torrent, dodging among the big rocks. The village itself had rather the look of a temporary summer camp, hastily thrown up, and abandoned years before. Now it was occupied again, one would have said, without having sufficient time invested in it to make it comfortable. There were not two sound pieces of glass in the windows of Back Creek, and the missing panes had been filled in with rags, sacking, or, at the best, thin boards which in turn had cracked again. The doors stood open, sagging from their hinges. Ricardo looked into interiors where the ground was naked, or where the flooring, perhaps, had been half torn up in order to supply fuel on the severely cold nights of winter.

The hunt for fuel had ripped away a large portion of the forest. Enormous stumps surrounded Back Creek, and one could tell by the color of the cuttings the number of years during which Back Creek had been a town. Beyond this ragged circle of clearing, the virgin woods began, huge beyond belief, making a secondary night beneath their branches. It was easy to see why Back Creek had become an ideal resort for criminals seeking to avoid the law, for the woods themselves offered an endless labyrinth through which whole armies of searchers might have passed in vain. And to complicate matters the more, canyons were split deep in the side of the mountain—looking as though they had been bashed out with the hammer strokes of the back of an ax.

A fugitive could have run on foot from the village and hidden himself from mounted men! Ricardo noted all these features with a most appreciative eye; and then he turned to Lew.

"We never can find our man," he suggested.

"If I can't go to him, he'll come to us," said Lew. "There's the hotel."

The hotel looked not like one building, but three or four heaped together in a jumble. One could see the lines of growth as the additions had been piled on hodge-podge. In front of it staggered a long veranda, and in front of the veranda were watering troughs, green with slime, and beaded with moss on the outside.

On this veranda no fewer than a dozen men were sprawled in chairs, smoking cigarettes, and looking out at the rough world and listening to the music which a gigantic Negro ground out of a small hand organ.

He stood in the dust of the rutted street and turned the handle of his organ, his head of tight, gray curls exposed to the burning heat of the sun, the back of his neck glistening with moisture. A short, disorderly, gray beard was kinked on his chin, and his tired, expectant face he turned up and down the veranda in hope of money.

No one gave any sign that they saw these appealing glances. Neither did they give any token that they were aware of Ricardo, who threw the reins of his horse to Lew and went up the steps to the veranda level. There he paused lightly and scanned the line up and down.

He received not a flash from a single eye in recognition. He drew from his trousers pocket a silver dollar. At the flash of it, twelve men jerked in their chairs, twelve hands leaped, and at the farther end of the line one man actually drew a Colt—though he hastily stowed it again in his clothes.

But in that instant, Ricardo had looked into more savage, fighting, human souls than ever he had seen or dreamed of before. He tossed the dollar to the huge, old Negro at the hand organ, made no pause to receive thanks, and walked into the hotel feeling that he was stepping through red-hot coals.

There was a little lobby, but not a soul in it except an iron-jawed slattern of a woman. A woman to keep a hotel in such a town!

But she was such a woman as could have kept the keys of a prison. The flesh on her face had shrunk with time to reveal the apelike structure of her head, and from under massive brows she glared at Ricardo out of red eyes.

"How d'ye?" And she shoved the register toward him.

"Good afternoon," said Ricardo.

At this, she laughed. "You're one of the high-flyers, are you?" said she.

She jerked the register around and scrutinized the signature which he had left upon it.

"Single or double?"

"Double."

"Them that ride double will break down the hoss!" she uttered. And then she led the way up a trembling stairs to the floor above. She took him to a dingy little chamber that looked to the rear of the hotel.

"How's this?"

"I can make it do."

"You better. It's the last in the place! Want anything?"

"No."

She went out, slammed the door, and strode down the hall with a step like a man's, while Ricardo made sure of his surroundings. His window sill was twelve feet from the ground. He could look to the side on the projecting shed which served as the kitchen, and six steps from the rear wall of the kitchen the mountainside began its upward flight, ending with the white helmet which sat at the crest, like a sun-filled cloud in the middle of the sky.

Lew came up with the packs at once. He whispered from one corner of his mouth, rolling his bright eyes.

"We come in a busy time," he said. "That's all the better. The more there is to talk about the less will be said. 'Tiger' Cheney and 'Lank' Morris is both here. I seen Paul, 'the Yegg,' and 'Little Willie' Smith that bumped off the two cops in Denver, last month. We got a sweet crowd, all right, but the main thing is that we got the crowd. We can hide in that!"

"Shall I stay close?"

"No, go and roam around. They'll expect you to. Walk up and down the street, then circle around the woods. Get a picture of everything in your eye. That's what a crook would do, you know. You won't have any trouble. A couple of those birds have spotted me. They don't know much, but they

110

know that I wouldn't be with any simp. They'll take you for something more than face value. Keep your mouth shut, or else talk about the weather. If anybody begins to kid you or work you up, sit tight and look him in the eye. If you find it too hard to do that, or you begin to get shaky, call his hand."

"Fight him?" asked the boy, keen with curiosity.

"With a gun. But if once they got an idea that you're backin' up, they might break you open to see what you're like inside. A killing ain't nothing in this town. Nothing at all!"

Ricardo took that careful advice and went down to the street. No one, again, noticed him as he crossed the veranda. There he paused to roll a cigarette, standing with his face turned a little toward the line of idlers, and his back against one of the wooden pillars which supported the veranda roof, the very attitude of a man who wants to keep his eye upon every neighbor.

He did the rolling, expertly, with a twist of his left hand—keeping the right almost always free, as Lew had cautioned him. Then he descended the steps, a little sidling, and turned hastily around the corner of the building.

Out of sight, he hesitated a single instant, long enough to hear a voice mutter:

"That kid ain't as pretty as he looks!"

"He's been there," drawled another.

And a ridiculously keen thrill of pleasure passed through Ricardo.

He went up the street as he had been directed, walking squarely in the middle of it; for he had read, somewhere, that the center of a street is the safest part of it. From the middle of a road, one can scan either side, and occasionally flash glances to the rear. And so Ricardo walked on as though he were one with a hundred murders upon his mind and prepared to fight out the consequences.

He made the tour of the town which Lew had directed. Then he returned to the hotel, and Lew met him on the veranda.

"There's a bird wants you back in the bar," said Lew. And he led the way.

Inside the hall, he whispered from the corner of his mouth: "You say no, you want nothing."

They went back into a barroom. Behind the bar was a

111

ruddy-faced man who smoothed the wooden surface with the palm of his hand. In the farthest, darkest corner stood a man with an old-fashioned, saber-shaped mustache that gave him an appearance at once sagacious and formidable.

"Your pleasure, gents," said the bartender.

The voice was oddly familiar to Ricardo, but he gave no sign. Lew was leading him up to the man of the mustache.

"You gunna ride inside or out?" asked the other.

Ricardo hesitated. He had no idea what this formula could mean.

"Some take their chances and others play it safe," said the other. "But I ain't peddlin' protection like life insurance. You please yourself, but I gotta hail everybody new."

"I'll ride outside," said Ricardo.

The other looked straight at him.

"You're young," said he.

"Just young enough," said Ricardo, and looked straight back.

And it was not easy; for it was as though a physical force were drawing his glance to either side; yet he remembered the caution of Lew, and narrowed his gaze and strove to beat down the barrier and look into the mind of the other.

Suddenly the latter grinned a twisted smile.

"What'll you have?" said he.

And Ricardo knew that he had succeeded in his second step in Back Creek.

25

⦿

Enter Perkins

They all drank—Ricardo only a small drink, which barely covered the bottom of his glass; and then the stranger left at once.

"What was it all about?" asked Ricardo of Lew.

The hunchback shrugged his rounded, thick shoulders.

"Ask the bartender," he suggested.

Ricardo followed that odd advice.

"What did he mean?" he asked.

"By what?" growled the man behind the bar.

"By riding inside, or out, for instance."

"That's a cinch," said the other. "He meant did you want protection and to stay inside the town, or out?"

"Is that it?"

"It is," said the bartender. "You take most of the boys that come up here, they got something on their minds besides hair. They got something to think about. Well, they got up a regular organization. They take care of newcomers that don't know the ropes. They work for each other like a lot of dog-gone brothers. That's what he was askin' you about."

"I may not be here long," said Ricardo. "Perhaps I can get along without it."

"You're pretty young," snarled the bartender, "and you don't know the town."

Ricardo had been in the act of turning away from the bar, but at this insulting speech, he checked himself. He was by no means inclined to take offense at everything; certainly not from a bartender! So he hung in mid-stride, noting a peculiarly wide grin of joy on the face of Lew.

Ricardo sighed.

"I don't know," said he, "whether you're insulting me or not, but if you are, we'll have our trouble now!"

The bartender smiled and nodded.

"You're doing very well, Ricardo," said he.

"Doctor Clauson!" murmured Ricardo.

"Hush!"

Ricardo could only stare. The worthy doctor was disguised in the most masterful fashion. Now he added rapidly: "The boys will leave you fairly well alone, now that you've shown that you're a man. That will leave your hand free to play the game with Charles Perkins."

"Where is he now?" asked Lew.

"In the back room beyond the door, playing cards."

"Now?"

"Yes."

Even the cool nerves of Lew were a little shaken by this announcement. He settled himself in the farthest corner of the bar and looked worried.

"He's been in here a dozen times in the last few days,"

went on the doctor. "And each of the dozen times he's looked me in the face and seemed to know me. A dozen times I expected to get a bullet through the head." Then he added: "He doesn't know you, Lew?"

"No chance of that, I think."

"He saw you at the house of Benn?" said the doctor to Ricardo.

"Yes."

"But you're one man he won't know. You've changed a good deal since that day," nodded the doctor, with satisfaction.

"Is he wild?" asked Lew.

"He's in the last stage," said the doctor. "He's taking to cards to kill time; and he's losing so much that he has to take to drink to console himself."

"Does he get drunk?"

"Not yet. He keeps himself in hand, because he has an idea that he'll die if ever he lets go. But the day isn't far off when he'll snap. We'll play a waiting game, I think, for a week or so. And then we'll take him with no trouble whatever."

Ricardo raised his head and listened more sharply. He knew that the doctor's morals were not of the highest, but it was hard to think that any man would wait until another was helpless with liquor before deliberately attacking him.

They had no opportunity for further conversation, for the door to the back room was at this moment kicked open and in came half a dozen men.

"You'll have this one on me, Charlie," said one of them, "and better luck to you afterward."

"You'll drink on me," snarled the voice of Charles Perkins. "I never drunk myself into luck, drinking liquor that another gent paid for. Line up and call for your own. Spin 'em out, bartender, and pronto!"

The doctor showed amazing skill, spinning the glasses rapidly onto the bar, where they stood in a straight, sparkling line.

"One for everybody, and that includes yourself," said Perkins.

The heart of Ricardo sank. He could steel himself to a good many things, but he could not be prepared to drink liquor bought by a man he intended to kill, if it lay within his power to do so.

So he steadied himself, and with faintly moving lips, he whispered inwardly that the time had come. Covertly, he touched the handle of his revolver. It was loose and easy in the sheath, and all was ready for the gun play which must surely follow.

In the meantime, the bottle of whisky was making rapid progress up the bar, being tipped at each glass, and thrust on until it reached Lew, whose pale, deformed hand clutched it when——

"Hold on!" barked Perkins. "Who are you?"

Lew dropped the bottle at that challenging shout. It rolled over the edge of the bar, spouting amber liquor as the doctor scooped it neatly up and out of the air and righted it.

Lew had spun about and faced toward the murderer.

"And who are you to ask me, Perkins?" said he.

Perkins strode slowly forward. The other men at the bar hurried back with scampering feet, for the voice of Perkins had been as loaded with danger as a gun.

"You're Lew Something-or-other," said Perkins. "I begin to place you, and I don't place you as no friend of mine!"

Lew did not retort to this.

Suddenly the left hand of Perkins shot out and he shook it almost in the face of the smaller man.

"You hang around to do dirty work for Benn. Is that it? You little skunk, is that what you do?"

Still Lew did not answer, and Ricardo, staring hard, was able to make out the reason. If there were a fight, and guns were drawn, whether Lew lived or died made small difference. But if he chanced to down the outlaw, then all the grandiose scheme of William Benn for the glorification of Ricardo was finished at a stroke.

So Lew said not a word.

"A yaller little rat, too!" suggested Perkins. "He won't answer back. Then, get out of here, you——"

He pointed toward the door—still with his left hand—for the right, of course, was being reserved for a necessary emergency.

Ricardo started violently as he saw what he must do.

"Perkins!" he called.

The outlaw jumped back to such a position that he could keep his glance upon both Lew and the new speaker.

"What're you?" demanded Perkins.

"You're hunting for trouble," said Ricardo, "and if that's what you want, why do you pick on little men like Lew?"

Charles Perkins looked at him with incredulous eyes.

"Are *you* nearer of a size to me?" he asked. "Why, you baby-faced fool, d'you know who I am?"

"You're Charles Perkins, sneak, robber, and murderer," said Ricardo, with deliberate satisfaction. "What else you may be, I don't know. Nothing good, I lay my bet."

A challenge more deliberate could not have been voiced, and for a trembling instant, Perkins was on the verge of a draw. Then he shook his head.

"I get the lay on the land," he said at last. "I start for you, and the hunchback there, shoots me in the ribs. Or, I start on him, and you split me open. And if the two of you got the nerve to start trouble with me, most likely you got somebody else planted."

He shouted suddenly:

"Where's a pair of gents that'll pull their guns and stand by me to give me fair play?"

From the card associates of Perkins there came no reply. They did not care to venture themselves in such a danger as this might prove to be, and now Perkins turned purple with rage and suspicion.

"Have you got your trap on me?" he asked. "Then, darn you, I tell you what I'll do. The next time that I lay eyes on either of you, I'm gunna have it out with you. No challenge first. No nothing. We shoot on sight. And that goes!"

He was backing toward the open door as he spoke, and now he leaped through it and was gone. Ricardo turned back to the bar.

"We might as well drink this," he suggested. "I'm glad to stand the round, boys!"

He felt keen, curious eyes upon him, and rejoiced to know that there was respect in them. He felt that he had come out of this part of the affair with some credit, but he knew that the plans of William Benn would not be strained to the uttermost if Perkins were to be maneuvered into a difficult corner. To a certain extent, the gunman had been forewarned. He might, as a matter of fact, straightway leave Back Creek. Ricardo told himself that, had he been in the boots of Perkins, he would have done exactly this.

The drink was taken. There was another round offered,

which Ricardo curtly refused. And then the gamblers scattered. The three were left alone again.

The doctor leaned over the bar.

"Now act fast!" he said. "Kid, get your horse and come back past the rear of the hotel!"

26

◉

Exit

Ricardo went on the run to do as he was bid. He was glad of any sort of violent action, for in his knees there seemed to be no strength, and his breath came short, and his face was cold. He felt that any sort of exercise was what he needed to start the blood pumping afresh.

He found his horse in the stable, jerked a saddle off the rack behind its stall, and quickly made it ready. The bridle he slipped over the ears of his mount, and now he was in the saddle and trotting toward the hotel. He went skimming past the window of the bar, and the doctor leaned out to him.

"Turn up the street!" muttered the doctor. "It's nine tenths in your hands now, Ricardo. Show Benn that I've taught you a few things worth knowing. And if you have to die, die shooting! Go on!"

These words were rapidly spoken, so that Ricardo hardly had to draw rein, and then he drifted past, into the street, and turned as he was bidden. He covered three of the snaky turns of the street and then had sight of Lew, mounted on a little mustang, a true mountain horse. He waved his hand frantically to the right.

"Up that way! Up that way!"

Ricardo took a curve at a gallop.

"And ride, kid, ride!" called the hunchback.

The whip stung the flank of the big horse, and he doubled his gallop through the meager and twisting lane, from either side of which branches reached out and whipped at the face of Ricardo. Then the trail pitched up a steep slope, and at the top of the slope, it forked to right and left.

He drew rein, for his horse was almost groaning with the great labor he had been forced through. Then Ricardo saw a form approaching through the trees on the run, leaping from side to side to dodge the trunks, very like a football player running through a crowded field.

Swerving into sight came a Chinaman, his pigtail afloat behind him, and he waved his hand frantically toward the left.

Ricardo glared at him. Was he friend, or was he enemy? At any rate, he sent the horse on the left side of the fork—the more gladly, because the slope was not nearly so stiff in that direction, and he could raise a gallop again.

The way began to pitch up and down like a choppy sea, when he reached the edge of a lofty wood, among the trees of which the trail was lost at once, and Ricardo, drawing rein in despair, was aware of a gigantic form standing beneath the next tree and watching him.

"Did a rider go this way?" asked Ricardo.

The giant—he appeared to be the same who played the hand organ in front of the hotel on the arrival of Ricardo—extended a vast arm.

"Go straight on till you come to a nacheral avenue runnin' to the left. Go down that avenue till you come to a clearin'. Tie your horse back in the trees, oil up your gun, and wait for what's gunna come to you quick."

And again Ricardo obeyed, though he wondered greatly what all of this might mean.

He rode straight on, flattening himself along the back of his mount to dodge the branches which were continually lurching at his head. On his left now opened what appeared to him a natural avenue, such as had been named, and he swerved his horse into it. As he did so, he had a distant glimpse, among the trees, of the gigantic Negro rushing after him with enormous bounds.

It caused him a strong misgiving, but he had committed himself to this action, and he could not draw back. The speed of the gallop was no less an impulse than the current of his own thoughts, which rushed ahead of him and strove to figure what was coming to him.

Charles Perkins? Or a trap cunningly laid and baited for

his destruction? Or was he himself part of a trap which was about to close upon that famous gun fighter?

He lurched into a clearing, as had been described to him, saw about him almost an acre of ground, carpeted thick with ferns and with long, rank grass and weeds. He gave it hardly a glance except to see that there was no sign of another man in the place.

All the prophecy which had been made to him had proved correct, so far; therefore, he obeyed orders with the strictest care. He led his horse at once into the thick of the trees and tethered it. Then he came out and stood for not more than a half dozen seconds, just outside the verge of the trees. Yet that waiting moment was printed deep in his mind, in such a way that it never could be forgotten.

To the day of his death he would remember how the pines stood up in a rigid circle, like soldiers on guard, and watched him; and how a thin, crystal puff of cloud began to untangle itself from a shoulder of the upper mountain and waft away across the sky; and how the snows gleamed on the forehead of Back Mountain; and how a white hawk tipped back and forth in its flight above the clearing. Water seeped across the clearing—from a spring, perhaps. He remembered afterwards that he was foolishly worried lest his boots should be spoiled——

And then a man came out on the farther side of the clearing and walked straight toward him.

Charles Perkins!

Ricardo clutched at his gun automatically; and then he remembered that honor would not let him take any advantage and he dragged his hand away again.

Charles Perkins hurried on to within thirty steps and then halted abruptly.

"It's the kid!" he said in a voice like the grunt of an animal. "It's the kid, by gum, and they've planted him here for me! Why, boy, I'm gunna split you in two!"

"Whenever you're ready," said Ricardo, "begin! You can make the first move."

"Can I?" sneered the other.

Then he changed his expression. "You act like an upstandin' kid," he said. "Now, between you and me, I don't see no reason why we shouldn't come to an agreement, do you?"

Before Ricardo could answer he went on:

"William Benn planned this. He sent you. I half remember seein' you in his house, one night, and if——"

He had been talking on more and more persuasively, more and more smoothly, but in the middle of the sentence his hand jerked down for his gun. In the first thousandth part of a second, Ricardo saw that he had been trapped by this commonplace treachery of the gun fighter's, and his heart bounded with fear and anger. In the second thousandth part of a second, he snatched out his own gun.

From the hip of the other he saw fire dart; a terrible blow glanced along his skull as he pulled the trigger of his own weapon, and he fell into darkness.

He gathered himself together at once and raised his head. No other man was in the clearing!

Had Perkins fled?

No, there he came, dragging himself forward on both hands and one leg trailed out behind him; he was coming on to finish the work which he had begun in such promising fashion. Ricardo made a vast effort—but his arms were curiously numb, and the revolver which he picked up shivered out of his hand.

He could only lie in a nightmare and watch death dragging rapidly toward him——

"Charlie!" called a deep and familiar voice from the edge of the woods behind Perkins.

"Who's that?" snarled Perkins, and twisted himself convulsively around.

A gun exploded; Perkins dropped upon his back and lay still; and Ricardo saw William Benn standing just outside the rim of the trees, the revolver leveled in his hand. And, as though the sight carried with it a healing and stimulating strength, Ricardo that instant recovered his nerve and control and was able to rise to his knees and then, staggeringly, to his feet.

In the distance, he saw the gigantic Negro looming and then heard the voice of William Benn:

"Stay back, Selim. Stay back and don't come near. We don't want this place littered up with footprints. This is all the kid's work—if he can live to collect on it. Ricardo, boy, are you hurt bad?"

Ricardo touched the ragged flesh along his skull and winced from his own fingers. Then he gasped:

"I'm well enough. It—it was—only a glancing bullet!"

"Thank Heaven!" said William Benn with real feeling. "I half thought it was the finish for you. You'll feel sick for a minute. Afterward, you'll be all right. Tear up your shirt and make some sort of a bandage around your head. Do you hear?"

"Yes," said Ricardo faintly.

"You'll be watched by us every minute till you're back in Back Creek with the body."

"Back Creek! Am I to take the body there?"

"Yes, yes! They'll never bother you, now. He had no friends. No more than a mad dog. But get the body back there. He's got two wounds in front. Fire one more shot. Fire it now!"

Instinctively, Ricardo obeyed, firing blindly at the trunk of a near-by pine.

"That will be proof enough for the whole world that you killed him without help!" said William Benn, and he laughed exultantly.

He went on.

"You'll find a doctor in Back Creek who will fix up your hurt head. Lie in the hotel for a couple of days to make sure that there's no poisoning set in. Then you can start back for the Ranger Ranch. You'll see no more of any of us, except Lew. But we'll be watching every minute. Good-bye, lad. You've done it more perfectly than I dreamed it could come!"

27

⊙

A Medical Friend

Badly hurt as he was, Ricardo listened with a sort of desperate attention to the strong, level voice of William Benn. He was only half conscious, in a state much like that of one newly awakened and still beset with sleep. He heard

Benn explain that he and the Negro could not come near, because if they did, their footsteps might be found on the place, and so men would come to know or to guess that more than one hand dealt death to terrible Charles Perkins. He understood this perfectly, and yet he could not understand why friends who were in sight did not come to him, who was in such desperate need of them!

They disappeared. He was on the verge of calling out after them, and only a hastily summoned pride kept him from it.

He went and looked in the face of the dead man. It was not pale. He had thought that a dreadful pallor possessed at once the face of a corpse, but Perkins was as in life, and seemed actually grinning in mockery of the crimson that streamed over one side of his face—a sort of stage effect, out of which he would presently leap up and slay the youth.

This thought made the brain of Ricardo spin, so that he covered his eyes with his hand; and though his wits steadied again, still he was nervous, and feared lest he should faint and die in this lonely place unless he hurried.

He must make the bandage first.

He took off his coat and then his shirt. He ripped this into lengths, and when he bound these tightly around his head he had a most exquisite thrust of agony that seemed like a white wave of flame consuming his brain. It was infinitely worse than the actual shock of the bullet, and it left him giddy, and a little nauseated. Thirst, too, suddenly ached in all his veins, so much so, that he would not wait for purer water, but kneeled down on knees and shaking hands and drank out of a pool that formed at the edge of the meadow.

When he stood up again the pain had abated a godd deal; he had more strength; and above all there was a sense that the bleeding had almost ceased.

Then he started about executing the orders of William Benn in detail. An odd irritation possessed him. They could help, if they would. They could do all these things in a trice, and with no effort. But though they played for seven millions, they chose to make him the butt at which all the arrows of pain and labor were shot!

And another emotion he felt, more and more intensely as his giddiness increased, was that he must hurry, even stumbling, through these present difficulties, in order to be received into the big hands and the comfortable wisdom of William Benn, later on.

While these half-delirious notions possessed him, he got his horse untethered and led it back to the spot where the dead man lay. But the brute would not come near. It reared and plunged and bore violently back on the reins; and even when it was at a distance, it bucked and carried on so furiously that Ricardo was afraid that at any moment it might break away from him entirely.

That fear made him weak, the thought coming over him that he would have to go on foot, with nerveless legs and failing strength, clear back to the village. He would surely faint on the way——

So he hesitated no longer, but having quieted the horse at last, in the entrance to the avenue through the trees, he mounted, and started back.

The horse wanted to fly at full speed, as it had come. Ricardo bore back on the reins, pulling, wrenching; but still, in scurrying starts, as though striving to escape from the blows of a whip, the horse rushed on and on, and the strength began to leave the arms of Ricardo.

At last he said to himself: "The horse has smelled death. His nostrils are full of it. That is why—of course!"

And, having said that, his own strength returned, in great part.

He had received a great shock, but it was more to his nerves than to his body. The impact of the bullet had not been so great as the emotions caused by the trip to Back Creek, and then the encounter with Perkins in the saloon, and finally the ride to the meeting point.

However, when he reached the front of the hotel, he dismounted with a stagger. The horse threw up its head and trotted on, reins tossing. Ricardo went painfully up the steps; not a man left the line of chairs to come to his aid. They hardly looked at him. One would have thought that it was beneath them to notice a man who had been foolish and clumsy enough to get himself wounded. He went on past them. He stood at the clerk's desk, with the brutal-faced woman behind it.

"There's a place in the woods out of town—you turn right up a trail. You come to a forking. You turn left—you reach a place where the trees of the forest are divided, like a row in an orchard. Do you know?"

"Well, I know," said she. "And at the foot of the avenue, there's a clearing."

"In that clearing," said he, "Charles Perkins is lying dead."

"He is, is he? And who killed him?" she asked aggressively.

He did not think to lie. But the thing had been taught him with such care that he answered almost instinctively,

"*I* killed him," he said. "His bullet only scraped my head," he went on, as if in explanation of the strange result of that fight. "It knocked me down, you see."

He was talking like a child, holding to the edge of the desk with both hands. There was a desperate frown on his forehead as he tried to remember exactly the manner in which William Benn would want him to tell this tale. He was simply reciting a half-learned lesson.

"And your bullet—it found his heart, maybe?" she asked with a curious earnestness.

There were others in the room. They had drifted in from the veranda, without haste. But already half a dozen were in sight, idling here and there, casual, apparently not interested.

"I shot him through the leg, the first time," said he. "When I opened my eyes again, I couldn't see anything, at first. I thought he'd gone away. Then I saw him dragging himself toward me. And I shot him through the face. He didn't yell," said Ricardo. "But he gave a sudden twist and fell on his back. He was dead. I tried to get his body back here. But my horse wouldn't go near the place. And I was beginning to get dizzy. In fact, I feel as if I'm going to faint right now. Can you get a doctor for me?"

The face of the woman faded, at that. Other faces slipped in between his eyes and the wall, and he was gripped by hands that sank deep into his flesh and hurt him cruelly. He heard voices, too. They seemed to be shouting to him from a distance, though he knew that they were speaking close at hand. Then he was being led somewhere, his legs trailing weakly. At last thick dust settled over his eye. A voice sounded in his ears like the boom of a breaking wave:

"Poor kid!"

"As a matter of fact, I'm not very old," said Ricardo to himself, and straightway was unconscious.

He was wakened by a sensation of red-hot fire scalding his wound. He jerked his eyes open and saw a face above him, contorted with interest and attention.

"You'll come through clean as a whistle, my beauty," said the doctor. "Here, stop kicking, will you?"

Ricardo recalled, suddenly, that he no longer was a boy in the family of Antonio Perez, but a grown man called Ricardo Mancos. He lay still and fortified himself with pride. The wound having been cleansed, the sewing followed.

"Why don't you swear?" asked the doctor after a while.

Ricardo turned his tortured eyes up to the other's face and laughed. The strain was gone.

"Why, doctor, this is nothing!" he said.

And he meant what he said. The physical pain was as nothing compared with the long nerve strain through which he had passed. He was suddenly strong.

And the doctor, with a grunt, continued his work.

When the sewing was finished, he went to the bandaging, and performed this with more careful hands, as though this were a work of far greater importance than the cleansing and the sewing of the wound. He stepped back, at last, and rubbed his hands together as he looked at the bandage.

"I remember a few things!" said he.

Then Ricardo, for the first time, saw that the man was dressed like an ordinary puncher, and that he had one of the most ugly faces in the world—a brutal, depraved face.

"I don't think that scar is going to bother you. It won't pull the flesh," said the doctor, "and it won't show. Your hair will cover it in no time. You're lucky, kid!"

"I was lucky to find you," said Ricardo, and looked up at him open-eyed.

"You're a good, game kid," said the doctor. "I never handled no gamer," he went on, enlarging his thoughts under the impression of the compliment he had received.

"In my coat yonder there ought to be a wallet," said Ricardo. "You take the wallet and help yourself to what you need for a fee."

"I'll dish out the coin to him," said Lew hastily, making for the coat.

The doctor caught him by the shoulder and whirled him away.

"You little sawed-off imitation of a half man," said the doctor roughly, "he told *me* to handle the wallet!"

"Let him alone, Lew!" exclaimed Ricardo.

And Lew backed against the wall, with a desperately wicked

125

look in his face, while the doctor dipped out the wallet and opened it.

"You got a good fat pile of coin here," said the doctor.

"Take what you want, doctor," urged the boy.

The other closed the wallet and dropped it back inside the coat.

"Well, kid," said he, "it's been a pleasure to me to take care of you! I wouldn't help myself to a penny. Write me down a friend, that's all."

28

⊙

An Insult to Nine Grand

"What are you thinking about?" asked the hunchback, after the doctor and all the others had gone.

"Well, you guess."

"About seven millions—and pretty Maud Ranger. She's gunna be a beauty, too, in another year or two. I know about women. She's gunna blossom. She's just in the bud now."

"I don't think she's so terribly good-looking."

"What do you know, a kid like you? I tell you, she's gunna be a knock-out. Look at her wrists, round and small. Look at the nape of her neck. Look at her eye, like the eye of a colt in a pasture, a hot-blooded colt that'll win races before ever it breaks down. Well, that's her. Oh, she's gunna be a beauty, kid. She's only a baby, now."

"And what difference does it make to me?" said Ricardo, suddenly irritated. "What will she ever mean to me? Her money will be stolen and after that, what will she have to do with me, Lew?"

Lew sneered with superior knowledge, superior talent, as it were.

"What a lot you know about things!" said he. "Is her money gunna be swiped at one swing of the hand? Not if I know William Benn. Gradual, slow and easy, he's gunna soak up the honey. Maybe he'll be an investment company, or something that has got all the confidence of the young husband of this here young and beautiful and trustin' girl."

Lew licked his lips and sighed.

"Whatever way he works it, you lay to it that William Benn is gunna do the trick proper and right. He'll cut deep, but he'll cut pretty. Now you go to sleep. You don't have to think. Benn and the doctor and me, we'll do the thinkin' for you."

Ricardo closed his eyes.

"One minute, Lew."

"Well, kid?"

"The big organ grinder—that was Selim, it seems. I heard Benn call him by name."

"You didn't tumble to that when you rode up?"

"How should I?"

"Is there two pair of shoulders in the world like Selim's, that's all that I ask you?"

"And there was a Chinaman who ran out and gave me directions toward the woods——"

"That was who?"

"I want to guess that it was Wong."

"You're a bright kid," said the other, ironically. "I always knew you had brains!"

He came closer to Ricardo and added in a different tone: "You got better than brains. You got nerve. With Benn behind you, you'll climb to the top of the heap. Why, kid, you'll be there inside of two weeks, maybe!"

Ricardo slept, but he dreamed bad dreams; twice in the night he awakened and stared at gloomy darkness. He was glad of the coming day; he was glad of Lew, who entered.

The hunchback explained that the body of Charles Perkins had been duly brought in the day before, the landlady herself taking charge of the work, and incidentally possessing herself of all the personal effects of the dead man.

"Who'll take them away from her?" asked Ricardo, surprised.

"Take away from her?" asked Lew, astonished by the question. "Well, I'll tell you, you poor sap, there ain't ten men in this town would dare look cross-eyed at her. She's a terror, plain and simple. She knows everything about everybody. She knows all about me, even!"

He turned green as he said it.

"Somebody will stab her in the back, one day—the ugly witch!" suggested Ricardo.

"Her skin'd turn a knife point," said Lew, with a whole-hearted conviction. "We ain't gunna talk about her any more!"

He scarcely had stopped speaking when the door opened, and the subject of their conversation stood in the doorway. She looked more like a female ape than ever, and she grinned horribly at Lew.

"You rat!" she said to Lew. "You rat that an owl had mauled and dropped because you're poison to eat!"

This gentle comment made, she approached the bedside and scowled down at Ricardo. He turned cold. He expected a more deadly blast from her, since she apparently had been listening at the door.

"D'you believe everything that this monkey man says to you, kid?" she remarked.

Ricardo managed to smile.

"No, you don't," said she. "Of course, you don't. You're only a kid, and you're a decent kid. But about the stuff that was on Perkins. You dropped him—the snake! You killed him, and you oughta have his stuff. There's nine thousand in this wallet. You put that with the price on him, and you'll have over twenty thousand. That ain't to sneeze at, eh? Here you are!"

She held out a money belt, several of the compartments fatly stuffed. Ricardo gazed at her in amazement and at the belt in horror. Amazement at her honesty, horror at the thought of taking that blood-stained money.

"I don't want it!" he said hastily.

"Hey!" yelled Lew. "Are you insultin' nine grand—and to its face?"

The hag turned on the hunchback. Two more ugly faces could not have been found in the world. Only to Ricardo there was one more dreadful, and that was the still, thoughtful countenance of the doctor.

"You're talkin' again, little man?" was all she said.

And Lew shrank from her as though her words had been so many deadly snakes.

Then she turned back to Ricardo.

"You don't want it?" she said gently. "And what d'you want done with it?"

"I don't know!" said Ricardo. "He has a wife—children, perhaps?"

"Who?"

"Perkins."

"Him? He never wasted his time!"

She laughed horribly. "He wasn't such a fool," said she. "He never had nobody. So that's out! You gotta take it, kid, even if it's powerful agin' your nature."

He shook his head.

"You keep it," said Ricardo. "You'll have poor fellows coming through here, now and then. They'll need help. You'll put them up and take care of them. That's one thing to do with the money."

This reduced her to silence, which continued for some time; during this interval she stared fixedly at Ricardo, her little eyes glittering into his, which opened wider and wider, bluer and more blue.

"Look here, boy," she said at last, "you got something on your mind."

"I?"

"You got something on your mind. I don't ask you what. But you're new at the crooked game. You still got a straight streak in you. Well, play to that. Play to that! You ain't got more'n one foot in danger. Draw it out while the drawing's good. But tell me once more—you want me to keep this money?"

"I do," said Ricardo rather faintly.

She drew herself up.

"I've had the idea," said she slowly, "that there wasn't man, woman, or child in the world that ever would put a lick of trust in me, but I'll tell you now that never a penny of this'll go into my pocket. I'll spend it on the down-and-outers, and Heaven help their miserable souls!"

She said this in a pausing voice, with a strange emphasis and emotion. Then she turned in haste and fled from the room.

Ricardo closed his eyes once more and breathed hard. And when he opened them, he found that Lew was sitting close to the bed, studying him with a curious detachment.

"I've been working it out," said Lew at last. "And I see that you're deep. The doctor's right about you! He's always right! You chuck the nine grand. Well, what's that to you? What's nine grand in the pocket compared to seven million in the hand? You go back to the girl and you're the modest hero. You've killed the villain. But you wouldn't touch the

129

blood money. You're above that. You gave it away to charity."

He laughed silently, with malicious admiration.

"How could the Rangers ever know about this?" asked Ricardo.

"D'you think a story like that won't have wings?" said the hunchback, almost savagely. "Man, the woman's so flattered that she'll have to tell every one, and show 'em the cash to prove her point. It's such a great thing to her that it'll almost make her think she's an honest woman. She's your slave, now. Well, and she's worth having in your pocket, too, almost more than nine thousand dollars. The whole range will know about this. And not by your braggin'! Why, the more I look into it, the deeper I see you are, kid. If Maud Ranger was a chunk of ice, she'd have to melt when she heard a yarn like this. She's gonna just blush and fall into your arms, kid, and ask you to take her money quick! And me, like a small-time crook, I never seen as deep as this in my life, before!"

He said this with a sort of unwilling admiration in his voice and in his frog-like face.

Ricardo raised his hand.

"I want to be quiet awhile," said he. And then he added at once: "Is she right? Is she right?"

He sighed: "I wouldn't take nine thousand blood money. But I'm willing to take seven million—and smash a woman's life! Ah, Lew, what sort of a rat am I?"

Lew rose with a gasp.

"Hey, whacha talkin' about?" said he. "Whacha talkin' about, kid? You ain't tryin' to make a fool of *me*, are you?"

He retreated as though threatened by a frightful danger.

"William Benn has gotta hear about this!" said he, and made for the door.

◉

29

A Missive and a Mystery

Strength came back to Ricardo very rapidly; he could have ridden away on the second day, but word came from William Benn that he should remain longer.

Lew interpreted the message of the chief in the following manner:

"You get potted and drop; you stick in bed a day and beat it. 'Just a scratch,' says everybody. 'He didn't do nothing much, after all.' But suppose you spend a week in bed? It makes you look pale and thin and weak. It snakes the sunburn off your face, and then people will say: 'This gent nearly got bumped off!' That's what you want. Besides, everybody's talking, now. The kid is a hero. Yarns about him come to Maud Ranger. Look how her brain will work! No matter how much she wanted Perkins killed, and no matter how well she likes you, the first thing she wants to do is to balk, because she says to herself: 'Now I gotta marry this bird! I'm tied up by my promise!' And a girl is like a dog; they hate a rope. It makes 'em savage. But you don't show up right away. All she gets is messages from other gents about you. The kid is a hero. He kills Charles Perkins in a fair fight. And then he won't take the head money! It gets her to thinking. What better kind of a man could she pick out? So she's all ready to melt into your arms when you blow back to the ranch!"

Then Ricardo said slowly: "Lew, I want you to go to Benn and tell him that I've got to see him here!"

Lew looked shrewdly at him.

"About what?" said he.

"If I could tell you that, I wouldn't have to see him."

"It's dangerous for him to come here, kid. You don't want anybody around here to know that you're thick with William Benn. It might start them all to thinking."

Ricardo nodded.

"He'll have to slip in at night, then," said he. "I've got to see him."

Lew argued no more, and that evening William Benn himself stood tall and grave in the room of the boy. Ricardo had rehearsed beforehand what he wanted to say. He said it now, rapidly, as though fearing that hesitation would inevitably prevent him from speaking at all.

"I've thought this thing over backward and forward," said he. "I can't go through with it."

He expected an explosion. William Benn said nothing, and because he was silent, Ricardo went on, more strained than before: "I can't go back to the Ranger Ranch. I can't face that girl. I never could hold her to her promise. Now you can blame me as much as you please. I know that I owe you a lot. I'm willing to try to pay you back in any other way. I can't do it out of her."

William Benn sat down beside the bed. Lew drew closer, behind his shoulder.

"Go back, Lew," cautioned the chief. "This is between me and the kid."

Lew drifted slowly into the darkness; but still his face was visible, hideously like the face of a frog.

"It's bad medicine to you, is it, son?" asked William Benn.

This reticence on his part frightened Ricardo more than any outburst could have done, but he nodded dumbly in reply.

"What's happened in your mind lately?" asked Benn.

"It's the thought of her," said Ricardo. "She's clean as a whip, Benn."

"Tell me," said the big man. "She's touched you pretty close to the heart. Is that it?"

Ricardo flushed.

"Certainly not!" said he.

"As a matter of fact," said the criminal, "you're a little dizzy when you think about her."

"I?" protested Ricardo feebly.

"You're in love with her!"

"No, no!"

"Well, why not? It's natural, isn't it?"

"A crook like me!" sighed Ricardo.

"You're in love," persisted William Benn. "You can't go back and claim her promise for that reason. Is that it?"

132

"Yes, yes, yes!" groaned Ricardo. "I couldn't look her in the face!"

William Benn got up and strode back and forth through the room for some time. He began to hum thoughtfully, and it made Ricardo think of the purring of a huge cat.

At last, Benn sat down by the bed once more.

"Very well," said he. "Write a letter to her and tell her whatever you please. I'll see that the letter is delivered. I'll only ask that you stay in bed here until you get an answer from her."

Ricardo gaped at him.

"Do you mean that?" he asked.

"I do."

"But after the work and the time and the money that you've invested——"

"Listen to me, Ricardo. You're too good a tool for me to throw you away on one job. Suppose I try to force you through with this business? Well, there's several millions in it, but the loot would have to be split between you, and the doctor, and me; besides, huge chunks of it would go to Lew, here, and to Wong, and Selim. Even the Negro would have his hand out for a share. And there are other expenses that would have to be considered. And, for a quick turnover, we might not be able to cash in a very large part of the estate. Too much of it is tied up in the stock of that bank, and in the ranch. But, above all, I wouldn't want to finish off with you in one stroke, Ricardo. If you're decent enough to want to be straight with the girl, you'd be decent enough to want to be straight with me. And there you are! Does that help you to understand my position any better?"

"I hear what you say," replied Ricardo. "But it's hard for me to believe everything. Am I really free to write a letter to her?"

"Of course you are! Where is there any writing paper? Lew, get some paper, and pen, and ink for Ricardo, will you? He wants to write a letter."

Lew slowly left the room. He came back and handed the materials to Ricardo, and as he did so, he favored the boy with the look of a basilisk on the kill.

"We'll leave you alone here," said William Benn more gently than ever. "Can you get me out of here unnoticed, Lew?"

"We can try," said the hunchback.

133

"So long, Ricardo," said Benn. "Is there anything you want, here?"

Ricardo thrust himself up in the bed. He reached out both hands and gripped the hand of William Benn.

"I vow," he whispered, "I'll pay down my blood to make a return to you for letting me off this!"

"Tush!" said the big man. "Don't have it on your mind. Just write your letter to your lady. Good night, kid!"

He went out of the room behind the hunchback, who guided him by devious and twisting ways out of the hotel, until they came to the rear yard, and there Lew clutched the arm of his chief.

"Is it straight, Benn?" he gasped. "Are you gunna let that young snake twist out of your hand?"

William Benn jerked his arm loose.

"Keep your fingers off me, or I'll make you!" said he roughly. "Be silent, can't you! I'm thinking."

He leaned against a tree. It was a stout young sapling. The forehead of William Benn pressed against the trunk, with his hands he laid hold upon two branches. And the hunchback saw the head of the sapling shake and shudder.

At last Benn straightened himself and spoke in a stifled voice.

"When he finishes that letter, take it off for him tomorrow morning," said he.

"Take it where?" asked Lew, thoroughly cowed by his master's exhibition of rage.

"Take it where it's addressed to go, you blockhead!" exclaimed the big man.

"To the Ranger Ranch, even?"

"You've heard me give you orders. Is that enough?"

"Yes," said Lew.

He was bewildered.

Then he dared to say: "Benn, I dunno that I foller you. I dunno that I make a big mistake, maybe. But are you gunna chuck it away? The whole of the seven millions, Benn?"

A shadowy fist leaped out at Lew, and he barely managed to duck the flying destruction and spring away. William Benn followed in a half stride.

"I've got a mind to break you open," said Benn. "You poison-puffed toad, you! Do what you're told to do. Don't answer back. And be hanged to you!"

He strode away through the darkness, and Lew cowered

134

as he looked after him. He had known this master of his for a great many years, and together they had been through almost all the trials that two men can endure; but never before had he seen William Benn exhibit such emotion as he had shown on this night.

Something, he felt sure, lay behind the actions and the strange words of Benn, who apparently was surrendering so quickly and so easily to the whim of the boy.

But, giving up all hope of penetrating to the heart of the mystery—since mystery there must be in the business—he returned to the hotel and went with a heavy heart to the room where Ricardo was now sitting up in bed, conning his letter, and adding to it little by little, more as though he were drawing a picture than scratching down words.

Now and again he raised his head, and Lew tried hard to catch the eye of the youngster, for he had bitter things to say, and many of them. However, on each occasion the glance of Ricardo probed nothing but his own thoughts, which he transferred again to the paper.

At last the missive was ended, sealed, and Lew held out his hand for it.

"I'll take it," said he. "I'll take it as willing as any gent ever took the rope that was to hang him!"

30

◉

The Letter

However unwilling Lew might have been to carry the message, he was a hard rider and, with an early start, he had the letter at the Ranger place by noon. He found that Maud Ranger was riding; and he had to deliver the letter to Mrs. Theodora Ranger.

She took it with a sour face.

"How's the boy doing?" she asked.

"How does anybody do that's shot through the head?" asked Lew grimly.

"Shot through the head? Of course he wasn't!"

"No fault of his that he wasn't," said Lew. "The young fool let Charlie Perkins trick him and get the first draw."

"Were you there?"

"No, I wasn't. If I had been, I'd have plugged the brute myself."

She smiled a little at his viciousness.

"How was Mr. Mancos tricked?"

"By talk, and by being a fool."

"In what way?"

"Fill your hand first—make the first move, is what he says to Perkins. Can you imagine that?"

"No," she said bluntly. "I can't. Maud will be back soon. You can wait for her answer."

"I'm not to wait for an answer. I got no orders to do that."

"Not to wait!" exclaimed Mrs. Ranger. "Ah, I understand. He's simply announcing when he's to arrive back here. Is that it?"

"How do I know what he announces?" demanded the dwarf. "I'll go out and feed with the boys. If there's a return message, you can send for me there."

And he went out to the cook house, while Mrs. Ranger went in haste to her husband.

He listened with a scowl.

"I'd give anything to open that letter," said she.

"A gun fighter's letter? You'd get me shot for that pleasure, then," he remarked dryly. "Besides, here's Maud. Let's see how she looks when she gets the message."

Maud Ranger, coming in flushed from her ride, took the proffered letter carelessly, tore it open—and suddenly sat down hard on the nearest chair. She looked helplessly up at her uncle and aunt. And then she offered the paper to them.

"I don't make it out!" she said, and her face was blank.

Mrs. Ranger seized upon the letter with an avid hand and read as follows, aloud:

"DEAR MISS RANGER: This is to let you know that I have met Charles Perkins, and that luck was on my side."

136

Mrs. Ranger commented: "As though he didn't know that the yarn was here years ago! Fake modesty, I call it!"

She continued the reading:

"The body has been buried here in Back Creek. My share of the receiving was only a scratch—which was lucky again."

Here Maud Ranger cried: "A scratch that ripped open the whole side of his head and put him in bed!"

Her aunt looked oddly at her.

"Don't be too sympathetic until you come to the end, my dear," said she.

She pursued the reading:

"As I started out from your place, I had intended to stop there on the way back, but now I think it best that I should not.

"You'll understand me, of course. I should have said at the time that I was not riding to Back Creek because of the promise which you made—which you were tormented into making—but Mrs. Ranger was so excited that my head was in a whirl; and I'm afraid you have been fearing that even if luck were with me when I met Charles Perkins, you would have to pay!

"Of course that is not to be considered; and again I apologize for having ridden away without letting you understand exactly how I felt about it."

"One moment," broke in William Ranger. "My own head is beginning to spin a little. Do I understand this letter correctly? Do I understand that this penniless young boy is throwing seven or eight millions out the window in this fashion?"

"I'm reading you the words as I find them," said his wife sourly. "I don't understand it a whit better than you do! What in the world can he have up his sleeve?"

She concluded the letter:

"You will be as glad as I am that this business is ended. Every one here is extremely kind to me. I shall soon be on the road again.

"Perhaps the first part of this letter was not at all necessary, but I thought it right to put your mind at rest.

"Ever sincerely,

RICARDO MANCOS."

137

Mrs. Ranger held the letter at her arm's length.

"It flabbergasts me!" she exclaimed. "I don't understand!"

"Nor I," said her husband.

Maud Ranger stood up and took the letter.

"I do," said she.

"And what do you understand, baby?" asked her hard-faced aunt.

"I understand that Ricardo Mancos is a gentleman."

"Tush!" said her aunt. "You know nothing about him."

Maud Ranger stamped in her impatient vexation.

"Nothing in the world is good or true, after you've handled it for a while!" she exclaimed. "I beg your pardon, Aunt Theodora, but I can't stand it! How could any one show more clearly what he is? He's a hero. You have to admit it. And he rode out there into that nest of outlaws simply to please a girl that he hardly had met. To please me—and for the sake of the adventure, I suppose. And to see justice done—and—and—I never heard in my life of anything half as noble and fine. I never did. Neither did you. Now confess it!"

"Stuff and nonsense——" began Mrs. Ranger.

But her husband cut in: "I agree with Maud. If everything is as it seems to be, then this fellow *is* a hero, and he is as straight as a ruled line. I confess I'm paralyzed. This is like something out of a fairy tale."

"Thank you!" cried the girl. "I'm glad that one other person is willing to understand him. I—I'm going to write a letter this moment to him."

"Maud, Maud!" cautioned her aunt. "You'd better wait until you've cooled off a little. Don't say anything impulsive."

Tears of excitement stood in the eyes of the girl.

"I won't wait. I want him to know exactly how I feel—this instant!"

"Will he be interested? His letter is cool enough," said her aunt.

"Do you think I'm going to throw myself at his head?" she demanded angrily.

And she flew from the room.

"Now," said Mrs. Ranger, "this is serious indeed!"

"Theodora," said her husband very gravely, "I know how you feel about the thing. But the truth is that you never would approve of any husband for our Maud except a man who had been picked by you beforehand. Isn't that true?"

138

"Perfect nonsense," she answered.

"But if this lad is what he seems to be, he's really one in a million."

"He's as poor as a church mouse. Mrs. Mancos told me so herself," said she.

"All the more reason," answered her husband, "that he should have credit for refusing to hold Maud to her promise."

"And who is he?" continued Mrs. Ranger, arguing, woman-like, by dint of many headings, and regardless of convincing answers. "Who is he?"

"A grand old family—no Mexican family older than the Mancos strain, I believe."

"Mexican family," she said pointedly.

"I won't try to convince you," said he, "only I advise you that if those two young people are going to lose their heads about one another, you had better stand out of the way, be-cause all your opposition will not accomplish the slightest thing. For my part, I'm going to encourage the match!"

"William!"

"I mean it. Here's Maud, again. Look at her. She's been crying over her own letter. Well, well, well!"

Maud came in, in haste.

"Where's the messenger?"

"I'll take your letter to him, Maud," suggested her uncle. "He's at the cook house."

"I'll take it myself," said the girl. "I want to see that hunch-back again."

And she hurried from the house without another word.

Mrs. Ranger peered from a window and followed her course.

"She's almost running," she commented. "And now the hunchback is coming out of the cook house. She's talking to him in a most excited way. Now she gives him the letter. Now she gives him something else. Money, I suppose! A lot of it, no doubt, by the way he raises his hat to her. I tell you what, William, that girl's heart is on fire at this moment."

"Let it burn," said her husband. "For my part, I think that there's only one way for a marriage to be built, and that's with love as a foundation."

"Love for a Mexican," groaned Theodora Ranger.

"And why not?"

"She's coming back," said Mrs. Ranger.

"Hush! What's that?"

"What's what?"

"Isn't that someone singing?"

"It's Maud," said she. "She's singing her heart out. Good Heaven, William, she's lost her head completely!"

31

◉

The Answer

In the dark of the day, Lew returned to Back Creek with the girl's letter; and hardly had Ricardo glanced feverishly through it when he asked eagerly for William Benn again.

"That's the walkin' of a tight rope—every time that he comes here to see you!" complained Lew. "But I'll take word to him. Kid, if ever these gents around here get wind of the fact that you're workin' hand in glove with William Benn, you can lay to it they'll be suspecting that you had a bit of help in the bumping off of Charles Perkins! Already they believe in you sort of because they have to; and here and there I hear a gent muttering that nobody has *seen* you do the trick! But I'll get Benn, if you gotta have him."

In spite of this warning, Ricardo persisted, and William Benn was brought, his figure looming silently through the doorway. He came to the bed and sat down with his knees and his great hands within the circle of the lamp, but his ominous face in the shadow.

"It's the letter from the girl, Ricardo?" he asked. "What about it?"

"Read it!" said the boy in a tormented voice.

"These things," said William Benn, "are best left between those that have the most to do with 'em!"

Ricardo reached out swiftly and laid a hand upon the arm of his companion. It was like a bar of corrugated steel, so thick and stiff was it with muscle.

"It's too much for my brain," said he. "I know what I ought to do; but I don't know that I have the courage to do it." He added: "Read the letter, and help me decide."

So William Benn unfolded the sheet and read:

DEAR MR. MANCOS: Your letter tells me nothing except that you are modest. But I knew even that, before. All really brave men are that way. I trust, however, that you'll not skip us on your way back to El Real. We all want to see you and talk to you. And particularly, *I* want to know all about Back Creek.

Do come. There are a great many things which it is a sin to leave unsaid. I want to say them to you in person and not in writing.

Having read this letter with care, the big man replaced it in the envelope and gave it back to Ricardo.

"And what do *you* think of it, lad?" he asked.

Ricardo sighed and touched his wounded head.

"I don't know," he murmured.

"You have a pretty fair idea, though."

"I want to hear you talk."

"She's interested, Ricardo. One can see that."

"Do you think so?"

"Don't you?"

"Yes!" said the boy with sudden frankness. "I think she is. What shall I do?"

"What are you tempted to do?"

"If I were an honest man," groaned Ricardo, "I'd chuck it all. I'd never see her again, except to tell her that I really didn't kill him!"

"And who did?" asked the other.

"Why, you, of course."

"When he was already down, half helpless."

"If you hadn't been there, he would have come on and finished me. You know that."

"How can you tell? In another minute you might have been yourself again; and polished him off."

The boy shook his head.

"Anyway," he continued, "I know that I shouldn't go back to her. Because," he added, "if I go, you go with me."

"Not a bit of it."

"You'll be in the background. I'll be in your hands. And if I

141

marry her, that means that her money will be in your hands, too!"

At this, William Benn remained silent for a moment, as though he wanted the words to answer themselves. He was entirely grave; there was no trace of the sinister little smile which so often showed itself upon his face.

Then, after the silence had continued for a long time, he said quietly: "There you are, Ricardo. You've worked out the thing perfectly. If you want to be entirely honest, you never see her again, and perhaps that's the best thing for you to do."

Ricardo groaned faintly.

"She's in your mind," Benn taxed him.

"I try to get her out," said Ricardo, "but the more I work to get her out of my mind, the more securely she's fixed in it."

"You can find greater beauties," said William Benn.

"Ah, what's that?" asked the boy. "Who wants to pick a horse because it's pretty?"

"No," agreed the older man. "Of course you want the horse that has the heart, and the bone, and the breed."

"And she's everything that she ought to be."

"She's a clean-bred one!" agreed William Benn.

"If you're crossing hot country—not even grass in sight—and your throat begins to get dry—and you think of dying of thirst—and then you have a sight of green on a hill—you're sure that there's a spring there——"

He paused, but William Benn gave him no help.

"Well," exclaimed Ricardo, "even if you knew that spring was on land you had no right to cross, would you have the heart to travel right on and not go near it?"

"Not I," said William Benn. "But," he added slowly, "I'm a crook, out and out. I want you to make up your mind for yourself."

"I try to figure it out," sighed the boy. "But the rest of the world is like the face of the desert to me."

He reared himself bolt upright.

"Darn her money!" he said savagely. "I wish she were a pauper!"

William Benn returned to his discreet silence and maintained it until Ricardo fell back, flushed and muttering.

"If you go on with her," said Benn at last, "I go with you, suppose."

"Ah, yes. There's no other way out of it."

"Between you and me, I think not. If you want to chuck

142

her, very well. I'll never say no. And I'll never throw the thing in your face. But if you go on with her, I think I have a right to my cut."

Ricardo sighed again, but he nodded.

"I couldn't double cross you," said he.

"Couldn't you?" asked Benn rather curiously. "No, I don't think you could. You're clean-bred, too."

"I? To turn her over to——"

"A band of crooks?" suggested Benn.

Ricardo set his teeth with an audible sound.

"No," went on Benn quietly, "you make your choice now. Either you play this game my way, or else you chuck her. I want to be fair with you, but I see the game in that way."

"You must be right," said Ricardo.

"Once in, you have to go straight on."

"Six weeks of Heaven," said Ricardo. "And after that she finds me out for what I am!" He writhed. "But when I see her come up in my mind, I turn to water, Benn!"

"Lad, you love her. And you have another way to look at it. Don't think that I'd simply raid the bank and run and leave you in the lurch. There are other ways and better ways. I could manage to soak out my share, and the share of the rest of the boys. Never more than half of the whole. Well, there would be an explanation. Bad investments. Investments made through that scoundrel, William Benn. She never need guess. There's still more than enough for the pair of you to live on. She loves you all the more because you've made a few mistakes in business."

"And I'm a lying hypocrite the rest of my life!"

"Not a bit," said William Benn. "The rest of your life, you're as straight as a string. And what a flying start you'll have!"

He enlarged on the last speech.

"Rich, happily married to a beautiful girl; known to have the nerve of a lion; respected by everyone——"

"Don't!" groaned Ricardo.

"And as for the past, I'll see to it that none of the boys ever gets any blackmailing idea in his head. Ricardo, when I first saw you, I knew that you'd be my luck; and I'll be yours, too. Will you trust me to wangle this thing through?"

"I'm a dog!" said Ricardo. "I'm a sneaking cur. But—but——"

"We come to a conclusion. Shall we shake hands?"

Benn stretched forth his hand; but Ricardo slipped from the bed and stood before him.

"I'm not logical, I know," said he. "But if I go through with this, there'll be the end of any good feeling between us. If this thing goes through, sooner or later it will cost us our blood. One of us will die for it. I tell you, I feel it in my bones!"

He spoke with such a savage gravity that the other retreated a little before him.

"Nonsense!" he said at last. "You've been in bed too long. Your nerves are out of kilter. Now, go back to sleep. Everything is going to go like a ticking clock."

And with that, he left the room, and found the frog-faced hunchback in the hall.

"Lew," he muttered, "find me a slug of whisky. I need a drink."

Lew stared at him, but the darkness of the hallway was too great to permit him to see the face of his master.

"Chief," he whispered at last, "you've failed with the kid. Is that it?"

"Failed? You fool!" cried William Benn. "I've won. I've taken half a dozen long shots, and I've landed on every one. But," he concluded, "it may be that I'll have to pay more than I'll ever cash in!"

32

◉

"Doctor Onate" in Charge of the Case

One week from the day that he went to his bed, Ricardo rose and left Back Creek, and Back Creek did him honor.

His hostess of the hotel gripped his hand and gave him a ghastly smile.

"You keep to short grass, kid," said she. "You ain't meant for the tall timber!"

And a score or more of ruffians, guilty of nearly every

crime in the calendar, gathered in the street and accompanied Ricardo and Lew out of the town with yells and whoopings. Then they drifted briskly across the hills. The horses so filled with strength, after their long rest, that they went like cloud shadows which dip over rough and smooth, unhesitant, and climb sharp slopes, and drop into ragged hollows, all with equal smoothness.

Nevertheless, having made rather a late start, they had to camp among the hills for lunch, which Lew carried with him. A coldness had sprung up between Lew and his companion, so that they spoke to one another hardly a word during the whole of the morning's ride. But while they sat among the rocks, they heard the sound of horse's hoofs on the rocks, like a steel knife tapping at half-filled water glasses, bringing forth a different note from each.

"See what it is," said Ricardo.

"See for yourself," said Lew without courtesy. "I ain't your servant except for show, you fool, and to keep you to the straight way!"

Ricardo made no protest at this insulting speech, but went out among the boulders and saw a horseman coming down the way which they had traveled, sometimes leaning a little in the saddle as he scanned the ground. The newcomer was dressed in elaborate Mexican style, with a vast sombrero, and with a great deal of metal-work on the band of his hat, facing his jacket, and down the seams of his trousers. He rode a high-headed thoroughbred, which stepped daintily among the stones, and that instant, being close, he looked up, and saw Ricardo.

He raised his hat by the crown and bowed to Ricardo, showing a handsome, olive-skinned face.

"Good morning, señor," said he.

Ricardo started at the familiar voice. He made a few steps to meet the stranger.

"Doctor Clauson!" he said at last.

The doctor laughed with more geniality than usual.

"If I can pass for one moment with you," said he, "I can pass for a week with strangers. I'm going to the ranch with you, Ricardo."

Ricardo submitted. It never occurred to him to question the superior wisdom of William Benn or the doctor.

So the doctor came into the halting place and nodded to

145

Lew. He explained the situation while he helped himself to the remnants of the lunch.

"I'm a friend of yours from Mexico. An old friend. I know all about you and your family, and your cousins, and everything else that people could care to ask. I heard what you had done at Back Creek, while I was traveling through this range, and I went at once to see what I could do for you. So that I'm accompanying you toward El Real."

Ricardo nodded.

"I'm a Mexican background which will make you seem more in place," said the doctor. "For instance, I knew your mother, a girl from America. That's why you speak English so well. I speak English myself as well as Spanish, because I was educated in the States. I'm the foil, Ricardo, to set you off and make you seem in place. In addition, I may be able to help you out with a touch of advice, here and there."

Lew put in roughly:

"Every horse needs the spur, now and then."

The doctor looked coldly upon the hunchback. "A kind mind you have, Lew," said he, "and a gentle touch."

He added at once, in a different tone: "But you've steered him through a good many troubles already, Lew. Don't think that we forget it!"

"I know how I'll be remembered," said Lew. "Me and the Chink and the Negro. We do the dirty work. We stop the gaps. And we get the spare pennies in the wind-up!"

"Tell that to William Benn," said the doctor coldly. "I ought to know better than to try kindness on a wolf!"

Afterward, when they started on, Lew fell to the rear, and then farther and farther, to let the dust of his leaders rise and drift over his head.

"Is it safe to badger him so?" asked Ricardo.

"Of course it isn't," said the doctor. "But a savage creature like Lew has to be handled roughly. Pat his head, and he'll take your hand off at the wrist. Smile at him, and he'll leap at your throat. There's no gratitude, no decency, no goodness in him. He respects two things: a brain clever enough to make money without work; and a hand strong enough to knock him down. Otherwise, there's nothing that he cares about. I know him fairly well."

"He could upset everything," said Ricardo.

"He could," admitted the doctor equably. "But nothing is free from danger in this odd little world of ours. You've probably noticed that. We have to wager our money as we can and take our chances. But I admit that there is a little too much surplus temperament in Lew to suit me. I never would work with such fellows. But Benn loves them."

"Loves them?" echoed Ricardo, startled.

"Loves danger," said the doctor. "Loves to pick up lions and tigers, and make them work for him. Loves to feel as an animal trainer feels, when he goes inside the cages, and the beasts fawn and snarl on him, and wait to sneak behind his back!"

Ricardo shivered a little at this unpleasant picture, but remembering Selim, and Wong, the Chinaman, he could not help feeling that the doctor was right.

"And what am I, then?" asked Ricardo, suddenly. "Wolf, or lion, or dog!"

"None of the three," said the doctor, turning his calm eyes upon the boy. "You're a tiger, Ricardo, and one day you'll probably tear out the throat of William Benn, and mine, too, for that matter!"

This he said in the most matter-of-fact manner. He might have been pointing out some casual feature of the landscape through which they were passing. And Ricardo shook his head again.

"I don't understand you and your ideas," he said.

"Of course you don't," said the doctor soothingly. "You're not the sort to understand such things. You don't even understand yourself. But one of these days you'll be surprised to find what I say coming true!"

"What, then, will make me into a tiger?" asked Ricardo.

"A good number of things. For instance, loving that girl and then having to lose her. If that ever happens and the news of it comes to me, I'll have a gun ready to drop you, Ricardo, the instant that you come within range of me!"

"Do you think I'd really attack you?"

"Some things a man knows. We expect you to make a great haul. But you're dynamite in the fingers, and we've lighted you with a short fuse; I don't know when you'll explode, my boy!"

Ricardo shook his head.

"Suppose you believe these things, really, why should you tell them to me?"

"For two reasons," said the doctor. "One is that a man likes to have others know how clever he is. The other is that

147

mere speculations like this will have little or no effect upon you, while you're in love with the girl."

Ricardo flushed.

"You don't like to have me speak about Miss Ranger, do you?" asked the doctor, smiling a little.

"I'm sorry," said Ricardo, "but I don't."

"I respect your wish," said the doctor, "and here we are, I think. Isn't that the place?"

The strange talk which he had been having with the doctor had taken Ricardo's thoughts completely from himself, and now, as they rode out of the mouth of a small valley, they saw before them the old, rambling ranch house. The boy was amazed, and he looked sharply aside to the doctor, half suspicious that the strange themes which the other had been pursuing in conversation had been taken up sheerly for the sake of diverting his mind, and keeping him from pondering nervously about the immediate future.

They came on at a brisk pace over the level ground of the larger valley and soon they were sighted by a cowpuncher who was starting from the barn across the fields. He viewed them only an instant; then he twitched his horse about and fled for the house.

"He recognized your horse—or the bandage around your head," suggested the doctor. "It's just as well to have people forewarned. Will they all be at home?"

It was a larger way of asking if the girl would be there, and Ricardo swallowed hard. Then he pressed his horse to a sharp gallop, and they hurtled up to the racks in front of the house.

As they dismounted, the dust of the halting billowing in a wave against the face of the building, the door opened, and through that dust came Maud rapidly. Her uncle loomed behind her.

"I'll bring them into the house, Maud!" he said hastily, and angrily.

She paid no attention to this suggested remonstrance, but went on until she came to Ricardo. She took his hand and looked earnestly and searchingly into his face, her glance lingering on the bandage about his temples.

"You've been badly hurt," she said gently. "I don't think we'll let you go all the distance to El Real to-day. But now come in."

The doctor was introduced as "Doctor Onate." He went

148

in with them, talking volubly, using his hands a great deal, after the Latin style, and being overpolite at every point. Once more Ricardo wondered at him—and feared him in his heart.

But he had little room in his mind for anything other than the thought of Maud Ranger.

She seemed to him miraculously changed. It was not only in her manner, which had lost all its boyish bluntness and become all womanly, but also her very appearance was altered. There was a delicacy in her face, he swore, that had not been there before. There was a softness in her eye, too.

33

⊙

Ricardo and Maud

He and the doctor were given adjoining rooms. The doctor came in and found Ricardo sitting near the window, with his head in his hands. When he spoke, the boy jumped up, trembling.

"Yes? Yes?" he asked.

"I came in to find out if you were ready to go down," said the doctor. "But I change my mind when I see you. You'd better take your choice between two things—either have a relapse and go to bed or else make up your mind to propose to the girl before you're an hour older."

Ricardo moistened his dry lips. He did not consider the first suggestion at all. He merely said: "How can I see her alone?"

"You won't have to think about that," said the doctor. "She'll arrange that you're alone with her before the day's half an hour older, I take it. See if I'm not a prophet. If you're excited about her, my boy, you're not a whit as excited as she is over you!"

It did not occur to Ricardo that there could be any truth in what the doctor said, for though he respected the great intelligence of Clauson, and his knowledge of humans, there was a profound conviction in Ricardo that Maud Ranger could look down upon any man in the world.

He went downstairs, at last. Theodora Ranger was there with her husband, and she pumped the hand of Ricardo once, up and down.

"You've done very well, young man," said the blunt lady.

They sat down together, and a silence began, which the doctor at once interrupted with a smooth flow of words, describing a hunting trip which he had once taken with the late lamented uncle of Ricardo Mancos, through country very much like that which lay around Back Creek.

Ricardo listened politely. He was too numbed in the brain even to admire the smooth inventions of the doctor.

Then Maud Ranger stood up.

"I'm going into the garden," she said. "I'm tired of this heat in the house."

At the door she turned:

"Do you want to come along, Ricardo?"

He rose, his heart in his throat. The doctor had been right!

Right, at least, in declaring that she was sure to find a chance for them to talk together alone. Right, perhaps, in saying that she cared for him, too!

They went out into the garden.

It was hardly worthy of that name. Six fig trees had flourished there and made shade, on a day. Three of them had died. Two were dying. Only the sixth remained healthy and strong. A broken picket fence betrayed the cause of this decline of the garden. Through it hungry cows or mischievous horses had wandered and chewed the bark off the trees, and trampled the meager fringe of flowers, and the garden plots.

They sat on a bench beneath the great fig tree, overarched with greenery which was turned pale as shallow water by the strength of the sun, shining through the broad leaves. She seemed in no haste to begin the conversation; and for his own part he could not find a thing in his brain to coin into words.

Once or twice he tried to venture speech, but his lips trembled, and he was afraid that his voice would tremble also; so he refrained and simply stared at her askance, and saw how her hands lay loosely folded in her lap, and how her eyes dreamed upon the distance, and how her lips were smiling with a smile which he could not understand.

"It's cooler here," she said at last.

"There's more breeze," said Ricardo faintly.

Then they were silent again.

"When you fell," she asked, "did you think that it was death?"

"I didn't think," said Ricardo. "There wasn't a great deal of time for thinking."

The chickens in the hen yards made a sudden rattling noise.

"A hawk!" said the girl. "There must be a hawk, somewhere. You hear the chickens?"

"Ah, I see the hawk!" said Ricardo.

"Where?"

"If you look straight up—through that gap in the branches."

"Which gap?"

"This one here. Do you see?"

They stood up and stared.

"You can see him balancing—he's turning now against the wind," said Ricardo, oddly excited. "There—just off the edge of that puff of soft white cloud—"

She, staring in turn, came closer still; her hair touched the cheek of Ricardo, and he trembled violently.

"I see it," said she.

Ricardo took her in his arms.

"I love you!" said Ricardo.

She put up a hand to defend herself—and then allowed that protective hand to waver and sink again.

"I love you!" said he, with wild joy as he saw that hand sinking.

She did not answer. She only smiled at him, and her eyes went slowly, searchingly, over his face—like a child staring at a toy—or again, like a painter taking a memory note to be drawn out hereafter.

"Tell me not to touch you—to step back from you," he begged her. "Forbid me, and I still can control myself; but if you let me hold you one more moment, I'll have to tell you ten thousand times over that I love you—and love you—and that I worship you. Are you mocking me? Are you laughing at me?"

She laughed, indeed, at this, but such laughter as Ricardo never had heard before from man, or child, or woman.

151

"Am I laughing at you?" she said. "Well, I'm not! I'm laughing at the world in which I might have missed you. But I didn't miss you. I found you. And so I'll keep you, too. In spite of the world, Ricardo!"

That made his mind fly off to the thought of other faces; he could see the demoniac grin of William Benn. But, resolutely, he shut those faces out of his mind and said to her earnestly: "I swore to myself that I wouldn't dare to say to you how I felt. Because I didn't want to presume on the promise you'd made."

"Hush!" she said. "What nonsense."

"It isn't nonsense, really."

"I want to know other things."

"Everything!" said Ricardo.

But his heart quailed as he spoke. For what worlds there were in him that he dared not let her view, or dream of!

"When did you first love me, Ricardo?"

He trembled.

"Tell me the truth. When you first came out here with me—you were dimly fortune hunting—hoping that something might come out of my money to you. Was that partly it?"

"Yes, yes." He groaned. "Heaven forgive my wretched soul!"

"Dear, dear Ricardo!" cried the girl. "Do I care what was in your mind at first? Of course, young men want to marry money. That's only being human, isn't it?"

"There's nothing but understanding and forgiveness in you," said he.

The barriers were melting in him. He felt the whole truth trembling on his lips, ready to burst forth; but he was checked by—the thought of William Benn.

"But I don't doubt you now," she said.

"Heaven bless you!" murmured the boy.

"Only, I want to know when you really cared?"

"I don't know. It's hard to tell. The further I rode away from the ranch toward Back Creek, the nearer I felt to you."

"I know!"

"You see, it wasn't like an ordinary journey. I had an idea that I was riding out to die. I don't want to seem to brag, though."

"Silly dear!" said she.

152

"But when the thing was over——"

"The fight, Ricardo?"

"I don't want to talk about it."

"Well, I'll never ask a word."

"But afterward, when I lay in bed, rather sick and upset, then I remembered your promise. I knew you'd keep it. Well, the idea was horrible. That I should take you by a bargain. Do you see? So I had to write to you, and as I wrote I knew that I was giving up what I wanted most in the world. It was a miserable business, the writing of that letter!"

"It was a glorious business," said she. Then she explained: "When I read it, then I knew!"

"That I loved you?"

"I guessed that. But I knew all about myself. It was almost as if—almost as if—well, as if your ghost had come with that letter and taken me in its arms."

"I love you," said Ricardo sensibly.

Conversation died to murmurs. They stood a long time in one another's arms, until an old brindle mustang, the color of a cow, came and jumped over the garden fence, and began to sniff here and there for a delectable mouthful out of that ruined greenery.

The two lovers watched it with eyes that swam with mirth and joy.

"Funny old horse, isn't it?" asked Ricardo.

"He's a dear old thing," said the girl.

"Clever, too," continued Ricardo.

"I'll never forget him," said she.

"I think I've seen him before," said he.

"Will he let us pat him?" she asked.

They went out, hand in hand, like two children. Ricardo went a little in the lead, holding out his hand; but when he came near, the mustang, seeing the shadow slide along the ground, tossed up its head, kicked its heels in the air, and rushed out of the garden and across the next field, with its mane shaken high, like the plumes of a helmet.

"How disgusting!" said the girl.

Ricardo looked with a vaguely hurt smile after the fleeing horse.

"He didn't seem to understand," said Ricardo at last.

"No," said the girl. "He didn't seem to understand. How odd!"

34

Señor Alvarado Guadalva

When they came back into the house, there was no need
for them to make an announcement with words. A foolish
joy shone in their eyes; they looked at one another as
though each were a dazzling sun of exceeding brilliance.
Theodora Ranger said, with her usual bluntness:

"You lost no time, young man. Nor you, Maud. You
young idiots are engaged, of course."

"I'm glad of it," said her husband. "Now I can wash
my hands of this whole business. I never was a rancher
or a banker; I never will be, either. Maud, I hope you're
happy!"

There was an inflection in his voice which allowed it
plainly to be seen that he did not expect his hope to be
fulfilled.

"I expected more trouble than this," said Maud frankly.

"Why make trouble?" answered her aunt. "One can't
ride a wild horse with a snaffle. Where are you going to
live, then? Here—or on the ancestral Mancos estates?"

"Wherever Ricardo wishes," said Maud Ranger.

"Wherever Maud wishes," said Ricardo.

They looked fondly upon one another.

"And when is the marriage to be?" asked the uncle.

"Soon," said the girl. "Because I hate long engagements."

"And so do I," said Ricardo.

"I thought you'd agree to that," said Theodora Ranger
gloomily. "Well, we can wash our hands of the whole
affair. The sooner the marriage, the better; then William and
I can go home."

"What's to-day?"

"Tuesday, isn't it?"

"Then, why not Thursday?"

"As good a day as any," said William Ranger. "You'll be a Mexican citizen by Thursday, then, Maud."

He made a wry face, as though the thought were almost too much for him.

And here a servant came in to announce that a gentleman was calling to see Señor Mancos.

"I don't care to see anyone," said Ricardo.

"This is a gentleman who has come a long distance," said the servant.

There was anxiety in his eye; he waited eagerly.

"I'll see him in another room," said Ricardo.

"By no means," broke in William Ranger. "Let us have him in here. Your friends are our friends, now, my lad!"

Ricardo frowned on the floor. But then he nodded. For of course no one could come for him under the name of Mancos except some emissary of William Benn. Almost immediately a scarred-faced Mexican entered the room. He looked a bucaneer of the sixteenth century; but he had the manner and the voice of a gentleman.

"You have forgotten me, Ricardo?" he asked gently.

Ricardo looked wildly into his mind. He never had seen that face before, he was sure.

"Of course I remember something but——" said Ricardo.

"Boys have no memories," said the stranger good naturedly. "Suppose I were to recall to you that I am Alvarado Guadalva."

As he spoke, his left eyelid fluttered ever so slightly, and Ricardo exclaimed with all the surprise that he could throw into his voice:

"Is it possible!"

The Mexican held out both hands; Ricardo, his brain spinning violently, accepted those hands with a strong grasp.

Alvarado Guadalva turned to the others.

"His father was my neighbor," said he, with a smile of explanation. "And yet I'm not surprised that he hasn't recognized me. When I last saw him, he was only a boy. Next, I have word of what he has done in Back Creek. Of course, being near, I came to see him! A Guadalva could do no less for a Mancos than to congratulate him!"

A flash of revelation broke upon the bewildered brain of Ricardo. This was one of his neighbors! He could have burst into huge, ironic laughter. But the next moment, he could have blessed his stars. From the Mancos of El Real, he had learned enough of the old home place in Mexico to be able to carry on some sort of a conversation. It was only wonderful that Guadalva seemed to feel not the slightest surprise at the complexion of this pseudo Mancos!

Maud Ranger, suggesting that the two would of course have a thousand things to say to one another, left the room and got the others out at once. It left Ricardo with the stranger, who, the moment that the door had closed, sank into a chair and turned upon the boy a singular smile of mockery.

"You see," said he, "that I intend to make no mischief."

That sentence ripped the hopes of Ricardo to bits. He stood transfixed.

"Don't be alarmed," said the visitor. "I'm a man of the world. And this goes to show that a small point will be the undoing, often, of the largest scheme. Chance blows our house of cards! Why should you have taken, of all Mexican names, the name of Mancos? Why not some other family? There are any number where blue eyes and yellow hair are possible. But never a Mancos! Bad luck, you see! And bad luck, also, which happened to bring to my ears that the young hero of Black Creek was a Mancos, and had blue eyes and yellow hair—and an uncle in El Real."

He broke off, and laughed softly.

"You must have paid something for his protection, eh?"

Ricardo sat down and rolled a cigarette. He needed something to occupy his hands; he needed something, no matter how trivial, to occupy his mind. With all his heart, he wished that William Benn or the doctor could have been in the room to overhear his conversation. But that was not to be, and he had to bear the full brunt by himself.

It was luckily not necessary for him to continue the talk. The other went smoothly on from point to point.

"Accident trips us up continually," said he. "I remember that I once sat in at a great game of poker. I had the deal. I had played quietly, waiting for a chance, securing confidence. Now I ran up the pack. I dealt a straight, a full house, a flush, and a royal flush. The betting jumped to the sky. I had a fortune there on the table. The straight flush went to myself. The other flush stayed with me, raised me again and again. I put everything that I had ever hoped to own on the table. He called me—and behold! I had dealt

156

him a flush, as I intended. But, by Heavens, it was a royal flush, and higher than mine!"

He laughed cheerfully.

"For two years I did not recover from that," said he.

Ricardo watched him cautiously. The man was obviously a rascal; he was taking pains to show Ricardo that fact, and thereby, perhaps, put him more at his ease.

"However," went on Alvarado Guadalva, "I haven't the slightest desire to spoil your game, as bad luck once spoiled mine. What I feel is that you and I should come to a quiet understanding. Don't you?"

"Yes," said Ricardo huskily.

"What should be my consideration. I haven't yet decided," went on Guadalva. "Perhaps you can suggest?"

"Your consideration for what?" said Ricardo.

"For what?"

The Mexican smiled and, when he did so, one side of his face was puckered by the scar.

"How much will she bring you?" he asked, with a gesture that invited frankness.

"How much will she bring me?"

Ricardo stared at him, blankly.

"I have eyes, of course," said the other. "I saw her way of looking at you. Such a look can mean only one thing. I dare say, even, that the wedding date has been fixed already! And I congratulate her. It is not every girl who has an opportunity to marry a hero!"

Ricardo saw at once that it was foolish to make denials. The whole household, of course, would know the truth at once. How could it be kept from this fellow, who obviously meant blackmail?

"As for the actual amount," went on Guadalva, "I suppose that you yourself know to a penny. Well, we must be contented with round numbers. You understand—Señor Mancos—I don't want to press you. I don't want to clip inside the ring. Not at all! Besides, I can be useful to you!"

"And in what way?"

"A thing to ask—and to answer!"

"Yes," said Ricardo.

"Very well, then. Families make inquiries about the men who are to marry their heiresses. But in this case, there is no need. Honest Alvarado Guadalva, the neighbor of the Mancos family in Mexico, knows all about you. When he has

157

been taken aside by the girl's uncle, he tells him a great deal about you. He puts every doubt at rest. That is a service, my friend?"

"Yes," said Ricardo.

"And as for the reward," said the other, "you see that I leave it to you."

Ricardo began to see.

"I need a little time to think this over," said he. "Suppose that we say five thousand dollars?"

The scar-faced man shook a gay finger at Ricardo.

"You have the true American business instinct," said he. "But let's be reasonable. Rumors says that the estate is worth—what? Seven millions? But suppose rumor exaggerates a little. Suppose we write it down as five millions. Now, you will see that I'm a reasonable man. Some people would want a considerable split, partly for their silence, and partly for their talk. But a small lump sum is all that I care to accept. Say one per cent of the total. Fifty thousand dollars is all I would ask, and yet that is not much, considering what is at stake. You agree that fifty thousand is not much?"

Ricardo smiled a little, and his smile was not good to see.

"I must have time for thought," said he.

"Certainly," said the other cheerfully. "Let's say, until this evening. You may think the thing backward and forward. In the meantime, you beg the señorita to let me stay in the house. I am such an old friend, and such a good fellow. A gentleman, too. You can see that for yourself! And, afterward, we come to our understanding. Perhaps you will want me here to see the wedding, even. But on that, I never would insist. In the meantime, command me, señor. I am at your service."

◉

35

Antonio Perez Hears Some News

It is necessary to go back, once more, to Antonio Perez, for his way is to cross that of his foster son again. It was the evening of a long and hot day, and Antonio Perez, all the day long, from early morning until the red of the sunset, had been working his three mules from the mill to the river barge, carrying sacks of flour, and back again from the barge to the mill, with sacks of wheat. For that work the pay was not high per load, but with three mules—all good ones— and a resolute driver like Antonio, the pennies mounted into dollars rapidly.

"Another week like this," he said to his wife when he came home that evening, "and I shall be able to begin to pay back Ricardo."

"Tush," said the Navajo woman. "Ricardo never would let you pay him back, because he has a heart larger than the sky."

Antonio smiled. Nothing pleased him so much as a compliment to his foster son. All his family knew this, so that if one of the other boys wanted his way, he began with a tribute to his foster brother.

The three were now employed, and all in the town. Pedro worked with Vicente in the quarry just under the hills, behind the town; they came home gray with rock dust every evening, with sore hands, and eyes half shut with fatigue. Juan, however, had found a better post, for he was in the carpenter's shop, and there he was picking up the craft with speed.

Now supper was ended, Mrs. Perez was busy cleaning the dishes. Her four men, in whom her heart gloried, sprawled in the doorway; or sometimes they got up and strolled back and forth, because there was not much wind stirring, and when one sat still, one felt the heat very quickly.

Just across the street was the blacksmith. He was, of all the men in the village, the very strongest, except for Pedro Perez, that lionlike youth. The blacksmith was too tired to rise and walk. He rolled against the jamb of his door.

"You have earned your supper, friend," said Antonio across the street to his neighbor.

Just then a rider galloped by, the shod hoofs of the horse tossing up clouds of dust which dissolved in the air and hung a stifling curtain across the street.

"These young fools!" said the blacksmith wearily. "They never can walk!"

"Young men care nothing for the comfort of their elders," said Perez.

"You have three good boys," declared the blacksmith.

"My boys? Well, they are what Heaven made them. I hope they will have a good end!"

"A straight sapling makes a straight tree," said the blacksmith kindly.

"Unless heavy winds blow, yes."

"Well, they will be honest. I know that. Ha! What a day! It is as hot as though the sun were still shining."

"You wear cotton underwear," said Antonio.

"It's cooler."

"Flannel is better. I always wear flannel."

"It will make your blood boil, Antonio."

"Here comes another of those galloping young fools!"

"Hey! Stop!" shouted the blacksmith. "It's my own boy, the lazy scoundrel," he went on.

The rider drew up and dismounted.

"There is news from Back Creek," said the boy.

"Ha? Who has been killed there? What wickedness have they been up to?"

"You guess who is dead!"

"How can I guess? There's not a man in Back Creek that doesn't deserve hanging!"

"That's true. But the rope will never claim them while they stay there."

"They knife one another in Back Creek, now and then. It is like a den filled with snakes. Who is dead now?"

"The greatest of them all!"

"The greatest what? They have all degrees of greatness. Robbers, pickpockets, cutthroats, safe-crackers, poisoners—who is the greatest?"

"The man who killed that rich banker. I mean, Charles Perkins!"

This caused a loud exclamation upon both sides of the street.

"Who did such a thing? What other murderer?" asked Antonio Perez.

"No other murderer at all."

"But he killed Perkins?"

"He did. He was only a boy. He had yellow hair and blue eyes. He killed Perkins!"

"Yellow hair and blue eyes!" cried Antonio Perez.

"Like your son, you mean?"

"Who else would such a description fit so well?"

"That's true. But——"

"Well, what did he do?"

"He fought this man—this Perkins. He was shot down, with a bullet scraping along his skull."

"But still he killed Perkins?"

"By shooting him straight through the head. It must have been a terrible battle. Well, Perkins is dead, at least. And the man who killed him—this will tell you what sort of a fellow he is!—refused to take a penny of the reward for the killing."

"How much was that?"

"Fifteen thousand dollars, some one said to me."

"Fifteen thousand dollars! Enough to make a man rich!"

"How many mules could you buy for that?" asked the blacksmith, chuckling.

"I could buy enough. I would make my three boys each drive a whole string of mules. I would buy other houses for them. We would live like kings. Well, some people are born to have the luck."

"If they shoot straight enough," cautioned the blacksmith.

"Yes, that's true. Hard work makes slow hands. I know that! But, yellow hair and blue eyes! What was his name?"

"Mancos is his name."

Said Antonio Perez, "Why do you start, Juan?"

"No reason at all," said the other.

"That is exactly the sort of thing that my Ricardo would try to atttempt," said Antonio Perez. "To go up to a town like that—I mean filled with poison and danger—and there to fight a terrible man."

"Your boy is not the only one in the world with blue eyes," said the blacksmith.

"Some day," answered Antonio Perez solemnly, "he will be famous!"

"May I live to see that day," said the other with a mock gravity. "Then our street will be famous, too. 'In that house, Ricardo Perez lived. His father kept mules!' "

Perez laughed in good nature at this, too.

"I will tell you something," he added, after a moment. "Already Ricardo is doing great things!"

"Tell me about them," said the cynic. "I haven't heard of them from other people!"

Antonio Perez, thus put upon his metal, said with some sternness: "He has sent me eight hundred dollars. That is worth knowing, my friend; also it is worth having!"

The blacksmith actually rose and stood up, in spite of the heat.

"Eight hundred dollars!" he repeated.

"Where else would I get the three new mules?" Perez asked. "Do such animals grow on thorn bushes?"

"But he is only a boy!"

"He has a brain?"

"And what is his work?"

"He works for a great merchant."

"Writing accounts?"

"What exactly he does, I don't know."

"You don't know!"

"No," muttered Perez.

"Father," said Juan, "let us go down to the river. It will be cooler there."

"Your boy knows something more than you do about his brother and his work. You see, he wants to get you away!"

"Bah!" said Perez. "Are you jealous of Ricardo, neighbor, and the money that he makes?"

The blacksmith said heartily: "I never wish you as bad a lazy son as I have, friend. Though I thought for many years that your Ricardo would be another such lazy one. I shall be glad if I am wrong. But you know what the proverb says. 'Idle hands find mischief.' You had better make sure about Ricardo."

Antonio Perez rose with something of a growl.

"You are right, Juan. By the river it will be cooler."

The two older brothers would have accompanied their

162

father and Juan, but Antonio Perez bade them stay where they were. He walked with Juan down to the river in the gloom of the evening. They stood where their dim images fell across the starlit surface of the water.

"Juan," said the father, "what is it that you know about your brother Ricardo?"

"I?" said Juan innocently. "I know nothing at all!"

"Did you bring me to find the cool of the water or to escape from the words of our neighbor?" asked Perez patiently.

"I was thinking only of the coolness," said Juan.

Suddenly the voice of Antonio Perez grew terrible, though it was not raised.

"Juan," he said, "I never have had to say that a son of mine is a liar. In the name of the saint who guards you, tell me the truth that you know about Ricardo."

Juan groaned aloud. And then he realized that that sound had betrayed him. He searched, with a dizzy mind, to find the truth; but he was too bewildered. Out of such small things had his father leaped to a conclusion!

"Father!" he exclaimed. "For the sake of Heaven, don't ask me any more questions! Let Ricardo be. Let him go his way. You never could change him a step. All I can tell you is this: That he still loves us."

Antonio Perez, after a little silence, lifted both his hands above his head, but he made no outcry. Then he said quietly: "Ricardo is doing some wrong. Tell me everything that you know!"

And Juan, his resistance beaten down by that weight of authority, told all that he knew, and all that he had reason to guess.

36

If Benn Were Here!

It was not exactly time that Ricardo had wanted when he asked Guadalva for a delay. It was rather advice. And of course he went to the doctor for that.

Doctor Clauson folded his hands and listened patiently to all that had been threatened.

Then he said: "This fellow means business."

"He does," said Ricardo.

"Don't speak except to answer my questions," said the doctor. "How old is he?"

"Guadalva?"

"Yes."

"About forty-five."

"How tall is he?"

"My height, almost exactly."

"And he wears a scar?"

"Yes."

"Is it a real scar?"

"A *real* scar? Why, I suppose so."

"You are a little young," said the doctor wearily.

Then he went on: "What is his voice like?"

"Deep, but pleasant."

"A deep bass voice?"

"Yes."

"Does it seem almost too big for his throat?"

"Ah, you know him!" said Ricardo.

The doctor sighed.

"I think I do," said he. "I know him, but I don't know how we are going to handle him!"

After a moment he added: "Fifty thousand dollars!"

"It is not so much," said Ricardo.

"Not for you," said the doctor slowly. "No doubt it's

not much for you. But for me, who have made and lost a good many times that sum, it seems enough to be worth saving. Besides, it would be only a beginning."

"He talked honestly enough about making the bargain," said Ricardo.

"That money," answered the doctor, "would only be a taste to him. He would come back to you as the bucket comes back to the well, and you could not keep on filling him forever. I think I shall have to try to persuade him. I wish," said the doctor, "that Benn were here."

"Shall we send for him?"

"Let him be. He would be here, true enough, if he didn't have other important business on hand!"

Then he added: "Have you arranged for Guadalva, as he calls himself, to stay here at the house?"

"Yes. That was easily done. Miss Ranger was glad to have—an old friend of my family."

The doctor smiled.

"You begin to show more heart, Ricardo. You begin to enjoy this game, I think."

"Our chances shrink," said Ricardo. "And of course I like it better and better."

He added: "Shall I walk out with you, this evening?"

"You shall stay home," said the doctor. "Stay home and sing for your supper!"

That supper was a very cheerful meal. Guadalva seemed a gentleman. He was full of talk about old Mexico and stories of the Mancos family. He had an inexhaustible supply, and there was enough wit and excitement in them to keep even Theodora Ranger bubbling. After dinner he was cornered by William Ranger, who appeared to be asking many questions in turn, and Ricardo could not help guessing that those questions were about himself.

Then he and Maud Ranger and her aunt and uncle sat on the veranda and watched the night thickening over the mountain, which was wedged against the stars. They spoke hardly at all. Only, now and again, he saw the girl turn her head slowly toward him; and every time his heart leaped wildly and pitched like a bucking mustang.

The Rangers retired early.

Maud only said: "Could you like this sort of thing? I mean, the wildness. But of course you could, because you were raised to it."

"Of course," said Ricardo rather feebly.

"And we'd make the house the center of the finest garden," said she.

Ricardo was left alone on the veranda and, while he waited, he thought he heard two faint sounds at a great distance, very much like the explosion of two guns. However, he was not sure of this.

The doctor and Guadalva had gone out long before. Certainly they were stretching their evening walk!

At last, he heard footfalls. He crouched lower, so as to look, more or less, toward the horizon's edge. And then he saw two forms coming past the picket fence.

They were coming back together, and he had hoped that the doctor might come back alone!

They were chatting quite briskly as they turned in to the house and came up on the veranda.

There they paused, Guadalva saying something about hoot owls and their odd habits—they had passed one of those weird birds in the dusk, it seemed. After that, he said good night, and the doctor sat down beside the boy.

"Did you scratch your hand on a cactus?" asked Ricardo.

"Why do you ask?" said the doctor tersely.

"It's all wrapped up, isn't it?"

"It's wrapped up," said the doctor, and made no further comment.

Ricardo, feeling that there was to be no exchange of information, now got up and yawned.

"I'm turning in," said he. "What are orders for tomorrow?"

"I'm sending for Benn. He'll have to come."

"He will."

"Guadalva is too much for me. He beat me, Ricardo."

He said this quietly, but Ricardo could guess, by the slightest of tremors in the tone of his companion, that the pride of the doctor had been humbled almost to the ground.

"He took you when you weren't prepared," hazarded Ricardo to make it easy for him.

"Prepared? Would I go walking with that scoundrel without being prepared? I'd rather walk with an acknowledged knife-thrower and half close my eyes!" He paused, apparently in bitter reflection, and at last continued:

"He knew me, Ricardo, and he showed that he understood I knew him. When I knew that, I saw that I must kill him, and I told him so. We fought rather a duel. We were both polite and made wishes for the other's good luck. Then we agreed that we would not try to get out a gun until a wretched hoot owl which was hunting over the valley floor should cry again.

"An unlucky signal for me! Mind you, I don't offer excuses. But the gun stuck a little as I was making the draw. And that Guadalva, as he calls himself, is a master. He was half a second before me, I suppose, and that's enough margin for the killing of three men.

"Cool and deliberate is this chap. He didn't even aim for my head or my body. What was the use, he explained later on, of having a dead man on his hands, and a dead body, either to conceal, or else to make a confession to the police. So he decided that I was to live."

"You mean to say that he didn't shoot for your body, but for your hand?"

"Not a bit of it. The man's too clever."

"I understand! I understand!" muttered Ricardo, as the force of this came home to him. "If you disappeared, he would have questions asked of him. And disposing of a body is no easy trick!"

"Do you think he's playing a lone hand against Benn and me?" asked the doctor testily.

"Ah, he has men with him?"

"Ah, hasn't he, though? But he has! Enough for most of his purposes, all of which are bad, I take it."

"Will you tell me his name?"

"I will not," answered the irritable doctor. "As a matter of fact, what good would it do you to know his name? Can you tell me any purpose that it would serve?"

"No," said Ricardo, "I cannot. As long as I have you to fall back on."

"He has done a neat job of me," growled the doctor. "No real harm. Except that he took a nip out of my wrist, and for ten days I won't be able to handle a gun again, at the very time when I most need to."

"And suppose you had killed him?" asked Ricardo.

"Perhaps I would have sent you out to bury him, in that case," answered the doctor coldly. "I'm going to bed!"

He got up from his chair, but did not pass through the door at once.

Instead, he walked slowly back and forth on the veranda, muttering a little to himself now and again. Ricardo felt that he must wait until the humor of his companion cleared, or until he had permission to depart.

The doctor, at last, stopped and tapped Ricardo impressively on the breast.

"We have our hands as full as they can hold," said he. "An unfortunate thing, too! Here we are with the prize in our hands, the ship taken, as it were, and the treasure simply not yet transferred into our hold; and up blows a storm which, for all I know, may blow us apart from the rich galleon, my boy—and we'll never have sight of the silks and laces, and the gold and the silver of that prize!"

He muttered softly.

"Benn should be here!" he insisted. "He was a fool to leave at such a time as this. An absolute fool!"

It was the first glimpse that Ricardo had had of any real weakness in the doctor, or at least, of any sense of inferiority to William Benn, or to any other human.

"I'm going to bed," said the doctor in conclusion. "You do the same, and if you know any prayers, say them all twice over!"

But Ricardo knew no prayers, and therefore he was soon asleep.

37

◉

A Gentleman's Agreement

Preparations for the wedding went on at a great pace. Theodora Ranger, although she did not appear reconciled to the marriage, now that it was inevitable, took charge of all that had to be done beforehand. She would have preferred a church wedding in El Real, but Maud would have nothing of this; and so the alternative was to make as much as possible of the old shack of a ranch house. Evergreen boughs were brought in from the hills. The house began to look like a bower. And Ricardo, watching all these things, felt like a man seized by a river and shot downstream to an unknown destination of incredible happiness, or incredible danger.

He tried to look about him, to be prepared and calm; but his brain was dizzy with this fate into which he had been rushed. But, on this morning after the doctor's evening excursion with Guadalva, other important news came in. William Benn was at last on the scene of operations. It was Lew who carried in word, and the message which Lew brought was, simply, that Benn could not raise fifty thousand dollars to pay the price of Guadalva. Would the latter give time?

"How can he give time?" asked the doctor bitterly.

But he called in Guadalva. With Ricardo, he talked things over with the blackmailer.

"We can give you thirty-five thousand cash," said the doctor. "Will that hold you?"

Guadalva listened with his usual polite interest.

"Thirty-five thousand is a great deal of money," he said seriously. "But, you know, if you have a good horse, you'd feel ashamed to sell him for less than a certain price."

He said this with an almost honest innocence, so that Ricardo prickled suddenly with anger.

"You can have our promise for the money that's to come afterward," said the doctor.

"Promises of honest fellows I always respect," said Guadalva. "But you understand, of course, the signed promise of the United States' treasurer—that's another thing."

"You'll trust greenbacks, then?"

"I don't want to seem hard," said the suave Guadalva. "But suppose something should happen to the promisers?"

"Suppose," said the doctor, still hunting desperately for an expedient, "we leave one man in your hands for surety. I'll go myself, for that matter!"

Guadalva shook his head.

"Your other friends might forget you, Doctor Clauson. That would be sad for you; it would be still sadder for me. I'm sure you can follow my reasoning."

The doctor rarely lost his temper, but Guadalva seemed to have learned the trick of upsetting him. Now, Clauson rapped his unwounded hand smartly on the table by which they sat.

"For the sake of the extra fifteen thousand dollars," said he, "you'll throw away everything—the thirty-five thousand you could be sure of, included. And the seven millions of this estate for us."

"You're angry," smiled Guadalva. "But you still have plenty of time. And you surely can raise the money—a wise man like yourself, and a great hand and head like William Benn, and a pillar of fire like Ricardo Mancos, here!"

He smiled again as he spoke the name, and he lingered on it with just a trifling hesitation, enough to make Ricardo hot with anxiety.

"You drive me mad," said the doctor. "How are we to raise the money?"

"It's not far to El Real," said Guadalva. "And in El Real there are banks—there are people with plenty of money in private safes—there is the establishment of your uncle, for instance!"

He nodded to Ricardo again.

"We rob the bank to pay you?"

"Robbing Peter to pay Paul," smiled the genial Guadalva, and his scar turned a rosy red on his face, and then grew pale. "I don't want to shock you or your feelings, doctor."

"Oh—much you care for my feelings!" snarled the doctor. He sat for a moment in earnest thought. Then he said grimly: "We'll have to get the money. We have until to-night say?"

"Or to-morrow morning?"

"To-night," said the doctor. "We'll make or break on that. I'll get in touch with Benn. We'll try to devise something. But afterwards, Guadalva, we'll all remember you for a long time!"

This sinister speech the other waved aside.

"That's my fortune in a good many parts of the world," said he. "I'm remembered by a great many people. I may even say that there are many who want very much to see me, and yet I can't spare the time to go back to them. Perhaps you all will come into the same list. Well, that's regrettable—but——"

He waved his hand again. Always the left hand. The right remained on guard, prepared. Ricardo began to see that this man had not crippled the terrible doctor by mere chance. He was a fighting tiger. The doctor, as a fighting machine, was nothing to him. Even the terrible hand of William Benn might go down before Guadalva.

"I'll tell you what we'll agree to," said the doctor. "This evening, just after sunset, William Benn will ride down to the river and meet you there. Do you agree? He will bring you the money—if we can raise it!"

Guadalva suddenly squinted at the doctor as though he were a sailor at the masthead, making a landfall.

"Very good, very good!" said he. "But I could do without William Benn. I'm a timorous fellow, doctor. Suppose a great fighting man like William Benn came down to the river in a bad temper. He might draw a gun, might he not? And he might shoot poor Guadalva. Which would be a great deal less in payment than fifty thousand dollars, for me! Am I right?"

"You're particular," said the doctor, pale with anger, but nevertheless half smiling at his appreciation of the cunning of the other. "Then tell us whom you will allow to bring you the money at the river?"

"I don't see the necessity of the river," said Guadalva. "I don't see that at all."

"Do you think that we'll bring you that much money into this house? Do you think we'll pay you before we've seen you started on your way?"

"Ah, yes, ah yes," admitted Guadalva. "I now can see the point of that. Otherwise, suppose I received the money, and on my way out of the house, from purest malice, dropped a word to Mr. Ranger—of course I understand perfectly what you mean. Very well. I'll pack and leave this evening before sunset. I'll be at the river in the flush of the evening. And who will meet me there with the money—other than William Benn?"

"Who d'you suggest?" asked the doctor.

"Why not your capable self, Doctor Clauson?"

"I'll never meet you again," said the doctor solemnly, "without a gun in my hand."

"Well, well," murmured the other.

He turned to Ricardo.

"Then why not my old friend, my dear old friend, Ricardo Mancos? Why should he not come down here to the river to meet me, and bring the money with him?"

"Ricardo? Why do you want him?"

"Because of the safeguard, doctor, if you must know. As

long as I have Ricardo in range, I don't think that I shall be bothered by any pot shots from the rest of you and your men. And so, you see, he will be my ticket to safety."

The doctor closed his eyes. A look of pain came upon his face. "You'd feel safe with Ricardo?" he asked, without opening his eyes.

"Ah, yes," said the other, "because I have an idea that I would be beneath the notice of the gun of the man who killed that terrible Charles Perkins—with his own hand—alone!"

He drawled out the last part of his sentence, and his eyes turned yellow with a sort of tigerish scorn and fury as he glanced at the boy. Ricardo stiffened and shuddered in his chair.

"Ah, well, then," said the doctor, "let it be what you want."

"He comes at sunset?" asked Guadalva briskly, releasing Ricardo from that flaming glance of suspicion, and scorn, and malice.

"He comes at sunset," said the doctor, in the voice of a hypnotized man.

"I suppose that's all we need to talk over?" asked Guadalva, cheerful as ever.

"I suppose it is."

"Good morning, then."

"Good-by, Guadalva."

The blackmailer left the room, and Ricardo turned a sick face upon the doctor.

"Well?" he asked.

"I wish Benn were here!" murmured the doctor. "But then, I don't see anything else to do."

"Than for me to go?"

"Yes."

"And you'll be able to raise another fifteen thousand dollars for him by night?"

"Of course not! Send you down to pay him with money, Ricardo? What do you think we are made of? Gold? No, no!"

"I don't understand," said Ricardo wonderingly.

"Why don't you?" asked the doctor, turning suddenly savage. "You carry a gun, don't you? We've taught you to shoot, haven't we? How else should you pay him than this way?"

Ricardo moistened his dry lips. He tried to swallow, and almost choked instead.

"I must kill him, doctor?"

"I tried to do it for you last night, and I failed. If you see any better way out of this, I beg you to take that way, my friend."

The doctor was coldly polite. He concluded:

"We have to pay for important things. There are no bargains in diamonds of the first water. And for seven millions one man already has died. Guadalva—we'll hope that he will be the last!"

38

◉

Fill Your Hand!

Through the cold cloud that settled over Ricardo, after that interview with the doctor and the blackmailer, only one moment of bright light broke through that day, and this was when he and Maud Ranger walked in the garden. She had little time to give him these days. She was full of preparations; only now and again she would come to him, her eyes misted over with joy.

What they said as they walked through the little, ruined garden was forgotten by Ricardo in his mingled confusion and happiness, but he remembered later how Theodora Ranger stopped him in the hall of the house and laid a hand on his arm.

"Whether you are good or bad," said she, "try to be good to her. She's worth it, boy!"

Ricardo smiled a sickly smile and went up to his room. He spent two hard hours that afternoon working with his guns. According to the precepts of William Benn, he carried two revolvers. One was slung in a holster, cow-puncher fashion, on his right thigh. The other was hung beneath the pit of his left arm, secured in the grip of a powerful spring, which was strong enough to sustain the weight of the weapon, and yet give it quickly to the jerk of his fingers.

This afternoon, he practiced all manner of ways of getting out those guns with speed. He had no skill with his left hand. Only with the right could he succeed. But because of the two weapons, his right hand could hardly be in a poorer position for making one of the draws.

The doctor, with a strained and serious attention, pondered upon this practice.

At last he said: "Put up the guns after you've cleaned and loaded them. There's no use working any harder. You may be as fast as he. You may be faster. But will you be as sure? Believe me, Ricardo, there is nothing in the world that will save us all except the killing of Guadalva; and there is no way of killing him except by your own grit. Tell me this: Are you afraid of him?"

Ricardo had been with the doctor so much that, for the sake of his pride, he would not attempt a deception. He said simply: "I'm afraid, yes."

"If you're afraid," said the doctor, "at the time when you meet Guadalva, he'll most assuredly shoot you through the head."

With that brief bit of counsel and warning, he left Ricardo to his own devices.

But the time did not hang on the youth's hands! It seemed as though the sun were rushing down the western slope with redoubled speed, and before long he had to be out.

Then he had to break away from Maud, who called to him as he started for the stables.

"I have to be alone," said Ricardo. "I have to ride and think. And if you're along, I'll be able to think of nothing but you!"

So he reached the stable and got horse and saddle and went down toward the river.

He did not go by the straightest way. For the horse was full of running after these days in the stable, and therefore Ricardo steadied that good half-bred runner for a mile sprint that brought the sweat pouring out; but at the end of that run, the horse was no longer dancing and prancing but went smoothly on and only gradually began to prick its ears at the sunset.

For when the sun goes down, horse and dog seem to

recognize a peculiar significance in the change. It is the hour when the beast of prey comes out to hunt. The dog is one of the hunters; the horse is one of the hunted. And so this fine fellow stepped more daintily, turning his head to every bush a little, as he passed.

Ricardo put him over the brim of the slope and rode straight down to the river's edge.

It was a river of crimson and gold, now; and where little points projected, cutting off the light, and where rocks poked up above the surface of the water, there were streaks of purple, like films of oil laid over the stream. In the quiet places along the banks, tall reeds were growing, and from these slight whispers filled the air, except when the rush of the stream made a greater sound.

By one great bush, the horse stopped, then sprang violently to the side, and Ricardo, sitting back with feet thrust hard into the stirrups, had a faint glimpse of a gigantic form in the shrubbery.

Selim!

Then the men of William Benn were scattered here and there across the river lands, and the hand of William Benn himself, perhaps, would be stretched out to succor him in the hour of danger, as it had stretched forth once before!

The coldness dropped out of the heart of Ricardo. It never occurred to him that perhaps the Negro giant had been placed there in semi-concealment for the sheer purpose of heightening his courage. But on he rode, so relieved that it was as though a great burden had been dropped from the shoulders of his soul. He turned at a sharp elbow of the river, and between a lofty bank and the verge of the golden stream, he saw Guadalva waiting for him.

Guadalva raised and waived a hand of greeting; and Ricardo rode up to within ten yards. There he paused.

"Have you an arm this long, my young friend?" asked Guadalva in his cheerful voice.

"I have," said Ricardo.

The other was silent, getting the force of this remark by degrees.

"I take it," he said then, "that you have come down to pay in something heavier than paper money?"

"I have," said Ricardo, short and grim.

"Ah, well," murmured the blackmailer. "I should have thought that the doctor and William Benn would be sharper-witted than this! Did they think that I would trust myself out here, without first leaving instructions to cover me?"

"And how are you covered?" asked Ricardo.

"With a letter in the hands of a trusty fellow. If I return by midnight to a certain meeting place, then the letter is burned. If I don't appear, the letter goes to William Ranger. Does that make a little difference to you, lad?"

Ricardo frowned.

He looked back into his mind, and wished mightily for the advice of William Benn.

But, when he turned the matter back and forth, it seemed to him that he was a soldier under marching orders; he had no right to change from the command which told him to come here and fight against this man for his life. What was his own wisdom, compared with that of the doctor and William Benn?

"You see, my boy," went on Guadalva, "that the best thing is for you to go back to those who sent you. I suppose you will find that they are not very far off. Take the money from them. Bring it here and bring it quickly. I've already waited longer than I care to do."

Ricardo said:

"Guadalva, I've thought you over back and forth. I think that you're lying about the letter."

"Do I lie about it? And what makes you so sure, my friend, my young friend?"

"Because," said Ricardo, "I don't think that you know any man in the world to whom you'd entrust a letter as important as that. He would open it—and know the secret as well as you!"

There was a faint exclamation of anger.

"Boy," said Guadalva, "I've warned you before. I warn you for the last time. Do you go back for the money or——"

"Are you ready?" answered Ricardo.

"Dios!" murmured Guadalva faintly.

They stared at one another, and the old flame of battle which had burned in Ricardo's heart so many times now flickered and flared wildly upward again. There was the world to gain, here, and very little indeed to lose—except his life! But, with this man gone, the last obstacle, it seemed, was brushed away. At one step he possessed himself of happiness, wealth, and the woman he loved!

"Are you ready?" he cried again, his voice turning harsh and hoarse as he spoke.

"Do you hear, boy?" shouted Guadalva, even more loudly. "You are throwing away your life—and seven millions! Don't think that the foolish stories about your fight with Perkins mean anything to me. I shall knock you over as a boy would shoot a rabbit! I'm offering your last chance to——"

"Fill your hand!" cried Ricardo savagely, and reached for his own weapon.

Yet he would not actually take any advantage of even such a practiced fighter as Guadalva; that jump of his hand was rather a feint, to make the other draw in real earnest. Guadalva answered with a lightning gesture; his bullet hissed past the face of Ricardo like the hum of a wasp down the wind.

The coat of Guadalva was crossed on the left shoulder by a narrow leather strap which ran down to his gun belt and supported the weight. Where it crossed the lapel was the point which Ricardo chose for a target. The shot followed that of Guadalva by a fraction of an instant. The force of the explosion jerked up the muzzle of the gun and, before he could fire again, he saw Guadalva sag to the side.

The Colt had dropped from the hands of the Mexican. He seemed to be half falling and half clumsily climbing down from his horse until at last he fell prone with a loose, jouncing sound, like that made by the dropping of a half-filled wine skin. He lay at the edge of the river. The puckering scar on his cheek made him seem to grin, and his right hand, thrown wide—for he lay like a cross in his death—was dipped into the blood-red sunset which flowed upon the face of the river.

Ricardo dismounted and looked curiously at the dead man. Then he stared at the fiery current. And looked higher to the smoke and flame of the west. And still farther where the house of Ranger lay in its nest of hills.

Suddenly he felt as though he had taken into the palm of his hand that house and everything in it!

39

The Vilest Thing in the World

A moment later, two riders came out of the brush not more than a quarter of a mile away and came toward him on the river path at a brisk gallop. From its scabbard beside his horse, he drew out his Winchester and held it ready across his left arm, for he could not tell whether these were adherents of Guadalva—the doctor had declared that the Mexican had many men in support—or cowpunchers of the range, or else emissaries of William Benn.

They were still a hundred yards away when one of the riders waved his hand with a shout, and Ricardo dropped the butt of his rifle to the ground with an instinctive exclamation of joy.

It was William Benn. He came on with a rush, leaped from his horse, and kneeled beside the dead body.

Then he stood up and, turning to Ricardo, he took both his hands.

"I thought, for two days, that we were going to be beaten; or bled dry. But the hound followed the trail too fast. And there he is! Dogs always should hunt in packs, or the wolves will cut their throats for them!"

He laughed aloud. Ricardo never had seen him in such ecstasy of pleasure. Then Benn stepped a little nearer to the loosely lying body and stirred it with his foot.

"There's all that's left of him, Ricardo," said he. "There was a machine for you! There was a fellow with his wits about him, and the nerve of a lion. But he's done. The watch has stopped ticking, and the works are so spoiled that they never can be started again. When I heard that Guadalva was after us, I was fairly sure that we would have the dickens of a time, but you see what's come of him!"

He laughed again, and then facing toward the brush, he whistled thrice, in sharply piercing blasts.

"Did you get him fairly away with an excuse?" said he.

"Yes," answered Ricardo. "He said good-by to the Rangers before he started."

"And where he was bound, he'll never arrive," said Benn grimly. "Ah, Ricardo, this is the best day that ever we put in. And you did it by yourself, with no backing, with no one in the background with a gun ready to help you!"

He smiled upon the boy, and there was no hint of the old maliciousness in that expression of his.

Ricardo had taken off his hat, and absently smoothed the wet hair back from his forehead. The last of the sunset light glowed upon him; it seemed to William Benn once more that living gold lay upon the head of Ricardo. And so he waved him away.

"Go back to the house."

"But the body?"

"I've thought of that—and here's one helper to take care of him!"

He pointed. Out of the brush came Selim, running with his gigantic strides. And presently a small form scurried out from the brush and came hastily toward them. It was Wong, his pigtail bouncing behind his head.

Ricardo waited no longer. He remounted his horse, and William Benn walked a few paces at his side.

"All but the last step is taken," said he. "We are closing our hands upon the money, lad! Keep your head high. Look straight before you, and remember that now I'm constantly with you. I would have tried my own hand at handling this Guadalva—but if he'd seen me coming, he would have ridden off as fast as horse flesh and spurs could take him. But from now on, I take a hand in the game. And we can't help but win. Do you understand? We can't help but win!"

With that refrain ringing through his mind, Ricardo rode on to the Ranger house and, just before it, he came upon the doctor, who was walking patiently up and down. He stood transfixed as the solitary horseman rode to him out of the dusk, and then he ran a few steps to meet the boy.

By his side he walked on toward the stable.

"You met him, Ricardo?"

"He's dead," said Ricardo briefly.

179

And saying that, he wondered suddenly why it was that the slaying of Guadalva had meant so little to him.

"Is everything well at the house?" he asked.

"I haven't been there for an hour. Of course everything is all right. The last thing I heard was word from your 'uncle' in El Real. Of course he'll be glad to come to your wedding. He wrote a note to congratulate his dear nephew!"

And the doctor laughed softly.

"The body?" he asked.

"Benn came to me. He and Selim and Wong are all out there!"

Again the doctor chuckled.

"We are in the last act," said he. "And all the actors are ready for the stage. There is no more chance of losing, now, than there is of the sun's failing to rise."

Ricardo left him and went back to the house, for the doctor refused to go in. His spirits were expanding to such an extent that he wanted to walk under the open sky, where the first stars were beginning to glow, and where Venus burned richly in the west. Ricardo went into the house and, at the very door, Maud Ranger met him.

She had a startled, tortured look.

"I want you to come here!" she said. "I want you to come into this room—oh, Ricardo, Ricardo!"

There was heartbreak in her voice, and he followed, heavy of heart, alarmed. The door swung open, and there he saw the picture he least desired. For, seated in a row upon four chairs against the opposite wall, he saw four swarthy men, one with iron-gray hair, and two mighty men, and one a slender youth with a face like the pointed face of a fox. Antonio Perez, and his three sons were before Ricardo!

He did not think of the loss of the money; he thought only at that burning instant of the loss of the girl. As if she were a cloud, his hope of her dissolved.

Antonio stood up, and his three sons with him, with eager and smiling faces turned toward Ricardo.

"We have found you at last, Ricardo," said the muleteer. "We have come a long way, my son!"

And he stepped forward, smiling, his hands outstretched.

Ricardo shrank back against the wall. He felt the tormented eyes of the girl upon him.

"Son?" he cried loudly. "To a smoky face like that? Son?"

Antonio Perez halted. His arms which had been stretched out in welcome slowly began to fall; his eyes were dazed, and the smile remained frozen upon his lips.

Maud Ranger threw a hand before her face.

"You see what it is, of course," said Ricardo. "There are scoundrelly blackmailers all over the world. And of course there had to be some impostor to try to separate us! Look at them, my dear. Could I be of their blood? There is the man and here am I! Is it possible that you take seriously what they say?"

She dropped her hand from before her eyes and stared at Antonio Perez and his three sons. Then suddenly, she clung to Ricardo her eyes desperately upon his face.

"Then it isn't true, Ricardo—what they say?"

"Never for an instant!" said he. "Great Heavens, Maud, how could it be?"

"It couldn't be," she stammered. "I should have seen at once. But I don't know why—the old man seemed so honest. He was so simple. He looked so happy when he spoke of you as his son——"

"There never was a really successful criminal," said Ricardo, "who did not understand how to lie with a good, bold face."

Antonio Perez faltered a little, and young Juan slipped to his side and supported him.

"We have made a mistake," said the muleteer in a dying voice. "Señorita, I am sorry. We all are sorry. We thought that it was my son, Ricardo. It is not! I only wish to go away and to make no trouble."

He went past her slowly, and through the door.

"Ricardo, Ricardo!" whispered Maud Ranger. "He may be a liar and a criminal, but he looks sick—and tired—tell them that we forgive the sham and that they can have food——"

Antonio Perez already was in the outer hall, but Vicente and Pedro heard these words, and Vicente turned like the tiger that he was.

"Food from you and in this house would choke us!" said he. "A glass of water here would be poison. And as for you, dog and traitor, you have killed our father—you have broken his heart!"

181

He seemed actually about to leap at Ricardo's throat; and the latter stood cold of face, attentive, scornfully interested, and watching like a hawk. Perhaps he was a little pale, but he kept himself in hand as Pedro, with an exclamation, grappled with Vicente, and led him out of the room, saying: "Vicente, Vicente, why should you try to ruin him? Heaven forgive the harm we may have done!"

"I curse the day that he ever came to our family," groaned Vicente.

"Hush," said Pedro. "We all have loved him and therefore if——"

The voices died in the hall; the outer door opened and closed, and they were gone.

Maud Ranger looked earnestly into the face of her lover.

"If that is all acting," said she, "I never have seen anything like it before. Never on the stage even. Ricardo!"

And that name was a cry of fear and pain.

"The goodness of acting depends upon the price the actor expects to get," said Ricardo. "Of course, those rats were hoping for a fat profit."

Then he added, savagely: "I am going after them. I am going to learn what the villains are——"

"Let them be," said Maud Ranger faintly. "I don't want to think of them again. Most of all, I don't want to think of the face of that man."

"It's my duty!" insisted Ricardo. "Blackmail? It's the vilest thing in the world!"

40

◉

Antonio Perez Speaks His Mind

When Ricardo left the house, in haste, he encountered the doctor, just coming in through the twilight.

"Where did they go?" gasped Ricardo.

"Who?"

"The four of them."

"The Mexicans? Yonder. Why?"

"All is lost!" groaned Ricardo, and dashed in the direction which had been pointed out.

He went crashing through a fringe of brush and there he came upon the group going slowly, for Antonio was supported between two of his sons. As he came up, he heard Vicente loudly cursing; then the familiar deep rumble of the muleteer, repressing his violent son. Ricardo came springing among them.

They stood before him silent. He was glad of the dimness which covered his face from their sight.

"Juan, Juan," he exclaimed, "you've done this! You've brought them here to ruin me!"

"It was no fault of Juan," said the muleteer. "It was my fault. First, I dragged from him that you were doing wrong since you had left my house. I made him tell me what he had learned about you. Then we all came. What else was so important as to try to save you from being a bad man? We gave up our work. We came."

"Have you come this distance on foot?" cried Ricardo.

"In the name of Heaven," said the other, "could I have used the mules to bring us here—when I knew that those mules were bought with stolen money? I gave them away. I shall begin my life where it was left off after the sickness and the trouble came to us. Because no good ever came from bad; rotten seed makes rotten wheat."

"I've never heard such talk," exclaimed Ricardo. "Juan, listen to me, if the others won't. Pedro, will you listen, also?"

"Ay, Ricardo," said the big man, "because you were once my brother."

"I am still," said he earnestly. "I still am your brother. You haven't understood. The girl in that house is——'

"I saw her cling to you. I saw that there was love in her eyes," answered Antonio Perez, "and of course I understood. You are going to marry her, and she is very rich— she is worth more than the cost of three villages like the one where we live!"

"You see!" said Ricardo. "And that was why I had to deny you. You can understand, now. But you thought that I'd forgotten you, too. You thought that I wanted to forget you. Never! So long as I have blood in my body, I never could do that. When I am rich, I am going to make you all rich. I am going to make all of you have whatever you want to have. That will be my pleasure. I am going to make my mother dress in silk and wear gold and emeralds. And for that very reason, I had to deny you all, tonight! I have had to call you——"

"Blackmailers!" snarled Vicente.

"Hush," said Pedro. "Let our father answer."

"How does it seem to you, Pedro?" asked the muleteer.

"I am not a very wise or a very old man," said Pedro simply. "I would have to do and think what you tell me to do and think. But I saw a very beautiful lady. She is rich, too. Why should not Ricardo marry her? Not that I want to have part of his good fortune. And if he marries her with a different name—well, he has as much right to the name of Mancos, I suppose, as he has to the name of Perez, because no one understands who he really is!"

"That is what you have to say," said the muleteer. "Now, Vicente, what is your voice?"

"I am too hot to talk," said Vicente. "I feel as though I could drink hot blood! I still remember how he sneered at us all—and he spoke about our smoky faces——"

"Hush," said Pedro. "Our brother was only talking, then, to save himself, and help us later on."

"Well, Juan?" asked Antonio Perez.

"Some men work with their hands and some work with their wits," said Juan, "and I saw Ricardo has fairly won his chance to marry that lady. He has been to Back Creek, and there he has killed a terrible man! After doing that, he deserves some sort of a reward. Besides, the lady loves him. Even I could see that——"

"Fox!" said the father. "You see all things—body and mind! But now I shall tell you what I think, Ricardo, since you have heard all your foster brothers speak. If your mother were asked, she would agree with them, because she wants fine things and plenty of money for you! But I tell you that workers in soot leave black marks. If you were to show me the millions of dollars loaded in solid gold bars upon the back of thirty mules, and offer them to me, I would not have them!"

His voice rose a little. When he was excited, he spoke like the roar of a lion.

"I would not have the thirty mule-loads of gold and give

184

up for it my honesty. I am an honest man. I never took a bribe. I never lied to gain by it. I never hurt a neighbor to make a profit out of him. I never have had my hands on dirty money, until the money that you sent to me, Ricardo —and for that I ask Heaven to forgive me, because I did not know that it was unclean!"

This profession of faith, spoken so simply, but in a great voice that rang with true emotion, seemed to crush and overwhelm Ricardo.

At last he said, faltering a little: "Father, I know that I am doing wrong. But you think that I am only marrying the girl because of her money. That is not true. I love her with all my heart!"

"Ha?" said Vicente. "If that is the case, then there is something else to say. Poor Ricardo, I am sorry that I said so many things against you."

He strode forward and found the hand of Ricardo, and wrung it violently.

"*I* am your brother again," said the impulsive Vicente. "Day or night, whenever you need me, I am your brother again, Ricardo!"

Ricardo swallowed hard. Tears were stinging his eyes.

Then he heard the muleteer saying:

"You love that woman and for that reason you think that it is right for you to lie to her. To marry her! What? You will be letting her marry a lie. You are not a Mancos. She will be marrying nothing. And yet you say that you love her! Ricardo, Ricardo, are you really a bad man, in your soul?"

"Father," said the boy, "I know that I am doing wrong. But afterward, I shall do right. If once this thing is finished, then I am going to do nothing but good the rest of my life. I am going to begin by doing good for you and my brothers!"

"I would rather see my three sons stretched here dead at my feet," said Antonio Perez, "than to see them wear so much as a bandanna bought with your money. Besides, I tell you this: A bad thing has no ending. It is like a lie. If a lie is to live, it must be kept working. It never stops putting out roots. Before long, it has become such a strong weed that it has spoiled the whole field of grain! Your bad sin is the same way. You think that you can manage it. You will find that it can manage you. It will drag you at its heels until your soul is black. Finally, you will be ashamed and ruined before men too! I hope that Heaven covers my eyes with the long darkness before I have to hear of that time!"

Then Ricardo answered desperately: "Will you listen to me when I tell you the truth?"

"Yes, yes," said the muleteer. "I would listen to you if I lay dying; and something in my heart is truly dying now, Ricardo, my dear son."

Ricardo struck his hands together with a groan.

"Do you see? I've given myself into the hands of clever and terrible men. If I did not go on with what they want me to do, they would kill me out of hand. I don't dare to turn back now, father!"

Said Antonio Perez:

"The world is talking a great deal about Ricardo Mancos and how he killed that Señor Perkins who had shot so many fighting men in his day. Well, you were a brave man when you went to Back Creek. Are you a coward now? You were not afraid of the hundreds of bad men in Back Creek. Are you afraid of the few who are around you, now?"

Ricardo was silent.

When he drew his breath it had a gasping sound, like a heavy sob, and Pedro actually groaned in sympathy and, stepping closer, he put his arm around the shoulders of his foster brother. Ricardo shuddered at that comforting touch.

"Ricardo," said the muleteer, "you have seen a great deal of richness and roguery. Tell me: Is it worth the five hearts who love you in the village, and who live in my little hut?"

"What shall I do?" asked the boy, brokenly.

"Go back to that house and fall on your knees before the girl. You love her. Therefore, it will be your right penance to tell her the truth—that your are a foundling—that you have been raised in the house of a muleteer—and that you have lied to her from the beginning. Tell her these things, and then walk out of her life. Throw the money out of your pockets. It is all dirty stuff. Come back to me. I shall show you how to work honestly. Good labor makes the soul clean. Water cleanses the skin, Ricardo, but sweat of labor washes the very heart. Go do the things that I tell you to do. I know that what I say is right and good. At this moment, when my heart is aching so terribly, I know that

Heaven would not let me say the thing that is not wise and true!"

Ricardo hesitated. He thought of William Benn, and his demoniacal grin. He thought of the cold, pale face of the grim doctor. And at last he though of Maud Ranger, lovely, and pure, and true. Then he heard the muleteer speaking out of the darkness:

"Go at once. The right road turns into the wrong one, often, if you walk too slowly on it. Pedro will go with you. Heaven bless you, Ricardo!"

Ricardo turned, and Pedro with him, and together they went slowly back through the darkness toward the house.

41

◉

A Changed Ricardo

The Ranger Ranch house had been to Ricardo the place first of great, wild hopes, and then of real confidence, and now it was to him more tormenting than a leveled gun.

He left Pedro at the entrance. On the veranda he found the doctor quietly smoking a cigarette.

"You're late for dinner," said the doctor.

Ricardo stumbled through the doorway without an answer. He felt like a drunkard, so greatly had excessive pain and sorrow of mind confused him, and so he stopped and half staggered when he saw before him in the narrow hallway William Ranger, and his wife and Maud herself, all busily laughing and chattering.

"Oh, hurry, Ricardo," said Mrs. Ranger. "You're late for dinner, boy."

He steadied himself by leaning one hand against the wall, and he looked upon them from the height of his agony as an eagle looks down upon lambs in a field.

"I'm not staying for dinner," he said. "I'm leaving. I'm only here to say good-by."

He saw the girl was still smiling, though there was no meaning in her expression. It seemed, nevertheless, a grisly thing that she should be able to smile like that.

"You're saying good-by?" cried William Ranger. "What in the world has happened?"

"I thought I could go through with it," said Ricardo, "but I can't. I'm here to confess everything. I'm not a Mancos. I was simply wearing a false name. I was trying to steal Maud. I——"

He paused, for as he said these things, he suddenly saw them. Fear leaps on the shoulders of the man who flees; so as Ricardo spoke the naked words of his confession, he saw suddenly the shameless and the cruel depravity of all that he had been hoping to do, and he was overwhelmed.

But he went straight on, only noting that Theodora Ranger had stepped hastily to the side of Maud and was standing now with an arm about the girl. But Maud Ranger was not either weeping or fainting. She stood only a little stiffer and straighter and confronted Ricardo and the truth about her lover with an invincible courage.

Said the boy:

"Everything was a sham. I didn't kill Charles Perkins. I shot the bullet that went through his leg and dropped him; but his bullet knocked me senseless. He crawled on toward me. I saw him coming and I was helpless, and then a friend of mine stepped out from the trees and called to him, and killed him when he turned. Everything was a sham. I never was real. I agreed with a gang of crooks who were helping me. After I married Maud I was to try to get hold of her estate as quickly as I could, and after that I was to share the loot with the others, half and half.

"I don't think there's anything more to say," concluded the dull, mechanical voice of Ricardo. "Antonio Perez told the truth. He is my father. My foster father. I'm going back to him, and Heaven forgive me for the harm I've tried to do to you!"

He stepped back through the doorway, suddenly. He heard a scuffling of feet across the veranda, and the doctor had him by the arm.

"What have I heard?" he asked. "What idiocy did I hear you talking in there? Have you gone mad? You yellow-hearted little rat, have you thrown away all of our money, and time, and work, and welched on us?"

Ricardo plucked off the hands of the doctor. He held the doctor's two wrists in one hand. With the other, he took him by the throat and jammed him heavily against the wall of the house.

"You and William Benn did this to me," he said. "I wasn't a bad boy when you found me. You taught me to play the devil. If you had two sound hands now, doctor, I'd pay you in full. As it is, I have to wait until we meet again. And then we'll settle everything.

"There's William Benn, most of all. I'm going to wait for the day when I see him, too. He and I have several things to talk about. Will you tell him?"

He cast the doctor from him. That formidable master, who had always seemed to him a sort of superman, now was less than a flabby child. He turned his back deliberately upon the doctor, who was making a choking, stifled sound of gasping, and went out from the veranda steps and into the night.

Pedro joined him.

"See, Ricardo," he said. "Already you are standing straighter and taller!"

Ricardo did not answer, but went on with Pedro until they reached the muleteer and the remaining two sons.

"I have done everything as you commanded me to do," said Ricardo.

"I knew that you would," said Antonio Perez. "Now let us go home. We have a long way to travel."

They walked all the way to El Real, never once stopping, never flagging in their steady pace. Before morning they were in the town; still in the first of the gray of the dawn they had slipped into an empty box car, and with that long, rattling train of empties they went jouncing and swaying down the track until they were back at the village which Ricardo had always thought of as home.

In the railroad yard, they dusted off one another as well as they were able.

"Your clothes look too fine for this town," said Antonio Perez thoughtfully.

"I don't think that people will stop me and ask me about my clothes," said Ricardo.

Something in his voice made the father and the three foster brothers look earnestly at one another, but not at Ricardo. He, straight, and lithe, and light-stepping, moved

189

with the rest down the side alleys into the "white" section of the town and, as they crossed it, two young fellows who were jogging their mustangs down the street shouted suddenly, and pointed.

"Ricardo's back!"

They swung their horses close and halted.

"Rich and famous, eh, greaser?" one of them asked.

Ricardo stepped lower and laid his left hand on the mustang's shoulder.

"Say that again," said he, and smiled up to the rider.

The latter's grin faded and died; his eyes widened; and he reined his horse slowly back.

That was all. Then Ricardo walked on with the rest, and they were undisturbed until they reached the Mexican quarter of the little town, beyond the river. There it became an exciting progress, for young and old ran out to see returning this youth of whom so many strange, so many great, things had been told of late. He talked to them cheerfully. He shook hands all around.

When they came opposite the blacksmith's shop, Ricardo was particularly cordial to the blacksmith.

"And you've got your pockets full of money, I suppose," said the smith.

"I haven't a penny," said Ricardo.

"Hello! And what have you brought back from your travels, my lad?"

"The knowledge that I've been a fool," said Ricardo. "Only that, and nothing more."

Again he continued with his family, and so they came at last to the little hovel which was home to them all. He stepped inside the door. The wife of the muleteer, sitting cross-legged on the floor, patting out tortillas with expert hands, jumped up and threw out her arms to him, and Ricardo embraced her heartily.

A great outpouring of talk ensued. And Antonio Perez, overjoyed, ran out to buy special provisions for a feast. A festival day began for them. Neighbors constantly were dropping in and staring at Ricardo, returned from the strange wanderings which had occupied him for so many months. Even the sheriff came.

He called Ricardo outside the shack.

"Now, my boy," said he, raising a cautionary forefinger, "when you were here before, you made a good deal of trouble in the town. You were a boy, then. It seems that you've grown into a man, in the meantime. I've just stepped by to warn you: From now on, no more fighting!"

Ricardo smiled coldly upon the man of the law.

"When I break a law," said he, "come and tell me about it. But," he added more coldly still, "don't come alone!"

The sheriff eyed him out of narrowed eyes; then he nodded, as though a former suspicion had been confirmed, and turning his horse, he jogged off down the street, a dusty figure. Ricardo watched him go.

Inside the shack, Mrs. Perez was whispering to Juan: "What have they done to our Ricardo?"

"In what way?" asked the youngest son.

"He was a good boy when he went away. Now see for yourself what he is."

"Not good?"

"Oh, good perhaps. But a tiger, Juan—a tiger. I almost tremble when I look at him. He never looks at one except straight in the eyes. Oh, there is an old soul in that young body of his. What have they done to him, Juan?"

"I don't know," said Juan, troubled by these questions. "He seems cheerful enough. He smiles a great deal more than he used to do when he was here."

"What are smiles?" asked Mrs. Perez, with a sad gesture of both her hands. "The last act of life is a smile, Juan. But what does it mean?" She added: "Hush! I'll talk no more about it. Let us all be merry and gay. Let us make Ricardo as happy as we can. But—there is going to be trouble—there is going to be great trouble. I'm afaird!"

But it was a great affair, that celebration. People came by half dozens, neighbors, and old friends; yet a whisper had passed through the town, and though all eyes looked at Ricardo, no one spoke to him very much, and then always as from a distance, respectfully.

◉

42

Time and Tide

In the cool of the veranda of the house of William Benn, the doctor made himself comfortable and placed his wounded hand where the sun poured in upon it, baking it, taking out the ache which lingered continually in it. William Benn himself lay back in a chair which was tilted against the wall. His grim face was tired; his eyes were almost veiled; one hand lay palm up in his lap, and the other dangled idly beside his chair.

"I don't mind a certain amount of silence," declared the doctor. "It's a good seasoning for most conversation. But you have something to say, Benn. Why not say it—as short as you please?"

William Benn fully opened his eyes, but he looked before him at his own thoughts.

"I don't follow it," he said.

"You don't follow what?" asked the doctor with impatience.

"A real hunch never goes wrong," said William Benn.

"Now what superstition are you talking about?" asked the doctor, shaking his head.

"The pot of gold," said the big man.

"Are you drunk?" snapped the doctor.

"When I first saw the kid——"

"I know. You thought he was what lies at the end of the rainbow. Another proof that there's nothing in these foolish ideas, my friend!"

Benn shook his head slowly, ponderously.

"You're wrong," he said. "Somehow it must work out. Only I don't understand."

"Did you see the young fool?" asked the doctor.

"Oh, I saw him easily enough."

"In his father's hut?"

"No. I saw him at work."

"At work!"

"Yes. In the flour mill—carrying and stacking sacks of flour."

"He'll never last at that," replied the man of thought.

"Tell me why?"

"Because he never was the working kind; and because he's had a taste of another sort of life."

"He'll not last at the work, but not for the reasons that you give," said William Benn.

"Supply me with better ideas, then."

"That's easily done."

"I'm listening, Benn."

"He's used up his good nature, doctor. He's got nothing left to him except bitterness and poison. When he saw me, I thought he was going to jump for my throat."

"If he'd tried that, it would have been a lesson learned for him!"

"D'you think so? I tell you, doctor, you underrate him. He's a bunch of wild cats. He failed to go through with a job for us. That was all. You hate him because he wouldn't do the thing that you wanted."

"A young jackass!"

"Why not call a spade a spade, since you like frankness? We were fools."

"Yes, ever to trust such a grand scheme to such a worthless rat!"

"Worthless? You're wrong again. We know him like a book—but we didn't see that there was an honest streak in him. An honest streak that beat us—an honest streak that beat him, even after he'd won the game! You admit that he had the thing in his hand. He'd sent off the four of them; he'd pulled the wool over the eyes of the girl again. And then conscience tackled him and beat him—where Perkins, and Guadalva couldn't beat him! Well, doctor, do you call honesty foolishness?"

The doctor was bitterly silent.

"I don't follow you, to-day," said he. "But did you try to get him to come back to us?"

"Suppose I said that he's coming back to us—that he chucked the work at the flour mill—that he's willing to throw in his cards with ours for good!"

The doctor sprang to his feet.

"Then we'll have a cutting tool that will open the way to millions for us, Benn!"

The other grinned.

"There you are! You'd value him highly enough if he *were* back with us. But he'll never come. He'll never come near us! He told me what he thought of you, doctor. He told me what he thought of me. He promised that if it weren't for the sake of keeping his job he would have blown my head off that moment. And he touched the gun he wore under his coat to prove what he meant. No, he'll never come back with us. He'll do his crooked work all by himself."

"Not honest enough to stay straight?"

"Man, he can't look at other people without a sneer. He has the poison in him. He's like a fellow with chilblains and rheumatism and gout all at once. He's on the fire."

"Because he hates to work with his hands, eh?"

"Because he loved that girl."

The doctor whistled.

"Loved her really? Loved her seven millions, of course. That's different!"

"You're too clever, doctor," said William Benn. "You see so far into things that you miss the main facts. He loved the girl. He loves her still. He's eating out his heart!"

The doctor chuckled.

"That's a picture that won't last."

"It won't, because he'll be in the middle of a grand fight before many days are over, and when that happens, you can depend upon it that he'll leave a dead man or two behind him as he starts for the tall timber. By the way, what's become of the girl?"

"Maud Ranger?"

"Yes, of course."

"She's starting for a trip to Europe. Italy, and Vienna, and what not. A little change of air."

The doctor smiled sourly.

But William Benn showed such great interest that he leaned forward in his chair and cried: "Do you mean that? She's leaving for Europe?"

"Of course. Why not?"

"But doesn't it mean anything to you, doctor?"

"And why should it?"

"Leaving for Europe! It wasn't enough for her to hear that her lover was a crook and a nameless man. She wasn't cured by that. She has to go halfway across the globe in order to try to forget."

The doctor shrugged his shoulders and then yawned.

"I see no point of interest for me and you," said he.

"When does she leave?" asked Benn.

"To-day."

"To-day!" repeated Benn loudly.

"Yes. What's wrong with that, Benn?"

"What time is it?"

"Four."

"And that eastbound train will be coming through in a half hour or so?"

"Yes. But it's always late."

"It's late," echoed Benn, "and that gives me a chance!"

He leaped from his chair and rushed from the house to the stable, where Lew hastily flung a saddle on a horse and dragged it out from the barn. Benn flung himself into the saddle and drove the animal at full gallop toward the trees. Through the narrow pass he went at full speed, and then, cutting out on the trail, he rode with reckless haste down toward the white city of El Real.

The hoofs of his horse beat heavy in dust or rang loud on pavement as he entered the town itself, and swerving down twisting alleys he came suddenly upon the open space in the midst of which stood the station, with the long steel rails running either way toward the horizon like flowing quicksilver.

From his dripping, foaming horse William Benn flung himself and sprang onto the platform. In the distance, down the track to the west, he saw a small and slowly growing smudge. The train was in sight, and his working time was not long.

Into the waiting room he strode and saw Theodora Ranger and Maud just rising from their seats; porters had their bags in hand. And through the little crowd he stepped, and passing the girl he managed to lean near her ear and murmur:

"Ricardo!"

She swerved, as a frightened horse swerves under the lash. And turning squarely about, she faced him with a white, desperate face and clenched hands.

He stood before her speaking rapidly:

"I have thirty seconds to tell you what should take a day.

I want to tell you the truth about Ricardo! I am William Benn—criminal!"

She closed her eyes, and then opened them resolutely.

"I've heard of you," said she.

"I found Ricardo. The yellow of his hair looked to me like a pot of gold. I thought my luck was tied to him. I stole him away from his home with lies. Then partly by giving him an easy life and partly by threatening him, I made him do what I wanted. I trained him to be a crook. I pointed him at a marriage with you. I planned the meeting with Perkins. He dropped Perkins; I finished the killing and managed so that Ricardo took the credit."

The train thundered outside.

"Hurry, Maud," called her aunt from the door of the station.

"Go on, go on!" she pleaded.

"I'm talking as fast as I can. You know how he denied his foster father."

"Foster father?" she echoed.

"Great Scott," said William Benn, "did you think he was the real son of the muleteer? Ma'am, he's as white as you are!"

She swayed, and caught at his arm to steady herself.

"Maud, Maud!" called her aunt again.

She shook her head. "His foster father!" she repeated. "And—and—what has he done?"

"He's gone back to the old life—he's gone back to his old labor! He's working in a flour mill, with trouble working harder and harder inside him."

"And what will happen?"

"He'll break loose. He's eating out his heart. There'll be a crash before very long, of course."

"Why is he eating out his heart?"

William Benn raised his forefinger and pointed it at her like a gun.

"I've got nothing to do with this any more," said he. "It's no concern of mine what happens to him, and less what happens to you. But if I tell you why he's eating out his heart, will you tell me why you're eating out yours?"

"Maud, Maud! We're late! The train—the train's beginning to move! Great Heavens, we're losing it. Maud, are you mad? Are you deaf? Do you hear?"

She did not hear. Instead, with a face suffused with glowing color, her eyes wide and dark, she stared into the face of William Benn. And then her lips parted slowly, and she smiled.

William Benn turned on his heel and strode away, while Mrs. Theodora Ranger rushed at her niece and shook her as though she were a child.

"Maud, Maud!" she cried. "What are you thinking of?"

"Heaven!" said the girl.

43

⊙

The Pot of Gold

The following night, William Benn and the doctor whiled away the hours with seven up; and the doctor had just made a mild sensation by shooting the moon twice in a row. At this, William Benn regarded him with his sinister smile.

"Crooked always—crooked even at home!"

The doctor did not deny it.

"Practice," he said, with a shrug of his shoulders, "makes perfect. Besides, you know the game as well as I do!"

"I do," murmured William Benn. "Of course, I know it! And I suppose, doctor, that I've done a lot more harm in the world than you. But still——"

"You won't go to so deep a perdition?"

"That I don't know. I don't prophesy! But I have a feeling that I——"

Selim appeared with his usual noiselessness.

"Lew," said he.

"Lew's come so soon?" said William Benn. "Send him in."

The hunchback came in and leaned against the side of the doorway.

"You little scoundrel," said William Benn, "why did you come back so soon?"

"Why not?" said Lew. "I finished my job."

"You finished?"

"Sure."

"What happened then?"

"Aw, the girl found him at the mill, all right!"

"And then?"

"Why, he come outside and talked to her for a minute."

"Darn you, go on! And then?"

"And then he went back to his work," said the hunchback, and yawned.

"And that was all?"

William Benn scowled angrily. "I don't believe it," said he. "But give back the change from that hundred I gave you."

"Sure," said the hunchback.

He took out a wallet and began to select from rather a thick sheaf of bills. The long arm of William Benn reached out and snatched the purse from him.

"You little cutthroat," said Benn, "where did you pick this up?"

"It was given to me," said the other.

"Given to you? Don't lie to me!"

"It was."

"By whom?"

"By a girl," said Lew.

"I'll wring your neck," said William Benn seriously.

"By Maud Ranger," said the hunchback, suddenly grinning.

"Ha!" said William Benn.

He added: "Go on, then and tell me what else happened."

"She met him again that evening."

"Where?"

"At his house."

"At the Mexican shack?"

"Yes."

"You don't mean to say that she went inside that hut?"

"Sure, she had dinner there with the whole family."

"Dinner!"

"She did. And a darn good appetite she had, at that!"

"Will you talk on?"

"There is nothing much to say. Except that after a while she up and made a speech——"

"She stood up and made a speech?"

"She sat down and made a speech. She told old Perez, the muleteer, that she loved his son, Ricardo. And that Ricardo loved her. And if he, old Antonio Perez, would give his free consent, she would like to marry this here Ricardo, if Ricardo was also willin'. And then——"

William Benn shouted. The doctor rose slowly from his chair.

"And then," said the hunchback, "I got too curious, and that feller Ricardo spotted me, and jumped at me in the dark, and carried me into the light of the shack the way that a cat carries a bird, and he laughed when he seen it was me, and told them a good deal about me."

The hunchback paused. Then he said with a grave air of importance: "This here Ricardo, he's a great friend of mine. So's his girl! Me, I'm gunna go live with 'em, and take care of 'em, if I can shake loose from the dirty work that I gotta do for you, Benn."

"She gave you that money?"

"That's advance wages," said Lew quietly.

"It worked, then, after all," said William Benn.

"It has!" said the doctor fiercely. "And by heaven, we'll follow him until we have our right share."

"Our right share!" said William Benn. "Doctor, you talk like a mighty sick man."

"Sick?" said the doctor.

"Ay," said William Benn. "A man that's got one foot in the grave!"

"By heaven," said the doctor. "I think you're with them!"

"D'you think," cried William Benn in a great voice, "that I'd let you rob me of the one decent thing I've done in my life? D'you think that, you palefaced fool?"

The doctor made no answer. His eyes narrowed with malice, and that was all.

"They sent along a letter to you," said the hunchback, and placed an envelope in the hands of Benn. He tore it open eagerly, and then he read aloud:

"DEAR BENN: We are going to be married to-morrow. We are the happiest people in the world, and, except for you, that never would have been. And except for you I never would have left the village, Benn; and you have done everything for me. No matter what the reasons were. My foster father is a very wise man. He says of this: Heaven uses men as he pleases, and not as they please! Well, I offer that as a suggestion; and I'm writing to tell you that we are your friends to the end of us and ours.

"Come to us soon.

RICARDO."

This he read, and the doctor laughed harshly, but Benn continued in a murmuring voice:

"You were right about everything, and the moment I found him again, I knew that my troubles were at an end. Yesterday I was the saddest girl in the world. Now I'm the happiest.

"God bless you, dear William Benn.

MAUD RANGER."

"And there you are," said the cynical doctor. "There's a fine mess of sentimentality and moonshine that you've earned out of all your work!"

"Moonshine?" said William Benn in a strangely hushed voice. "No, no, man. It's the pot of gold!"